Jav WIL
14.75
JUL   2014

The People

vs

Cashmere 2

The People vs Cashmere 2

Karen Williams

www.urbanbooks.net

Urban Books, LLC
97 N18th Street
Wyandanch, NY 11798

The People vs Cashmere 2 Copyright © 2014
Karen Williams

ISBN 13: 978-1-60162-606-6
ISBN 10: 1-60162-606-1

First Trade Paperback Printing August 2014
Printed in the United States of America

10 9 8 7 6 5 4 3 2 1

Distributed by Kensington Publishing Corp.
Submit Wholesale Orders to:
Kensington Publishing Corp.
C/O Penguin Group (USA) Inc.
Attention: Order Processing
405 Murray Hill Parkway
East Rutherford, NJ 07073-2316
Phone: 1-800-526-0275
Fax: 1-800-227-9604

Acknowledgments

Whew! Where do I begin? Let's just say that I feel incredibly blessed to have come up with this concept that just managed to fall into my lap. *The People vs. Cashmere* has always been a novel dear to me. When we talk about these young girls who are out there selling their bodies against their will people fail to realize that these young girls are being sexually exploited right smack dab in our neighborhoods. Reality is that the average age of the girls out there is thirteen! And almost all of these young girls are being sexually exploited against their will by a pimp. I thank God legislation is being changed to tackle this issue. I also wanted to shout out people like Rachel Lloyd and Nola Brantley for really striving to make a difference, fighting for our young girls, and trying to eradicate commercial sexual exploitation and domestic trafficking.

I always tend to shy away from doing a sequel unless there is a really good reason and the concept is a good one. But this concept was an amazing one that I loved. And it felt so good to revisit some old characters that, since I created them, just seemed to stick with me. What was just as exciting as revisiting old characters was creating new ones like Dominique and Meka. I don't want to give it away before you read it but the lives they live now may be a bit surprising to you. We never really know what happens after a novel ends. We just tend to believe and sometimes hope that it is as happily ever after as the ending often is. But that is not always the case. Believe

Acknowledgments

me when I say there are some twists and turns so you're gonna need a seat belt for this one J. But again, I strive to bring the depth and intensity for you guys. So I hope you guys enjoy.

I want to thank my children, Adara and Bralynn. Love you two!

Thanks to my mother and my sister Crystal.

Hey to my nieces, Mikayla and Maydison; my nephews Omari, Jeff Jr.; my cousins Donnie, Devin, and Mu-Mu; and my goddaughter La'naya . Hey to Tammy, Shauntae, Ray, and Eric.

Thanks to my friend Lenzie, with your crazy self!

Hey to my best friend, Christina. Christina four words: "For The Weekend Baby!" Lol. Only she will get this inside joke.

Thanks to Sheryl, Gwen, Linda, Tracy, Christina, Talamontes, Pam, Carla, Sewiaa, Ronisha RIP, Shameka, Valerie Hoyt, Tara, Pearlean, my second mom! Dena, Angel Williams.Thanks to Lamartz Brown, Sandy, Johanna Jo Jo Collier, Sharlene Smith, Papaya Flagstaff, Shawnda Hamilton, Just Read Book Club, Fundamentals, African American Writers On The Move and SLYCE Book Club. I appreciate all the love and the support.

Smiles to Bernie, and Patrice for always uplifting me.

Thanks to my editor, Kevin Dwyer. He's the best in the business.

And to my fans. (Clearing my throat Part 2) . . . The past year has been kinda tough. You guys always keep me on point and always inspire me to produce the best work I can. I know for a fact that if I didn't have you guys cheering me on that I wouldn't have completed this novel. So I thank you guys.

And finally, *The People vs. Cashmere 2* would not be complete unless I continue to encourage those around me. To those that are going *through it*. Know that darkness

Acknowledgments

is temporary and we are always guaranteed a new day. And while you're waiting for that new day, you may find people around you that continue to keep you down or even rejoice at your suffering. They may be the one who caused your suffering. Keep pushing on and know that these individuals are merely using your temporary struggles to build themselves because they in all actuality have nothing else. They are nothing else. Continue to use all of what they throw at you for motivation and soar because I know you can. Trust me I am not exempt from experiencing this. As I said before, use the haters as fuel, keep going. And in the end, thank them like I'm doing here . . . (Clearing my throat part 2) . . . To those who tried to tear me down, your attempts just weren't successful. Know that truth is always revealed. I'm not mad at you, I'm praying for you. You may want to keep in mind that I've got a ray of light around me and you aren't dimming it.

Chapter 1

Cashmere

"Black Mitchell! Wake your motherfucking ass up!" My gun was aimed at his sleeping form.

As soon as I saw a speck of white in his eyes, as his lashes touched the bottom of his brows I wasted no time in pumping those bullets into that sorry motherfucker as his body jerked to and fro. In fact, I emptied the entire clip. I enjoyed seeing all the bullets pierce his flesh as smoke filled the air and blood started to seep from his body. But still, despite the fact that he was no longer breathing and his eyes were wide, I loaded another clip and emptied it as well, ignoring the terrified screams of Dominique. I smiled at his dead body for a moment then as my daughter continue screaming I looked over at her tear-soaked face.

I lowered the gun.

She stood to her feet.

"Dominique. No!"

Before I could grab her, she ran toward the bed and threw her body over Black's. She started bawling.

I rushed over to her and grabbed one of her arms. "Get off of him, baby!" I started crying. What had he done to my child?

"How could you, Mom?"

"I had to, baby. I—"

"You killed my father!"

Chapter 2

Seven months before, New Years Eve Night, 2011

Cashmere

I covered my ears at the sound of our dresser mirror shattering from Demarco putting his fist through it. I wanted to go to him and help him as he looked down at his bleeding hand. But I knew he wouldn't want me touching him. So I just sat on the bed and cried tears as he wrapped a towel around his hand and looked at me hatefully. Seemed like every day I was crying. No wonder I couldn't get pregnant. I was always super stressed at all the arguing between Demarco and me. And I really didn't know where we stood. But one thing I knew for sure and that was that he hated me. My baby hated me. And I loved him. I loved him like I did when I was eighteen. When I was going through all that mess with Black after I had gotten out of jail. Throughout it all he had been there for me loving me unconditionally. Even when he found out the truth about my past: that I had been a prostitute, addicted to drugs, who went to juvenile hall for murdering my sister at the age of thirteen. None of that mattered to him. He stayed by my side and never left it.

After the trial Black was locked away and no longer a threat. Demarco and I moved in together. We both bought a house in Inglewood, the city where he opened up another hair salon. I worked as a hair stylist there and cared for my man. Things were perfect. Demarco also opened a shop in Long Beach and one in Marino Valley. So he was always busy and business was thriving. I had a huge rock on my hands and bitches who worked at the salon were so, so jealous. At least twice a day I would hear, "What's so special about her?" And I would chuckle. I had calmed down a lot and wasn't the hothead I used to be who was always willing to fight at the drop of a hat. I thought it was Demarco I had to thank for that. He was always so calm, so happy and smiling. He was my peace. Then a few months into us living together, I found out I was pregnant. Now while I was far too young to have a baby, I was still excited. I gave birth to a little girl named Dominique. My mother and her commissioner retired from Lancaster Police Department and bought a house down here in Carson to be closer to me and her granddaughter. Now my baby, she was absolutely perfect. She had my coloring, my eyes. That was my partner in crime there. Seemed like after I laid eyes on her, everything in my world made sense. It just did. And I was the most doting, paranoid mother ever. Without a doubt, no one was going to be able to let any type of harm come my baby's way. When I was twenty-four and Demarco was twenty-nine we got married in Vegas. Thing was part of me knew he had drifted apart from me. And part of me also questioned whether we should have gotten married. And when I asked him he told me, "It's the right thing to do." But it wasn't. Life for us was not good. He drifted further and further away from me. Like he resented me. And what didn't make the situation better was the fact that I couldn't get pregnant again. And Demarco felt like I was doing this on purpose. That I deliberately didn't want to give him a baby.

I thought about how loving he used to be toward me. A tear couldn't drop without him wrapping his arm around me and kissing them away. Now he would see me sobbing and would say. "Good. I'm glad you're hurting, bitch!"

Things between us had changed around the time Dominique turned five. He became more angry and hateful toward me and more distant. But I continued to play the role, pretending that my marriage was good and we were happy. The chicks at the shop thought I was so lucky to have such a fine and successful man in my life. But if they only knew. Despite how much I faked the funk, we were in a miserable marriage. Yet still, I loved Demarco and I was so desperate to save what we had. Because of the resentment he harbored I sometimes didn't think it was possible.

His yelling snapped me out of my thoughts. "Get it right, Cashmere! You don't run me. I go as I please. I have always been my own man until I let myself get pussy whipped by you. But those days are over. And truthfully I don't want to be around you. I mean if you want to know the fucking truth, Cashmere! This shit is your fucking fault. Things between us will never be right. And you know why. If you had done one simple thing we wouldn't be like this."

"What was I supposed to do, Demarco?" I demanded.

"What did I ask you to do?" he raged.

When I didn't respond he got all up in my face. I was so hurt at how he was coming at me.

"Answer the fucking question, Cashmere!" He now had his hands gripped around my shoulders and he was shaking me.

I started crying and said, "Get your hands off me, motherfucker!"

"Man, I should slap the fuck out of you." He shoved me away. I lost my balance and fell on the floor. I just lay on the floor crying. It had no effect on him. It never did anymore. That made me hurt more.

Suddenly, his phone started ringing. He stepped over me and grabbed it off of the dresser top. "Hello?" He paused. "What's up, Dame?" He looked over at me in disgust, shook his head, and said, "Man, yeah, I can get out. Because this shit right here is for the birds. I got no time for it at all anymore." He paused. "All right, I'm heading out now. I'll meet you up there."

He grabbed his wallet and keys and shoved them along with his phone in his pants pocket.

"Where are you going?" I demanded. I got up from the floor.

"Bitch, your reign over me been gone a long time ago. Don't ever ask me what the fuck I do!"

He stepped past me like I was trash on the floor or dirty laundry that he didn't want his legs to touch.

Chapter 3

Dominique

Things between my parents were super weird. I tell you, I just didn't get why my daddy hated my mommy so much. But more importantly, I didn't get why he acted like he hated me. To tell the truth it seemed like it came from nowhere. When I brought it up to my mom she would tell me I was tripping. "Look at your baby pics and see the love in your father's eyes!" She would always shove a photo album in front of me, with pics of me as a baby with him and her in them. I don't know; that's just one thing I never saw in his eyes: love. But love was something my mother gave me in abundance. I knew my mother deeply loved me. She told me every day that I meant the world to her. Although my dad didn't pay me any mind; I might as well have been invisible. Even when I got good grades it meant nothing to him. I could also play the cello so good that my mom would come in my room, lie on my bed, and close her eyes and listen to me like she was at an actual concert. But my daddy never showed any interest. He wouldn't come to my concerts at school (so I stopped playing), or to any of my open houses, teacher conferences, or when I graduated from elementary or junior high school. Funny thing was I was a real good student. My teachers always said I was a joy to have. I knew my mother felt the same. I just wished my dad did as well; nothing meant more to me than having my father's love. I needed it. I would always remember my mother talking about how much her daddy loved her and how much he treated her like such a princess. I wished my daddy loved me like her daddy loved her. I would do all kinds of stuff to win him over. Like baking him cakes, to washing his car. When he would nap I would take off his shoes and socks and massage his feet. He would always wake up, look at me, jerk away, and snap, "Go play." Then finally, I gave up.

Despite my relationship with my father, our life was pretty decent. We lived in Inglewood, CA, in a nice and organized five-bedroom two-story house. My mom did hair for a living and, boy, was she super good at it. I was amazed at all the hairstyles my mom could do. My hair, which was long like my mother's, stayed nice. In fact, we looked a lot alike. I was dark like her with her set of gray eyes. Life was really simple. Our family was a triangle with me at the tip and and my mama and daddy at the base. I went to a private high school where I was pretty quiet. My mom said I was worse than a church mouse. I just wasn't a very social person. Sometimes other girls at school would pick on me or make fun of how quiet I was. I hated it and it made me even more closed off to people. I thought back to the last time a senior girl had shoved me down some stairs. I came home crying. The other two times she had put her hands on me, one time pulling my hair and the other time she smacked me, I kept it from my mother. But this time I couldn't. The fall had me limping. My mother, furious, called my grandmother and the next thing I knew we all drove in my mother's Cadillac Escalade to the school. The whole way there my mother drove like a bat out of hell. On the way there my grandmother urged, "Now, Cashmere, we are going to go in there and be ladies. No yelling or cursing; we are going to conduct ourselves with class."

Right.

When we got there, they cursed out the entire school office. "Why the fuck are you letting little bitches at this school bully my fucking grandchild?" my grandmother demanded. I wondered how her husband would feel about the way she was acting.

When the staff in the school office didn't respond, my mother spied the principal's office. "Come on." She pulled me with her and with my grandmother in tow, we walked directly into the principal's office. In a quick motion, my mother swiped all the items off his desk while my grandmother took a fighting stance waiting for the principal to react.

"Mrs. Pena."

"Shut the fuck up! Let me tell you something. My daughter don't bother anyone. So whoever the bitch is who put her hands on my daughter needs to get up in here now and there needs to be some type of corrective action. There are kids killing themselves because of bullies. So guess what, Principal? If my daughter slits her wrists because she getting picked on I'm going to come in this bitch and slit yours!" she threatened.

His eyes bulged. "I have spoken to—"

"Naw fuck that. Let's be clear, you pasty-face mother-fucker. We're not paying your punk ass seven hundred dollars a month in tuition for other girls to pick on my child. Come on, Dominique."

Needless to say the girl ended up being suspended and she never bothered me again.

When I got out of my shell and would visit my friend Jada's house, I saw how it was so different from my household. She actually had a close relationship with her dad that I wished to God I had with mine. In fact, I spent more time over there than I did at my own home. Jada had revealed to her father that my dad never really treated me with love. So I thought that was why he was so nice to me.

I stood on their doorstep and before I could knock Mrs. Douglas opened the door, prepared to step out but paused when she saw me.

"Hi, Mrs. Douglas."

She gave me a warm smile. Mrs. Douglas was the color of butterscotch. She was a very pretty woman in her forties with a petite frame and a bob that framed her face. My bestie, Jada, had the same haircut. But Jada looked more like her father.

"Hi, sweetness!" she said.

I stepped back and lowered my balled left fist that was about to knock on the door, to let her pass. Before she did she planted a kiss on one of my cheeks. Whenever I met adults, teachers, family members, and parents of my friends, they always tended to call me this. My mom as well always told me I was the sweetest kid in the world. I wondered if my daddy felt the same way. Probably not. It was crazy because I loved my mom 100 percent, my mommy seemed to love me 100 percent, and it seemed my daddy loved me 0 percent and hated me 100 percent.

"Jada's inside. You going to have to wake her behind up because I'm sure she fell right back to sleep." She walked past me down the steps. As she walked toward her Benz she turned back to me and said, "My hubby gave me some shopping money. I was surprised. That's a nice little treat this Saturday." She ended her sentence with a giggle and unlocked and opened her car door.

"I asked Jada if she wanted to go with us but she said she was too tired." She hopped in and closed the driver's door back.

"'Kay," I said with a smile.

She rolled her window down and backed out of the driveway. "See you later, honey."

I waved at her as she backed out of their driveway. She was such a nice woman and was always sweet to me. Made me feel a little bad about the secret I was keeping from her and Jada.

I turned and opened the door to their house and stepped inside the living room. I called out my friend's name. "Jada."

When she didn't respond I walked toward her room. I walked quickly and nervously. Once I made it to her door, my hand reached out for the knob. But before I could grasp it I felt two hands cup both of my breasts and felt a kiss planted on the side of my neck. I closed my eyes as pleasure and shame filled me.

"She's 'sleep. Don't wake her until we done," a husky voice said in my ear.

I was silent but I didn't pull away from Jada's father.

"Why didn't you come to my room, baby?" he asked me.

He spun me around and kissed my lips while rubbing one of his hands between my legs. "Has someone . . . ?" He gripped between my legs aggressively.

I shook my head.

"Good."

He yanked one of my arms gently and tugged me toward his bedroom.

I protested. "Mr. Douglas, I told you. I don't want to do this with you anymore. I feel bad about what I'm doing to your wife. It's wrong."

Still he was stronger and as a result managed to pull me into their bedroom, and closed and locked the door. Then I was at his mercy as my body betrayed me. But still I continued to tell him no as he peeled away my clothes.

As he did he said, "Mrs. Douglas don't give a fuck about what I do, pretty baby. She been checked out of this marriage. Now. You know I love you." When he had me naked, he sat down on their bed and sat me on top of his lap.

"This is wrong, Mr. Douglas. Please stop making me."

"Be quiet, baby," he told me gently. I gave in again. Despite the promises to make the last time the last time.

"If your daddy won't be a real father to you, you know I will," he always said to me. "You make love to me better than my wife ever could."

So I gave in all the way like I always did knowing I would feel guilty later.

I stared at Mr. Douglas. He was brown skinned with a black-and-white goatee. His head was completely bald. He stood six foot four so he towered over my five foot six frame. And he was ten years older than Mrs. Douglas so he was old enough to be my grandfather. Still it didn't stop him from taking my virginity about five months ago. He said he wanted to wait until I was a little older before taking it. And I had let him take it. I always let him take what he wanted despite the fact that I had promised myself I would no longer do this to Mrs. Douglas, to Jada, to myself. Thing was Mr. Douglas always showed me the love and attention my daddy never did. He made me feel so wanted that when he first started touching on me, when I was twelve, I didn't see it as wrong because he said it made him feel good. And I wanted to make him feel good because that was how he made me feel. And I felt it had to stop because I always walked away feeling shame. But I loved Mr. Douglas like he was my father. And the things he did to my body felt good. But it was hard to look Mrs. Douglas in the face anymore. And if Jada had a clue she would never forgive me and I would lose my best and only friend forever.

I stood and started grabbing my clothes when he asked, "How was school, baby?"

"It was okay I guess."

"How did you do on your test?" he asked

"I aced it," I said with a small smile.

"That's my girl." He sounded really proud of me. I went into his bathroom and washed up quickly. I then put on all my clothes and left his bedroom. Then, like I normally did, I waited in the living room and sat down on the couch like I just got there, and waited for Mr. Douglas to get dressed and go into Jada's room and wake her up.

A few minutes later Jada and I were watching music videos and laughing. Jada and I were so opposite. I was the shy, quiet one and she was the loud and wild one. A song came on by Young Money, "I Can Make Your Bed Rock." "That's my shit, girl." She got up and started dancing. She pulled me and forced me do it with her. "Come on with all that butt!" she joked. I laughed and copied the moves she did while she continued to hit me on my butt. I laughed. One slap was so hard I screeched and fell on the couch.

"Oh! I'm sorry!" She laughed and fell on top of me on the couch. She hugged me. "I didn't mean to hurt my bestie!" I giggled and hugged her back. I hoped nothing ever came between us; she was my only friend.

When she pulled away she said, "Hey, you know Nathan's boy Manny wants to holler. And, girl, he is super fine. Puerto Rican and black."

I shook my head. Mr. Douglas forbade me from having a boyfriend. I couldn't tell her this but I thought of another excuse. "I'm not ready to start dating."

"Why not? Come on, girl, you are no fun!"

"What's so fun about having a boyfriend?"

"Nate licked on my titties and the other day he finger banged me behind the gym." Her eyes were wide in emphasis.

If she only knew the things her father and I did.

Chapter 4

Dominique

My mom, as she normally did, made a really good meal for dinner. She made Fettuccini Alfredo with tender chunks of marinated chicken and big fat shrimps. She made broccoli spears and parmesan and garlic bread to go with it. My mom was such a great cook. She always took the extra step to make things good for my father and me. Instead of buying a bottle of already-made sauce from the grocery store my mother made hers homemade, mixing freshly grated parmesan cheese and heavy cream with real butter. Man, nothing compared to her Alfredo sauce. She would sauté her marinated chicken with Creole seasoning, onion, peppers, parsley, and garlic. She would then throw in the shrimp when the chicken was done. I knew all of this because since I was little, I would come in the kitchen and watch her cook. She ignored the phone and all distractions, even me. Well except for a few smiles and winks. Her marinara sauce took eight hours to make! I always asked her why she went through all the trouble and she would say, "I'm cooking with love, little girl. One day when you have a family you'll understand." My mom was the best. I 100 percent loved her. I smiled and watched her as she poured her melted butter concoction over the bread and placed it in the oven. But Daddy, he never seemed to appreciate how long my mother slaved over the oven to cook us meals after being on her feet all day.

Dinner today was like any other day. We ate in silence. Although the food was really good, I couldn't determine if my daddy liked it because he ate it with a frown on his face. When my mom tried to engage him in conversation he all but ignored her. When my mom rambled on about work and how this was the best the Alfredo sauce came out it got no response from him other than a shrug as he chewed on a broccoli spear. My mom looked my way but I was practically scared of my own shadow let alone trying to broach my daddy for conversation.

"How was school, D?" my mother asked me.

My dad gave me a sharp look that my mom saw. It made the plastered smile on my face waver a little bit.

"Good." I bit into my garlic bread. It was really good.

"And you went to Jada's house? What did you guys do?"

Flashbacks of Mr. Douglas passed before my eyes making me drop my fork. It fell on top of my plate with a loud clatter.

"Christ!" My dad shook his head at my clumsiness.

"I, ah . . . We watched some music. That's all."

My mom arched a brow at me.

"You can't watch music," my dad snapped.

"I mean music videos," I said nervously.

There was an awkward silence. Then my mother said, "Well I made homemade caramel pecan cake for dessert."

I gave a little clap making my mother laugh. My mother was also good at baking. To tell the truth, I didn't know what my mom was bad at besides not getting my daddy to be nice. He responded no way shape or form at the dinner table other than anger.

She waited for a reaction from him about the cake. He gave none at all, didn't even look her way.

"Let me get it for you guys." As my mom rose from the table and walked into the kitchen, I watched my dad wipe his mouth and drink the last of his grape juice and stand to his feet. I wanted to remind him about the cake my mother had made but when I said, "Daddy," he ignored me and continued out the dining room.

My mom walked back into the dining room. "Okay. Here this bad boy is." My mom proudly set the cake on the table, along with extra plates, a knife, and forks. When she looked up and saw Daddy was not at the table she instantly looked disappointed. Her whole face crumbled. And I knew she was holding back tears.

"The cake looks so good, Mom," I told her. I wanted to make her feel better.

"Thanks, D."

"Let's take our pieces in the living and watch TV, Mom," I suggested.

She gave me a half smile and nodded. I watched her cut us both a slice and place them on small plates. I went into the kitchen and poured us both glasses of milk then I followed her into the living room. But once we were seated in front of our sixty-inch flat-screen TV to watch the new version of *Sparkle,* my mother didn't eat a single bite of the cake. She just sat with a sad look on her face as I ate mine. To redirect her thoughts I asked, "Mom. How did you say you learned to bake so good?"

She managed to give me a chuckle. "I told you when I was about your age, I dated a guy whose family owned a bakery and we baked all sorts of goodies together." I always asked her this because no matter what she always had this far-off look with a blush, I guessed because she was thinking about the guy.

"Mommy, how come Daddy hates me so much?"

She closed her eyes briefly. "I think all his hatred is reserved for me."

"Mom. When I go over Jada's house, it's different. Jada and her father have a relationship. They spend time together, her talks to her, even gives her hugs and kisses. Jada's dad even shows me more attention than my own daddy does. I wish thing were different. I wish my daddy loved me, Mom."

"Daddy loves you, Dom."

"Mom, I really don't think that he does."

"Your dad is just dealing with a lot of things right now. He's at odds with the both of us. Eventually he will come up out of this."

I used to believe that he did. But for so many years it had been like this. I didn't want to tell my mother but I didn't believe Daddy would ever change. He would always hate me. But why?

"Did I do something wrong to him?"

"No, and your daddy does love you. Who wouldn't love Dom?" She tickled me under my chin and pecked me on one of my cheeks making me smile. And that was the end of the discussion.

Chapter 5

Cashmere

I tried my best to keep my patience as I listened to my mother run her mouth on the phone. So many years had passed after all the stuff that had happened to me. I mean, we were cool. The thing was I was never super close to my mother anyhow. I was a daddy's girl. Always had been. There was nothing like a father's love. So I felt so bad for Dom that she couldn't experience with Demarco the love my father had showered on me. Truth was, Demarco was taking his anger out on Dominique and me. He was also dealing with his issues with an open bottle at every opportunity. I couldn't relate to how my child felt because I had always gotten love from my daddy. My mom loved me but growing up with her, she was too infatuated with material things. And even though Demarco and I made good money it never really meant shit to me.. So my mother and I never related and never had much in common. But we were cool. We had managed over the years to get along somewhat. Since we had reunited when I was eighteen she had consistently been there for me when I needed her. She was a decent grandmother as well, although her idea of being a good granny was showering Dominique with expensive-ass gifts, teaching her how to be superficial and materialistic, and getting on my damn nerves every few minutes. But I will say that at the drop of a hat, she was always willing to be there should I or Dominique need her.

But today, she was asking for too gotdamned much, as she babbled on about the importance of family and forgiving since she was now a devout Christian and all. Her conversation was agitating the fuck out of me.

"Cash? Are you listening to me?"

"Yeah, Ma."

"Now, honey. You know your aunt had this planned and you agreed with me over a month ago that you would come. I'm not sure why today is the day you are trying to get out of it. Yes, my sister is not the nicest person. But that breast cancer really changed her. She even started going to church with me. And she personally invited you, Demarco, and Dom."

I watched Dominique walk into my room. I was pretty sure she could hear my conversation. I was too pissed off to care.

My mother just didn't understand. Truth was, I knew my mother was right. I should have forgiven my aunt. But I couldn't. I also didn't want to be around her fat ass. At the age of thirteen, I was a baby! And she was the only family I had left. She put me out in the streets. I just couldn't help but think that if she hadn't done that to me I would have never been taken by my sister, Desiree, drugged, raped, and then pimped out by Black Mitchell. I knew what my sister had done to my aunt was wrong. But that was what my sister did. I didn't have anything at all to do with Desiree sleeping with her husband.

I looked at my own daughter who sat on my bed and stared at me. She was innocent, precious. A baby. And that's what I was when I was thirteen and my innocence was taken from me and my aunt could have prevented all of that. Her jealousy and insecurity prevented this. Instead of accepting the fact that she had a dirty, nasty-ass husband she instead turned her back on her niece. And as a result I suffered mercilessly. It could have all been prevented. Yes, I was now in my thirties but the scars from what I had endured were still intact.

There were times where I still had nightmares from being out in those streets and I woke up either screaming or crying, or simply couldn't go back to sleep. In the past Demarco would hold me, stroke my hair, kiss my cheek, and tell me I was safe. But eventually he would just turn over in disgust. Despite this I knew I was supposed to forgive, to get past it, and I had, to a small, small, certain degree. But I just didn't want to be in my aunt's presence. Or her bastard husband's.

But when my mom kept rambling I said, exasperated, "All right! I'll go. Damn!" I ended the call and looked at my child. "Go get dressed and do your hair."

"Okay, Mom." My daughter obediently got up and went to her room.

It was now January and still winter so I pulled on a long-sleeved top, a pair of skinny jeans, and a pair of Uggs. I tossed my hair back in a ponytail. I hoped my aunt's bitch ass didn't trip and I hoped if she did I would be able to keep it together. But who knew, maybe she really did change. If she did then I was sure I could completely let the past go and try to build a relationship with her. And even hopefully my child could be close to her great-aunt. After all we didn't have much family out here and all in all I realized long ago that family was important.

Chapter 6

Dominique

I had put on a long-sleeved shirt, a pair of skinny jeans, and the new Jordans my mother had bought for me for Christmas. My hair like my mother's was thrown back in a ponytail. My mother played the new Marsha Ambrosia album as we drove to my aunt's house. I liked it. She had a pretty voice. My mom looked at me as "With You" played and busted up laughing as I had my eyes closed, singing along with Marsha. I giggled along with my mother.

"Seems like just yesterday you were obsessed with Miley Cyrus, Justin Bieber, and Raven-Symoné's music."

I laughed as well. When the song switched to "Far Away" it instantly changed from a happy mood in the truck to a sadder one and by the bridge, "And every minute you're gone I'm missing you so / I can't believe that you're far away," my mother looked so sad. I knew why. I didn't have to ask. The song brought her back to Daddy. It had to. And even though he wasn't far away, meaning she saw him on a regular basis, it seemed like he was because he was so distant from her. I saw it so I knew she had to see it and feel it.

Once we got there, I watched my mom park behind my grandmother's Porsche truck and turn off the ignition before taking a deep breath.

As my grandmother made her way toward the car she waved happily. I waved back but my mother ignored her.

"You okay, Mom?"

"Not really but come on, baby."

We both unsnapped our seat belts and got out of my mother's Escalade truck.

My grandmother may have been in her fifties but she looked easily like she was in her thirties. She wore a weave that came down to her butt and had her nose and belly button pierced. She was very pretty, and curvy like my mother, and stylish. She carried the Gucci and Louie Bags and even wore red bottoms. She had bought me Michael Kors, Louie, and Gucci bags. Once we went shopping, I told her that girls at my school wore Coach bags and shoes, and she said Coach was for hood rats and refused to purchase any Coach items for me. Every gift that came from my grandmother was name brand. Even down to socks. She told me for my eighteenth birthday she was going to take me red bottom shoe shopping. "Every girl must have a pair of red bottoms, sweet girl. And I'll make sure you get them." My grandmother was really something else. But I always felt that the relationship between my grandmother and mother was a little strained. Often my mother seemed like she hated my grandmother. But it seemed like all the relationships around me for some reason were. They knew the truth; I didn't. But I loved my grandmother. She was always kind and nurturing toward me.

"Hey!" My grandmother rushed up to my mother and gave her a hug and kiss on one of her cheeks. "Hey, Dom Dom!" She then hugged me tightly, pulled away, and kissed me on the cheek as well. Then she looked me up and down hitting me on my butt. "Girl, you are too skinny to have all of that booty!"

I blushed as she smoothed out my ponytail and puckered her lips and blew air kisses at me. "I tell you, you should, just like Cashmere, be thanking me that you got all my good looks and curves." She bent closer to my ear and said, "I would say you got something else good from me too. But I'm a lady of Christ and can't speak like that! But Cash knows very well what I'm speaking of." She then clapped her hands together and cracked up laughing making my mother roll her eyes at her.

Just then my grandfather, Hank, walked toward us. "Hi, ladies," he said.

"Hey, Hank," my mom said. He kissed my mother on one of her cheeks.

"Hey, Grandpa." I said. He kissed me on one of my cheeks as well

"Hey, sweetheart." Although my grandfather and my grandmother moved out here I had to admit that I saw my grandfather more when they lived in Lancaster. But my grandmother was always coming around but my mom always acted like she didn't wanna be bothered by her. My grandfather was distant. But I wished my daddy treated me like my grandfather treated me. He also had his real grandkids and I knew he wasn't my blood grandfather.

"Now let's go inside. I heard she had this catered so the food should be really good."

"I'm sure," my mother mumbled. My grandmother held on to one of my hands and we all walked to my great-aunt's house.

Once inside I sat down next to my mother on one of the couches. I was glad I had worn a pair of pants because the couches were covered in plastic. I looked around the room. The thing that was weird was the fact that there really were no people there. The only one I saw was my aunt's husband, Bryon. I had met him only a few times. My mother pretended she didn't even see him as he came our way. My mother looked at him in disgust as he hugged on my grandmother while Hank put a gift on the dining room table.

I gasped when one of his hands grazed my grandmother's backside. "Don't play, motherfucker," she whispered as she sashayed away.

My eyes were now wide. My mother gave him a look as he had his arms outstretched for her.

"Cashmere, all grown up and beautiful! Hot damn!"

"Hello," was all my mother had gotten out dryly. She stood next to where I sat.

He then turned to me. "Little Dominique. Looking all fine just like your mama."

"Moth . . ." my mom bit off.

"I'm just giving you ladies a compliment. I know how you get, don't trip. *Respecto* baby. Trust."

"Cool," my mother said dryly.

"Hi." I gave him a small smile.

My mother smiled at my shyness.

That's when we all heard, "Hey! Hey! Hey!"

"The lady of the hour is here!" Bryon yelled.

I watched my great-aunt come into the living and pose in the center of the room. Bryon rushed over to a boom box and pressed a button. "The Wobble" came on loudly in the room. I watched my aunt do the steps; she was incredibly off. My mom mumbled, "Are you fucking serious?"

"Hey!" my aunt yelled as her and her husband struggled to do the steps.

I watched my grandma join in and pop her butt up and down. Bryon's eyes stayed on it while he danced with his wife.

After a few minutes and my aunt was out of breath, Bryon cut the music and my aunt said hello to my mother and me. "Hi, Cashmere," my great-aunt said.

My mom gave a mere nod.

I didn't miss the exchange of hatred between the two of them.

She then turned to me. I hadn't been around my aunt too many times growing up. Only at a few gatherings at my grandmom's house and at her anniversary party. So I can't say that I was all too comfortable around her.

"Well hello, Miss Dominique. I would say you look like your mom but you don't."

"You wish *you* looked liked me," my mother snapped.

Before my aunt could reply my grandmother whisked her sister away. "Now let me see your new crystal."

"Okay," my aunt said seeming unnerved by the comment.

As they stared in the wooden cabinet at all the objects my grandmother stood like she was transfixed and said, "Wow. This stuff is just beautiful."

"My mom needs to knock that shit off," my mother mumbled to me.

I stifled a giggle.

"What's the value of it now?" my grandmother asked.

"Well last time I did my inventory it was up to two thousand."

"That is just amazing," Grandmother said, which was strange to me because my grandmother had purses that cost more. It seemed like she was being a little fake. But my mother said that they never really got along so they were trying to mend their relationship because of my aunt's last bout with cancer.

When we sat down to eat the fried rice and gummy orange chicken I noticed my great-aunt continued to give my mom menacing looks, as she chewed the food distastefully. I mean it was gross but my mother made it very obvious that it was while we all played it off.

"I thought this shit was catered," she mumbled to my grandmother.

My grandmother gave Cashmere a stern look.

"How y'all like the food? I had it specially catered," my aunt chimed in. It was funny no one else was there besides us although it was supposed to be a party.

"She know damn well this shit is from that Chinese takeout down the street," my mom told my grandmother.

"Problem, Cashmere?" my great-aunt asked.

"I didn't say shit," Mama said.

"Yes, you did. Say what you gotta say, Cashmere."

My mom stared her down. Then she started laughing at her.

"And just what the hell is so funny?"

"You."

"Cashmere. Stop," my grandmother whispered. But it was like no one was at the table except my great-aunt and my mother. And my mom seemed like she has some stuff to get off of her chest.

"Do you really believe that you have more worth than a pile of shit?" my mother demanded of my aunt.

My grandmother placed a hand over my mother's and slyly pinched her hand.

"Why yes. I do. I have a husband I've been married to for over thirty years."

"Who is less than a pile of shit."

That got my aunt. It seemed like she took more offense to Cashmere insulting her husband than insulting her. My mom always said that no one was able to talk about Bryon the bastard but her. I remember hearing her tell my grandma that.

"Little girl. You may be cute, live in a big house, and have a Mexican husband but we all know at this fucking table that you living a lie."

Then my aunt turned and looked pointedly at me. My mom looked my way nervously.

"I don't have to throw insults, Cash! Alls I got to do is tell the truth. Matter fact, why don't you tell her the truth about her life? Or are you gonna keep her in suspense? Like y'all mama did?"

My mother stood to her feet, rattling the table. "Hey, Aunt. Shut the fuck up! One titty or not I won't hesitate to lay hands on your fat ass."

"I wish you would."

"That's it!"

I gasped when my mother lunged across the table and wrapped her hands around my aunt's throat. Plates and glasses fell to the floor.

"Cashmere, stop!" my grandmother yelled. She grabbed her arms in a tight squeeze until she released her hold on my great-aunt's neck. My grandma pulled her completely off the table. My mother yanked away from her and walked a few feet away from the table.

My aunt held her neck furiously.

"Catch, motherfucker!" My mom picked a plate off the floor and flung it at my uncle Bryon. It hit him in the side of his head then fell on top of the table.

"Bitch!" My aunt stood but my grandmother shoved her back in her seat.

"Come on, Dominique!" My mother grabbed one of my arms practically snatching me from the chair and yanking me away from the table.

"You ain't shit, Cashmere; and, little girl, if you ever want to know the truth about your life come and see me!"

"Don't listen to her, Dom. Shut the fuck up!" my mom yelled in rage as she raced out of there. I had to run to keep up with her.

Once we got to my mother's truck she unlocked the door and we both hopped inside. My grandmother ran outside to my mother's window. My mom rolled her windows down and said, "I'm never coming back to that bitch's house. And don't you ever fucking ask me to!"

Before my grandmother could respond my mom sped off.

The drive was really quiet and my mother looked so mad I was scared to say anything to her. But I did want to know what my aunt was talking about when she said if I want to know the truth about my life. I mean I loved my mother to death. She was the best. Surely she was not hiding anything from me. But why would my aunt even say what she said? Then I thought back to my mom saying that my aunt was shady and unhappy. Then I reminded myself of how great my mom was. I came to the conclusion that my aunt was just trying to be mean. You didn't have to be young to be messy. And plus that was my only second time being around my aunt. But I was around my mother all the time. I had no reason to question her as a person. If there was something my mother kept from me I was sure it was for a good reason. Not for anything bad like my aunt was trying to imply at that table. My aunt was probably jealous that my mom was so beautiful and had the best of everything.

So when my mom turned to me and said, "Listen, about what she said . . ." I simply placed my hand on her free hand and said, "Mom it's okay. You don't have to explain. I just know that she is one mean lady."

I saw my mom breathe a sigh of relief. Then she said, "Yes, she is. Okay."

"I'm so lucky you know how to cook, too."

To that my mom tossed her head back and laughed. "Speaking of food what do you want to eat for dinner? Because I know for a fact that I am hungry."

"Don't matter, Mommy." I gave her a soft smile and she stroked my right cheek before driving on a green light.

"Let's get some fried fish, shrimp, and some oysters for Demarco. He's over at the shop in Compton today."

My mother drove to Rosecrans and pulled into the driveway of Central Fish Market. We went inside hand in hand. Not like mother and daughter but like best friends. I giggled and kept up with her, happy that my mother's anger at what just happened had washed away.

When we got to the counter a brown-skinned chick with very slanted eyes ended her call and looked at us with a smile on her face. "What can I . . . Cashmere?"

"Yes?" my mom said confused.

"You don't remember me?"

"No, sorry. I can't say that I do. I do hair so I see a lot of faces daily."

"Two words: Black Mitchell."

At those two words my mother's face got flushed and she started stuttering. She looked at me fearfully and said, "Dominique, go sit in the car. I'll be out when the food is done."

"Okay, Mommy," I said obediently. She tossed me the keys and the lady scanned my face quickly before her eyes widened. I smiled at her, looked away, and I started walking toward the door like my mom said.

Once in the car, I saw my mother carry on a quick conversation with her before sitting down. But my mother seemed uncomfortable.

Once she came back to the truck with the food she had a troubled look on her face. My mom set the containers of food on the back seat and sat in the driver's seat. As she snapped her seat belt I asked curiously, "Mom, who's Black Mitchell?"

"A man from my past. Dom, I'm not trying to keep you in the dark but you just have to trust that there are some things you don't need to know now. You're too young. But when you are older I will tell you, I promise."

"Mom, you don't need to promise. I believe you. If there is something you don't feel I need to know now I trust you on it."

"Aw, girl, you are just too sweet." She winked at me and I blushed.

She turned on the ignition and pulled out of the restaurant. "Now let's go surprise Daddy and take him some food."

Chapter 7

Cashmere

I knew I should have gone with my first mind and not have gone to my aunt's event. One thing was for sure. My aunt had not changed and she was a messy, miserable bitch. I was glad that I had gotten my daughter out of there before she played dirty and spilled the beans about my past just to entertain herself. The last thing I wanted was for Dominique to know about my past: my drug addiction, the cutting issue, or the prostitution. Hell, I didn't even want her to know the facts that surrounded my sister's death. I wanted to keep my daughter sheltered. When she was older and an adult then I would tell her. But not now. And seeing the lady in the fish market was also a close call. That was Meka. She was one of Black's prostitutes when me and my sister worked for him. I was just glad she didn't spill the beans on another secret. Maybe it was a bad idea to even come back here. One thing was for sure, if I did ever come back I wouldn't bring my baby. I put in the new Frank Ocean CD as Dominique requested and drove toward the shop in Compton.

Demarco said he was going to be at the Compton shop fixing some things that would take all day. But when I pulled up to surprise him with the food I noticed his car wasn't there. *Weird.* Then I thought maybe he stepped out to get something. "I'll be right back, Dom. Sit tight." I hopped out and walked inside.

I waved to all the ladies doing hair and walked into Bev's little office. Yep, she was still working there and was like a second mom to me. I love Bev to death. I walked in her office. She was adding something up on a calculator. "Hey, babe!"

"Hey, Bev." My voice didn't have the happiness hers had in it. Casually I asked so she didn't suspect anything was wrong, "Has Demarco been here today?"

"No, girl. I haven't seen him in a couple days, matter fact."

I blinked rapidly. He had said he was there yesterday as well.

"Give me one second, Cash. Don't leave. I want to speak to you anyway."

"Okay." I sat in the chair across from hers. She walked out of the office. While I waited for her, I texted Demarco and asked him where he was.

He texted me back: At the shop in Compton. Why?

My heart sank. I just didn't get why he would lie to me. I was convinced more than ever now that he was fucking someone else. I wondered if he loved her. Looked at her the way he used to look at me. Kissed her the way he used to kiss me with passion. Now all I seemed to get from him was a courtesy fuck. Where he seemed to have to get drunk to even touch me. It was always quick and awkward, cold, if he could get it up. And I never said anything. And thinking of him with another woman made me ache. Sad part was it didn't for a second, for an ounce, stop me from loving or wanting Demarco. Yep, I was fucking pathetic.

Bev walked back into the room interrupting my thoughts. She took one look at my troubled face and said, "Uh-oh. Is everything okay?"

I had known Bev since I was eighteen. I knew I could trust her but not with this. I didn't want to speak my worries. It just might make them worse. All in all I didn't want to think the worst of Demarco, either. I mean I had my suspicions but really what woman didn't? Especially with the problems we were having.

"Bev, I'm cool. Just tired."

"Well you gotta stop stressing, Cash. How you gonna give that man another baby if you always stressed out? When he does come in here he's wearing the same face you wearing now. What's going on with you two? I remember when you guys used to be so happy together. Seems like that was so long ago. I can't remember the last time I saw you or him smile. I thought marriage would make it better."

I gave a tight smile. "I know, Bev. I'm just going through so . . ." I turned my back on her so she couldn't see the tears in the corner of my eyes.

"I can tell. But I wish you two weren't. You used to have a beautiful thing. Don't forget about that. Fight for it."

I wiped my face as the tears trickled down. I couldn't stop them. Nor the sob that racked my shoulders. Damn I missed what we used to have so much.

"You can fix this, Cash. No doubt."

I couldn't even look back at her. Because I had serious doubts that I could. "I'll talk to you later, Bev." I waved with my back still to her and walked out of the shop with my head down so no one could see I had just finished crying.

Chapter 8

Dominique

I stopped by Jada's house after school and again found myself in Mr. Douglas's bed. He did the things to me that always felt so good. I wondered if I'd ever be able to break away from him.

When we were done he held me and said, "Damn, baby, you really needed to relieve some stress. What's going on? Anything you want to talk about?"

Truthfully there were some things I wanted to talk about. Like what my aunt had said at her dinner party. Why my mother was so angry at her. I know she didn't like her. But was there something more that my mother wasn't telling me? Was there some secret she was holding over my mother's head? Yes, I knew that I had said that I would trust my mother but as more days went by I found myself curious. I wondered what he would think of it.

But as I talked Mr. Douglas did what he did. I wondered if he was fully listening. Wasn't no real way to tell until we were done. Because then I'd have his full attention.

As his hands gripped me I closed my eyes to the pleasure, pain, and shame. I heard Mr. Douglas groan.

Then out of nowhere he shouted, "Jada!"

My eyes shot open and before I could do anything, she grabbed me by my ponytail and slung me off of her father to the floor. I peered up from the floor and watched my best friend look at me and her father hatefully.

"Yeah, y'all thought y'all was gonna get away with this again. You not slick, Daddy. This time you must have forgot to drug me so you can do it to my best friend. I just so happened to walk in the kitchen and saw you! So I didn't eat that! When you went to let her in I snuck in your closet. I wish I had remembered to get my phone and record it!"

Mr. Douglas scrambled into his boxers.

"I'm calling Mom! And when she get here, Dominique, she gonna beat your ass!" Jada ran into her room at a fast pace.

By the time Mr. Douglas had his boxers on and raced to her room it was already locked. Still he beat on the door. "Honey."

After a few seconds I heard Jada's door open and her yell, "Daddy! I can't believe you cheating on my mama with my best friend."

Jada was now standing in the bedroom doorway with Mr. Douglas next to her. She entered the room as I reached for my dress but was stopped by Jada who rushed toward me and kicked me in my head with a booted foot. I moaned low in my throat scared to make a sound although in pain and fell back to the floor.

"Jada, stop!" Mr. Douglas said.

"Don't tell me what to do, Daddy!" she spewed hatefully. "Get out of here! Matter fact don't. My mom called her two brothers and they on the way to fuck you up for cheating on her! Daddy, I hate you."

Mr. Douglas looked fearful at this point. He dressed in a rush and retreated toward the door. Jada tried to block and he shoved her out of the way. I sat up fearfully.

"Yeah, he got away but not you."

"Jada, please," I whispered with tears in my eyes. My heart was pounding and I couldn't stop shaking.

"Bitch, don't talk to me!" She grabbed my face between her hands and started pummeling me on top of my head.

That's when I heard yelling from the living room. It was a woman's voice and men. Next I heard Mr. Douglas's voice and he was howling while Mrs. Douglas continued to shout at him.

A few minutes later Mrs. Douglas came in to the room. "Where is that little slut?" I heard her yell.

I didn't bother going for the door because Jada was blocking it. Mrs. Douglas walked in and before I could even take a second breath they both commenced whipping on me. A man came into the room and put me in the full nelson while Mrs. Douglas attacked me, throwing a series of punches.

"You fucking bitch! I let you in my house and you got the nerve to be fucking my husband!"

At the reminder of what I had done, Jada spit in my face. The man holding me elbowed me in my side so hard I couldn't breathe for a second and slid to the floor. I closed my eyes and curled up into a ball as her and her mother tag teamed me. Seemed like forever that they beat on me. My right eye was swollen shut to the point I couldn't see out of it. My nose was bloody and my lip was not only busted but there were several knots on the inside of my lips. Jada continued to pull and tug at my hair with all her might until strands were caught in her fingers and off my scalp. I cried and took it all, not just because I was scared to fight back but because I knew I deserved it. When they were done, Mrs. Douglas said, "Bitch, now get the fuck out of my house and don't ever come back around here! When I see your mom I'm fucking her up on sight just because she had a ho-ass daughter like you!"

I nodded and Jada gave one final kick to my back. At that I took off running out of the house. I cried all the way to my house.

I wanted to say sorry. I wanted get down on my knees and beg Jada and her mom to forgive me. Jada was my only friend and I felt bad for hurting her. But I simply ran from their house all bloodied and bruised.

Chapter 9

Cashmere

I sat in the living room and took a deep breath. Dame, Demarco's friend, had come over to fix the toilet. In all actuality I had dropped one of my hair clips in the toilet and flushed it, messing up the toilet, and I had called Demarco and made it seem like a big deal in hopes he would come home and maybe we could spend some time together and even talk about us and making our "us" better. But when I called him he huffed out an impatient breath like I was bothering him and said Dame would come over and fix it. I couldn't say anything to that because if I said never mind he would know I had bullshitted, and the hair clip really did mess up the toilet. Dame brought his snake and unclogged it in a matter of minutes.

I also had still not confronted Demarco about how he had lied about being at the shop in Compton. I didn't want to make him mad; and, I really didn't want to know what his answer was because it would hurt me.

After Dame fixed the sink he came and sat down next to me and we started chatting. He like everyone else noticed how unhappy I was looking. Dame had been close to Demarco for a long time. He worked with Demarco at all the shops. He fixed any maintenance issues we had. So when he sat down next to me I knew I should have told him to leave but I was so down and out I started speaking on the issues Demarco and I had. For me there was nothing like

being able to talk to a man. I mean this is what I missed
all these years about no longer having a father. But with
Demarco I never felt any sort of void. Because he filled
every void that I had. At one point he was the best.

After I talked his ear off about our problems, Dame
listened patiently and said, "Well, Cashmere, I don't
think Demarco hates you," he assured me. "The man is
just stressed is all. The best thing you can do in this situation is give him some space. He's a Pisces. He'll come
around. Just continue to be the good and fine woman
you are, Cashmere. Don't turn your back on him. 'Cause I
notice you kinda been letting yourself go lately. Like right
now for instance, your hair not combed and you need
a manicure. Come on. A woman can't slip up on stuff
like that. You be whipping those girls up at the shop and
neglecting yourself. There is always someone willing to
take over for you. It's fucked up but it just is what it is."

I chuckled despite the situation. But I swallowed as
I mulled over the last of his comment, about another
woman willing to take my spot. Hell I believed it.

"But I will say that Demarco not dumb. He has a fine-
ass woman and he is not trying to lose that by fucking
around."

"Are you sure?" I asked hoping he would confirm my
hope that he wasn't.

"No. He is drinking a little more and he don't want you
to know about that because you know how you women
nag."

I chuckled again.

"But that man ain't fucking around. After dealing with
all that bullshit with those bitches at the shops who wo—"

The living room burst open and Dominique ran into
the living room and threw herself into my arms sobbing.

I screamed when I lifted her face and saw it all bruised
and bloodied. "Dominique! What happened to you?" I
demanded.

She wouldn't speak, just buried her head in my chest like a small child who had just seen a monster. I pulled her face out of my chest and demanded of her again, "What happened? Who did this shit?" My eyes started tearing up at seeing my child all bruised. Dame even asked and she wouldn't respond.

"Dominque." I shook her gently. "Who?"

Silence.

I stood and pulled her to her feet. "Tell me!"

She closed her good eye and whispered, "Jada and her mom."

"What! Let's go!"

"No, Mom. Mrs. Douglas's brothers are there."

"I don't give a fuck." I paused, took a deep breath. "I'm calling your father." I grabbed my phone and dialed his number and got no answer. I even texted him that it was an emergency and he didn't respond. A few seconds later he called back.

"I need you to come home. Dominique was attacked."

He paused, took a deep breath, and said, "I'm busy! You handle it." Before I could respond he hung up.

I swore silently and pulled my daughter with me toward my living room door. Adrenaline was pumping through me so I ignored Dame as he called my name.

"I'm coming with y'all," he said.

Chapter 10

Dominique

When we were on their doorstep, I stood back as my mother walked up the steps, to the door, ignoring Dame, who asked what she was about to do.

To his question she mumbled, "He will see."

My eyes were wide and my heart pounded in my chest.

"Times like this I wish my sister were still alive. I know she would do some serious damage with me," my mother said. She banged on the door until Mrs. Douglas opened it. Before she could say anything my mother yanked her out of the house.

I watched as my mother put a serious beating on Mrs. Douglas while Uncle Dame stood back and laughed. I knew he was waiting to see if another man would come back out and intervene. But I guessed her brothers had both left because no one came out to stop Mrs. Douglas from the butt kicking my mother effortlessly gave to her. A beating that made me feel bad because it truly was my fault. I had deceived Jada and her mother. They were nothing but nice to me and I had been foul to the both of them. Now my mother was taking a risk of going to jail to avenge me. I didn't deserve her to take those kinds of risk. Not when I caused this.

But what was funny, not in a comedic way but in a weird way, was that Mrs. Douglas was so powerful when she and Jada had attacked me. But now she looked so powerless as my mother continued to assault her. I mean my mother gave it to her good. Then Jada flew out the door. My mother spun around just in time and slammed Mrs. Douglas to the ground. She landed in a sharp thud and she struggled to get up. As she struggled to get up, Jada rushed toward my mother. My mother simply took Jada and tossed her. "You better get the fuck on," my mother threatened Jada. Jada got up and continued toward her. My mother took her by her hand and flung her onto the pavement. Jada screamed out in pain. Mrs. Douglas made her way to her feet again and lunged toward my mother. My mother took a fighting stance. "Come on. I'm ready for you, hoe!" my mom said.

I looked away as Mrs. Douglas took another ass whipping from my mother. Soon Mrs. Douglas backed away from my mother and said while panting, "You. You don't know what that little bitch did."

My mother ran up on her again and smacked her in the face. "Her name is Dominique. Nothing could have been worth you putting your hands on my child and hitting her like she is grown. She is thirteen!"

"She's been sleeping with my husband!"

From the corner of my eye I saw my father approaching.

At Mrs. Douglas's comment, my mother went after Mrs. Douglas again. "Lying bitch!"

"Cashmere!"

My dad ran forward and grabbed my mother by one of her arms before she could assault Mrs. Douglas further.

I shook my head fearfully as my mother cast a look my way. She tried to snatch away from Daddy but he held her firmly. "Stop this shit before you get arrested!" he yelled at her.

"She has been!" Jada yelled.

My mother ignored him. "Fuck y'all and your lies. My daughter not sleeping with your husband. Stay the fuck away from my daughter."

My daddy snatched my mother and pulled her until she started walking on her own. "Shut the fuck up!" he ordered.

My mother's eyes bore into his as he pulled her out of the yard but she said nothing. My mother turned to look at me.

"Come on, Dominique," Dame said. He put his arms around my shaking shoulders and I walked back with him to the house.

When we made it home Dame left and my father went off on my mother while she cleaned up my bruises. He continued to go in on her as she cooked dinner.

"What the fuck is wrong with you, Cashmere? You not a kid anymore. You a grown-ass woman with a kid and you running around putting your hands on somebody."

My mother paused on the chicken she was rinsing off. "Did you take the time to look at Dom's face? Shit, while you going off on me."

My dad walked up to my mom and shoved her into the sink. "I don't know who the fuck you think you talking to, bitch, but you better watch you motherfucking mouth."

Instantly my mother's eyes got watery at how rude he had just treated her. But instead of standing up for herself she hung her head in shame.

"I'm not those bitches in the street. Shut the fuck up talking to me like that." His voice raised an octave. "Got it?"

My mother wiped her tears away and turned back to the chicken. "All I was saying is Dominique got beat up pretty bad and I'm not buying that Dominique slept with her husband. Dominique is only thirteen. She is innocent. Why would she do some shit like that?"

"Look. I got a lot on my mind. I don't have time to worry about what Dominique do and don't do."

"But—"

"Period point blank. Now I gotta get back to handling real business."

As strong as my mother had been with Mrs. Douglas and Jada, she looked so weak now with my daddy. But I was weak all the time so who was I to judge? I walked up the stairs and went into my room. I lay on my bed and cried. I knew sooner or later what I had done would catch up with me. And now I had lost my only friend. I cried into my pillow feeling horrible.

Chapter 11

Cashmere

Demarco stayed gone for two days. And for every bit of those two days I blew his phone up. He never answered though. It made me sick to my stomach. Maybe he was leaving me for good now. That after all these years he had finally had enough of me. The thought of that brought more tears to my eyes. I didn't go to work for those two days but I did call all the shops nonstop to see if he had gone to any of them. He hadn't. I was such a wreck that I continued to call Dame nonstop. He would be cool and always pick up. But he really couldn't do anything for me. The only person who could change things was Demarco. Matters of the heart could fuck you up, boy. 'Cause my ass could not get out of the bed, period point blank. I had no appetite at all and always a sinking feeling in my stomach. My mother had to come over and take Dominique to school. Good thing she was a big girl and could heat up a frozen pizza. Literally every other second I was dialing his number.

I cried my eyes out in my bed wanting to throw my phone into the wall. That's when I heard my mother knock and without permission come into my room.

"Hey, Cash, you feeling better?"

Dominique was with her. I turned my back to her and wiped my face before turning back around in my bed to face her. Before responding, I told Dominique, "Go do your homework."

"Mom, you okay?" Dom asked.

"Yes, I am."

"Okay, I'll check on you again. Soon." She walked out.

My mother closed the door and sat on my bed next to me. "Is this about Demarco?"

"Yes. He hasn't been home in two days and I don't know if he is dead or alive." Despite not wanting to divulge the problems I told her anyway. "I don't know what to do."

My mother huffed out an impatient breath.

"That's all you have to say, Mom?"

"Honey, you don't want to hear what I have to say 'cause if you want my help just know I'm going to pray that nigga out your life."

"Yeah? And why the fuck would you do that?"

"Because. Look. I don't know where you get this shit from, Cash. One thing about me is I always keeps it moving. When a man acts up he ain't got to wait around for me to bounce. I'm gone. I don't take no shit. I'm too pretty and too good of a woman. You are too. I don't know where you got this low self-esteem from. How many years are you going to take Demarco's bullshit? He don't want you and he don't love you, Cash. You got to let this shit go. What, you think you deserve this treatment?"

I sat up in the bed and pierced my mother with a hateful look. "Well I'm sorry if my self-esteem is so low that I won't leave Demarco. Maybe if I weren't raped, drugged, and prostituted as a teen then maybe just maybe my motherfucking self-esteem would be as high as yours!"

"Here you go throwing that in my face again. I have said sorry to you countless times and you keep bringing it up. If you forgave me for abandoning you and your sister years ago then you shouldn't bring it up now. Cashmere, all I'm saying is you don't deserve to be treated this way.

You want me to agree with how you're handling this and I'm not. The marriage is a mess plain and simple. It is not going to get better. You need to divorce Demarco bottom line."

The sound of that word, "divorce," caused a sharp intake of breath in me. The thought of divorcing Demarco made the pit of my stomach twist and turn to the point where I thought I was going to throw up on my bed. The thought of leaving Demarco was worse than the pain I was feeling because of how he was treating me. She just didn't get that!

"You know what, Mom, just get the fuck out!"

"See how you talk to me? When I'm only showing concern. What y'all going through shouldn't affect the respect you have for me. I'm your mother."

"I lost respect for you long ago and never quite got it back," I bit out hatefully. I knew I was wrong for speaking to my mother that way but I needed to lash at her so she would leave and stop telling me what I didn't need or want to hear: the truth. But I swallowed an apology and turned my back on her.

"Fuck it then," she mumbled. "I'll go home to my husband where I'm appreciated."

I didn't bother to respond. Just waited for her to get out my room and close the door behind her.

I texted Demarco and asked him where he was and he texted back: Where I'm at. I cried more tears and through my phone. Images with him with another woman popped into my head. I wanted to escape the pain I was feeling. I went into the bathroom, pulled out my NyQuil, and chugged down a capful so that I could go to sleep. That was the only thing that would stop the pain I was feeling: sleep or death.

***

The doorbell ringing woke me out of my NyQuil slumber. Feeing groggy, I slid out of my bed and walked out of the room, downstairs to the living room. I hoped it was Demarco and that he had maybe lost his key. But once I opened the door I saw it was Dame instead. He smiled at me. "Hey, Cash."

My smiled had dropped and I mumbled, "Hey. Demarco's not here."

He stared at me with narrowed eyes. "You okay? You don't look good."

I didn't bother to answer. I just turned my back on the door and went to sit on the couch. I held my face in my hands and heard the door close. Dame walked into the living room and sat down across from me. "You didn't answer me. Are you okay?"

I instantly started crying knowing I sounded like a damn fool as I gushed out, "Do I look okay? Demarco ain't been home in two fucking days." My shoulders started shaking and I bawled like a baby. Images of him and another woman came in my head again. I stood and went to the bar area we had in the living room. I grabbed a bottle of Cîroc, opened it, and took a swig. I had to find some way to get those images out of my head before I went insane. I sat down next to Dame and tossed some more down my throat, wincing as it burned going down.

Dame grabbed the bottle out of my hand. "Girl, do you realize it's ten in the morning?"

"What the fuck you expect me to do?" I cried miserably. "My husband didn't come home last night."

"Well shit, Cashmere. Don't you think you should be calling the police instead of getting faded? D could be dead right now."

I thought about the text message. "That man ain't dead. Right now he's probably lying up with another woman."

He took a deep breath. "So that's what this is about. Girl, that man loves you." "Well he has a fucked-up way of showing it."

"Well he is going through a lot right now. Stress from the shops and all. And you know he wants a baby."

"Well I want a baby too. I can't make the shit magically happen. Don't you think it bothers me?"

Dame said nothing, just wiped the tears off my face and looked at me in a gentle manner. Made me feel a little comfort because it was the way Demarco used to treat me long ago. "One thing I know for sure is that you are a beautiful woman Demarco is lucky to have and it pisses me off that he is treating you this way." He reached over and kissed me on my cheek. Then somehow, his arms wrapped around my waist and his lips were now on mine and he kissed me.

Despite all the alarms rang off in my head, his lips on mine felt good. So without any bit of hesitation my lips opened and welcomed his tongue inside. One of his hands rubbed my butt and the kiss intensified. For intervals our tongues played with each other's, making me moan out of hurt, loneliness, and horniness. The desperate need for attention from a man. He whispered against my mouth, "What are we doing?"

Then he pulled away. He covered his face with his hands and started laughing. "Man, I can't believe I just did that shit."

I looked away as guilt washed over me.

He stood to his feet. "I've always had a little crush on you, Cashmere. Demarco always knew, too. But he always said that ain't a man he knew who didn't once they laid eyes on you. It's probably going to be the same for little Dom. I mean you are beautiful. And I don't like how Demarco has been treating you. But at the same time, he is my friend and we work together. I never had any intention to do what I ah . . ." He cleared his throat. "What I just did. So let me get out of here. But if you need anything call me or text me. And if he don't come home

by tonight you need to call the police. If you don't want
to be bothered with it then I'll call for you. But in the
meantime I'll keep hittin' him up and if he answers I'll tell
him to call home."

Crazy, I never guessed in all these years that Dame
secretly wanted me. He covered it up really good. I didn't
know what to tell him, so I said simply, "Okay, Dame."

"Later."

Funny thing was I didn't have a crush on Dame at all.
I had no attraction for him. Not because he was unat-
tractive but because I loved my husband and wanted my
husband. But hell I was lonely, depressed as hell, and the
kiss he gave me felt good. 'Cause I ain't had no tenderness
like that from a man in a while. But I knew I could never
tell Demarco about it. I just sighed and hoped he'd come
back home to me. When I started thinking about him
being gone again all I could do was assume that he was
with another bitch and making love to her in a way he just
couldn't do for me anymore for his own personal reasons.
That shit caused another headache and more tears. So I
went into my room, drank some more Nyquil, and went
back to sleep. For the rest of the day I slept off and on.
Every time I woke up I took another dose to go back to
sleep. I sent Dom a text telling her to order a pizza and to
get money out my purse.

I was awoken in the middle of the night by a movement
in my room. I opened my eyes and watched Demarco
strip down in the middle of the floor. Naked he walked
into the bathroom and I heard the shower going.

I sat up in the bed groggy and slipped my feet to the
carpet and stood to my feet. I walked into the bathroom.
I watched him through the glass shower doors. He was
lathering up his body with soap and scrubbing between
his legs. I closed my eyes and shook my head disgusted.
Could he at least have some motherfucking couth than to

be gone for two and a half fucking days and wash his dirty dick in front of me?

He turned and saw me in the bathroom watching him. He frowned at me, and then poured shampoo in his hair. I watched his curls uncoil and become silky straight. I gave a half smile despite the situation, because I was taken back to that day when I was eighteen in his shop, washing his hair, and thought about how much he had pursued me back then and wouldn't take no for an answer. My, how times had changed. I wondered if he'd ever pursue me like that again. Now he was out there pursuing someone else. So probably not. I wouldn't be surprised if he divorced and left me. Did I want that? I asked myself. No. Even if he admitted to me that he was actively fucking someone else? The answer was still no. I needed Demarco. He was my world. He rescued me and loved me despite my past, what I was. I'd be a fool to think another man could or would. Like they said, "You can't turn a ho into a housewife," and that was exactly what I was. Whether it was against my will didn't matter. I had no confidence at all to try to date and fall in love with someone else. I'd be too ashamed to divulge my past. And in all actuality I loved Demarco so much. I couldn't lose him and couldn't live my life without him.

My heart was pounding wildly and I demanded in a calm tone, "Demarco, where you been?"

He rinsed his hair, turned the water off, and grabbed a towel. Demarco was now thirty-five and was even more handsome now than when I first met him. He got better with time. He dressed well and worked out so he still had a nice body. I was sure there were a great many who would welcome his attention. I wondered if he was fucking someone from one of the shops.

He stepped out of the shower and paused in front of me. "Move." I did and he brushed right past me into our bedroom. I followed him and watched him dry off and throw on a pair of boxers.

"I asked you a question."

Still nothing. He simply tossed the towel on the floor and got into the bed.

He laid down and turned his back to me.

I was sick of this shit. I walked up to him and shoved him." Answer me! Where the fuck were you?"

Still nothing. I continued to shove him but it rendered no response from him. I dropped to my knees in front of him and started bawling. "Can't you see what you are doing to me? This shit hurts and I don't deserve it!" I cried pathetically on the floor in front of him.

He didn't even open his eyes. And within a few minutes I heard a slumber coming from his lips.

My pleading was hopeless.

Chapter 12

Cashmere

The morning brought nothing any different from Demarco. He never once offered an explanation for being gone all those days. And I didn't bother him again for one because, in all actuality, I didn't want to make him angry and then have him leave again. I knew it sounded stupid as hell but that was what I felt I needed to do to keep him. I loved him and I needed him. I didn't think I would function properly in this world without Demarco even if he was dragging me through the mud. Eventually something would give and he would love me again. I just wished to God I could get pregnant. I knew that would fix this shit.

I went to the shop the next day and tried to pour myself into my work hoping that it would take my mind off of things. But everyone at work knew something wasn't right about me. They could see the pain and despair I felt even though I tried to cover it up with a smile.

I put my client under the dryer and went outside to call Bev. I knew she could help me find some sort of clarity about my situation if I could just open up to her.

She answered on the second ring. "What's up, Cash?"

"Hey, Bev. Listen. I need your advice. What can I do to make Demarco love me again 'cause for long I swear he don't."

"The man love you, Cashmere. You two are just at a crossroads."

I confessed to Bev about how Demarco was gone for two and a half days.

"Do you want to vent or do you want to hear my opinion?"

I thought of the shit my mother had said and told her, "Bev, if you gonna say that he cheating save it. My thing is it sounds stupid for me as a woman to say but if he is doing it I don't think it's gonna stop me from wanting that man. Bev, I can't imagine life without him. That's what kills me because maybe just maybe I'm supposed to leave Demarco but I don't know if I could, ever."

"Then keep fighting for him. Cashmere, give him his space, but keep loving him. No marriage is ever smooth sailing and you guys been married for a cool minute. These years may be the hard ones and after you get over this hump it will be happy again. But you just gotta hold on. Tonight why don't you go home and cook his favorite meal? No nagging. If you say you don't want to leave him then don't even bring up him being gone for the past two days. Just give him a hug and a kiss. Offer to draw him a bath and give him a massage. Reaffirm to him that you love him and that you are committed to making your marriage work."

I nodded as she spoke. She was right. And she made me feel like this shit could get better. "Thanks, Bev."

"All right, baby. Call me if you need me."

I ended the call and went back inside. I put my iPhone back on my dock and put it on shuffle. The song changed from Anita Baker to Luther Vandross's "Here and Now." It made me get a little teary-eyed because it was our wedding song. I smiled and thought about that day. All it did was reaffirm that I wanted to at all costs save my marriage.

***

When I got home I cooked his favorite meal: stewed oxtails, rice, cabbage, and cornbread. Then pulled out his mother's recipe for caramel flan he had given me years ago. Dominique wasn't trying to eat any of that. She made herself a tuna sandwich, did her homework, and went to her room to watch TV. Normally, I would hang out with her but I wanted to get myself together. Earlier, I had one of the girls at the shop put some pretty curls in my hair. I showered, shaved, put on lotion, and sprayed myself up so I smelled yummy, and threw on a sexy black dress that complemented my curves. I had texted him and told him I was making him a special dinner and to please come home as soon as he could. He replied: Okay. Which was a little hope that tonight could go good.

I sat on the couch and, every couple minutes, I peeked out the window to see if he was coming. He was an hour over the normal time he came home. Still I waited and I kept the pots on top of the stove on low so the food was still nice and warm when he came home and the oven on low to keep the cornbread warm.

After another thirty minutes I got up to turn off the food so it didn't dry out. That's when my phone rang. I grabbed it off the coffee table and answered it recognizing Demarco's number.

"Hello, baby? Where are you? I'm . . ."

My voice trailed off because I heard a woman moaning and shouting between moans, "Demarco! Demarco!"

I looked at the caller ID as if wishing that it weren't so. That this call wasn't coming from his number. But logically speaking, say it was another number. That number was still calling my home and the caller was still saying my husband's name.

"Whose pussy is this?" a masculine voice said. And, yep, you guessed it.

That was my husband's voice. And I knew in that moment that no matter whatever happened between us he could never deny that he was in that moment making another woman scream. So the truth was right in my face. It was clear to me that he was cheating on me. Now could I still hold fast and true to what I told Bev? That even if it were proven true that he had been cheating I'd still want him? In that moment I just didn't know. I was too hurt and too traumatized by what I was hearing on the other end of the phone.

"Awww. Damn. I'm cuming."

"Me too!" she moaned.

"Damn I needed that shit. That bitch was getting on my motherfucking nerves."

"Anytime, baby. Don't even think about her ass."

I closed my eyes as sobs racked my body.

The next day, I was glad that Dominique was in school most of the day so she didn't have to see me like this: a drunken mess who had been drinking since she had left for school. By ten I finished a whole fifth of tequila. Around lunchtime I opened another bottle. This time I chose Everclear. I knew that mixing liquids wasn't good but I needed to not feel. I'd rather be throwing up than cry.

But when the alcohol could do nothing for the ache in my heart I called the only person I knew could make me feel better: Dame. I needed to talk to a man. No woman could do anything for my pain. In times like this I really wished my daddy was still alive. I knew he could help me deal with this. But Dame was the only male figure I could talk to. And he had direct ties to Demarco.

As soon as he heard my voice and me say desperately, "Can you please come over?" he said, "I'll be there in ten minutes."

And as soon as he walked in the door he took the Everclear bottle out of my hand. "What's wrong, ba . . . Cash?" he asked me. He looked so concerned. The type of concern Demarco didn't show anymore.

I heard him about to say "baby." But I ignored it because I needed a male ear, someone who cared because at the moment my husband didn't. "Demarco . . ." I took a deep breath and closed my eyes. "Demarco is cheating on me." I spoke between sobs.

He sat down next to me. "Wait," he said firmly. "You may be getting all worked up for nothing. How do you know? For sure?"

"He accidentally called home and I could hear him and another woman having sex."

He sighed. "Damn. I'm not advocating what he did at all, Cash, so don't think I am. But if the nigga was going to do that dumb shit he should have squared all damn corners. If you ever decide to cheat on wifey, she should never know. This shit is really pissing me off. Nigga out here acting a damn fool. Demarco is fucked up for what he is doing to you."

I covered my face with my hands and cried into them.

"Awww don't cry." He pulled my hands away from my face and wiped away the tears running down my face. "I really hate seeing you hurt like this."

He started rubbing my back. Then his free hand cupped my face in his and he started kissing me. First it was an innocent peck. I shoved his chest back some but he resisted. And then, I didn't push my line against his resistance. Instead my mouth opened to his tongue. A part of me didn't want him to go away from me. I was lonely, vulnerable, and just a little horny. His hands slid up and down my arms then they cupped my breasts.

I pulled away. "This is wrong, Dame."

"Let me make you feel good and take your mind off all of this." He gently shoved me down on the couch. A hand went into the crevice between my legs and slipped under my panties to my pussy. And I sang like a canary. I needed him to do that in that moment. It instantly got creamy and wet for him, as he let his fingers gently stroke in and out of it.

"You don't know how long I wanted to do what I'm doing right now."

As good and as vindicating as it felt, I knew I couldn't continue with it.

So I yanked his hand out of me. "Dame, move."

His eyes were hooded with desire and he placed his hand right back on my pussy. "Why? Wasn't it feeling good?"

I ignored the question. We had gone way too far and I had to shut this down. My temporary moment of weakness was over. My hands reached for his shoulders to completely get him off of me. But he was big like Demarco and wouldn't budge. "Come on, Cashmere, let me taste you. Please. Demarco ain't gotta know. This what this nigga get anyway for treating you bad."

I tried to tune out his words. "No; now please get up." I shoved against him and still nothing.

"I want some of you at least just one time. I won't take it. But I want you to offer it to me."

I shook my head indicating no. "You need to leave."

And, that's when the door to the living room burst open and Demarco rushed in. He took one look at us on the couch and lunged toward Dame. When Dame saw him he jumped up and flew back with his hands in the air.

"Man, I told you she was a hoe. Once a hoe always a hoe. You can't trust her, man."

I gasped. Demarco had told Dame about my past.

Demarco punched him.

Dame placed a hand over his mouth and then looked at his hand that was now covered in the blood leaking from his mouth and looked at Demarco shocked.

Dame slammed Demarco against the wall. He balled up one of his fist to hit Demarco but he didn't. "Nigga, what the fuck you hit me for? You the one who told me to do this shit! The last thing I would ever do is fuck with a chick who used to sell her pussy for money. She is ruined! Her insides are probably rotted out."

I cried from the couch bitterly as he talked about me. Damn I wanted to cut on myself to stop the pain I was feeling. Why would Demarco set me up? Did he not have any belief in me that I was a faithful wife to him? I only did what I had done tonight because of the way that he was treating me. I shook my head over and over again in shock.

Demarco yanked away from him. "A kiss is all I said. And I told you to forget about it because I would be working late and wouldn't be able to pop up to catch her and you come over anyway nigga? And shit went a whole lot further. So yeah. You were being tested too. Any man that was always trying to down a man's wife even if she wasn't worth shit is doing it for a reason. I'm not dumb. Get the fuck out, Dame!"

"Fine, choose that rat bitch over your boy!"

Silence and no one moved.

"So before I leave, tell me this, 'cause I have bills: are we still cool or we done over that bitch?"

Demarco ran out of the living room. I panicked and raced after him. He was going into his office where he kept his guns. I watched him snatch his nine. *No!* My heart sped up. I blocked him. "Demarco, what the fuck are you doing?"

He roughly shoved me out of the way. "Shut up, bitch."

Dame approached us. When he saw Demarco's gun he froze and placed his hands in the air. "After all these years we been friends you gonna get a gun? What you gonna kill me over this slut?"

Demarco stood still as a statue and mean mugged Dame with his gun aimed. Then after a few seconds he shrugged and dropped his hand at his sides. "No. You right. I'm not gonna kill you. 'Cause you dead to me already, nigga. Get the fuck out my house."

Dame shook his head like he was hurt. "D?"

"Get the fuck out!"

Dame sighed heavily, turned, and walked away. The living room door slammed with his exit.

Defeated with the entire situation I went back into our bedroom and sat down on the bed.

Seconds later Demarco stood in the doorway. When I looked up at him he smirked at me in disgust and shook his head at me. "I always knew you weren't shit."

In rage I grabbed my iPhone off the nightstand and threw it at him. It hit him in his arm. "You piece of shit motherfucker! You talking? You were fucking. I heard you and her, you bast—"

Demarco was on me in a flash and slapped me so hard I flew across the room.

Chapter 13

Dominique

When I came home from school I heard nothing but yelling. Uncle Dame whisked right by me with blood on his face.

"Uncle Dame, you okay?" I asked him.

He wouldn't give me eye contact, just mumbled, "Bye, baby," and walked out the living room door.

I could hear my mother and father yelling. I walked up the stairs and toward the hallway and hid in a corner so I could peer into their room. My mother was hitting my father.

"Cashmere, stop!" After every couple hits my dad would either shove her or hit her back. But it didn't stop my mother from hitting Daddy again and again.

"You mothafucka!" she screeched with so much pain in her face after he punched her in her face. She started screaming and continued assaulting my father. Finally he growled, grabbed my mother by her forearms, and threw her so hard she flew into their closet.

I cried at the brutality he was showing my mother. You don't treat your worst enemy the way he was treating my mother. But I was too scared to go inside their room and defend her. I buried my face in my hands as the tears poured from my eyes. Her head and right shoulder slapped against the closet door. My mom just sat there with her head tossed back and sobbing. Her mouth was open but there were no sounds coming out. Her shoulders shook violently like she was having a seizure.

My dad's breath was coming out in hard pants. When his breathing calmed down he said, "I'm not happy in this marriage. I hate you and I want out. And you know why."

"Why?"

"If you had aborted her, maybe we wouldn't be here today. She had placed the strain on our marriage and made me resentful toward you. I hate even looking at her. You knew that and yet you still chose to go on with that pregnancy."

My mother started bawling. "If you couldn't deal with the fact that Dominique was not yours and accept her as your own then why did you stay all these years, Demarco? Why did you marry me?"

"I prayed day and night while you were pregnant that it was my baby. But after so many years when she started looking like him more than you, I . . . At the end of the day, I thought my love for you could surpass my hate for her. It didn't. When I see her, I see a pimp. I see Black: her daddy. I hate her as much as I hate him. And then I thought maybe if we had a child together that would change things. And the one thing I wanted more than anything you couldn't give me! You couldn't give me a baby. Maybe if you had I wouldn't feel the way I feel. I can't love something that's not of me!"

"But she is of me and of you-"

"Half of you and half of motherfucking Black!"

My mom closed her eyes and she let out a long moan.

I gasped and place a hand over my mouth. Demarco wasn't my daddy. Someone named Black was? Tears poured down my cheeks. I cried silently. How could my mother do this to me? How could she pass another man off as my father? In that moment for the first time in my life I hated my mother just as much as Demarco hated her. She had robbed me of the truth. How could my mother have done this to me? I looked up to my mother. I thought she was perfect. And she wasn't because she was a liar. I shook my head bitterly. Pain was spreading into my heart. And I couldn't help the tears that poured down my face.

"Because I loved you so much, Cashmere, I thought I'd grow to love her. But I didn't and I won't."

My mom continued to cry pitifully. I cried as well and watched him pull out suitcases and pack his stuff. After he had what he needed packed he said, "I've been talking to a lawyer. I'm going to file for a divorce first thing tomorrow. Just so you know."

"Demarco, please," she begged. "I can fix this. Put those suitcases down, baby." She stood up, grimaced in pain, and blocked the doorway.

He wouldn't even look her in her eyes. "This is over. We took this shit too far. I can be man enough to say that I should have never married you. But now I'm doing the right thing by leaving you."

"Please!" My mother got down on her knees and pleaded with him while crying uncontrollably. She was crying so hard I thought it sounded like she was hyperventilating.

But it did nothing for him. He simply shoved her out of the way and walked out of the room. I could hear my mom screaming for him.

As he stepped out of the room into the hallway I stepped out of the shadows. He saw me, paused for a moment, then continued.

"Daddy?" I called.

He kept walking.

More tears poured out of me as I chased after him outside to our long driveway. With more guts than ever I chased after him. "Daddy, is it true? You're not my real father? Tell me the truth please. I'm begging you, Da . . . Demarco, please tell me who my father is."

He got in the truck like I wasn't standing there and drove off leaving me in the driveway crying like a lost kid who couldn't find their mom in a grocery store.

My mom didn't even come out of her room. And it was just as well for me because until I knew the absolute truth I just couldn't face her. I couldn't even believe that was coming out of my head. I loved my mother to death. But to find out that my mother had been lying about my birth father . . . I didn't know if I could ever look at her the same way or even forgive her for that. Who knew, maybe if she had told me who my real father was he would have given me the love Demarco never had. It made sense that he had treated me the way he had over the years. I wasn't his and he plain-out hated me. And now I wanted answers, the truth. I didn't think my mother was capable of giving me this because for thirteen years she had lied to me about who my real daddy was. So how could I believe anything she had to say now?

I remembered all that night as my mother continued to cry. I lay in my bed and racked my brain for where I had heard the name Black. It came to me after a few minutes: the lady at the fish market was the one who had said the name Black Mitchell. Then I also thought about what my aunt had said about if I want to know the truth.

So the next morning I got dressed and skipped out on school. I figured out how to ride the bus to Compton. My mom was still so out of it that I hadn't heard a peep out of her. By the time I made it out to Compton it was too early to go to the fish spot. During the long bus ride all kinds of thoughts ran through my head. Tyler, The Creator could not take me out of my thoughts as he played on my iPhone. Besides the fact that this was the first time my mother had ever hurt me or made me mad, I didn't think I could look at my mother the same. Why would she lie to me? Did I know my mother? Really know her like I thought I did? I never would have thought my mother would have kept such a big secret from me. Parents are a part of a child's identity. Maybe if she would have told me I would have not been hurt by how hateful Demarco had treated me because I would have understood why. I also would not have cared because he wasn't really my father. Nor would I have spent my whole life trying to impress him and win his love. I urged myself not to make any assumptions or have any type of hope until I found out the truth. I knew two people who could give it to me. One of those persons I figured since she offered would give it to me easily: my aunt. The other would be the lady in the fish shop.

After I got off the bus and walked to my aunt's house I took a deep breath as I walked up the steps. I almost expected her to not be awake since it was still early. But not even three seconds after I pressed the doorbell the door flung open and I was met with a set of angry, bloodshot eyes.

She made my heart speed up. I swallowed hard, my eyes wide.

"What you want?"

I licked my dry lips.

"What you slow or something? What are you doing at my doorstep? Huh?" she demanded. Her voice got louder with each word.

I held my hands up as if in surrender. "I . . . I didn't mean to bring you trouble, Auntie. I just needed you to talk to me. I wanted the truth. You said—"

She held up a hand. "Say no more. Come inside. I'll give you all the truth you can handle, little skinny girl. The question is, can you handle it?"

Chapter 14

Dominique

I sat on her couch that was covered with plastic. My aunt waddled toward me with an empty jelly jar filled with water. She shoved it in my hands.

"Here. Drank that. 'Cause when I'm done your ass gonna need some type of nourishment. 'Cause what I'm about to say ain't for the faint of heart."

"Thank you, ma'am."

She narrowed her eyes at me when I said that and gave a grunt. I took a couple sips and set it on top of her coffee table.

"When your mother was thirteen and her sister was seventeen they came to live with me after your grandfather was in an accident and your grandmother abandoned both the girls. This was a very difficult time for me because I tried to be a very loving aunt to the both of the ungrateful bitches."

My lips curled at her calling my mother a bitch. But I kept quiet.

"Look like you want to do something to me, little gal."

"No, ma'am," I said quickly. "I just don't like to hear people call my mother out of her name is all." I mean that was still my mom. She deserved more respect than that.

"Well once you find out what the bitch did you gonna be calling her out her name!"

I also never knew my grandma had abandoned my mother and her sister. I was also told that my mother's older sister had died in a tragic car accident.

Her nostrils flared out. "Now where was I? Your grandmother stole her husband from me when we was younger. I was a God-fearing virgin and he was courting me. Back in my day before this twirling, twerking, and hippy hop bullshit, men were real and they knew how to treat a decent lady. Anyhow, your grandmother, being the little slut she was, must have put it on Desmond something good because he left me and married her. She was carrying someone else's bastard seed. And you won't believe who's seed she was carrying: Her uncle's. Yes, I know, your God-fearing grandmom married to that police commissioner was fucking our uncle's brains out. Truth was she seduced him."

I looked away disgusted.

"He a man, what you 'spect? You throw a dog a bone they going to gnaw at it. And well, my uncle gnawed at her even though it was like lying with a serpent. But anyhow Desmond, he always was a dummy so I suppose it's betta he ended up with her and not me. Anyhow your grandmother made that man work day in and day out so she could have the finer thangs."

My mother had never really talked about my grandfather much, just said he was a good man who passed away when she was thirteen.

She went on. "He ended up getting into an accident, becoming a paraplegic, and could no longer fit the bill. Your selfish grandmother ran off and left him and them girls. I gave them a home and guidance, something their hoish-ass mammy wouldn't 'cause she was too busy running the streets, getting that big hole between her thighs filled with filthy, disgusting peckers."

"What happened to my aunt?" I asked.

"Oh you mom must have not told you. Shut up now and stop cutting me off! Now them girls, your aunt Desiree and your mammy, did everything under the sun from selling dope to stripping. Then your aunt slept with my husband. Cashmere was on her way to do it too except I put a stop to it and they both ran away. I guess I provided too much of a stable, wholesome family and it scared them." She looked away.

"Anyhow, both them girls set up shop with a pimp as black as the night. I ain't never seen a blacker man walking around. They got involved in using dope. Yep! I said it! Your mother was a druggie just as bad as those you see walking the streets begging for change or selling they ass. Then she got mad at your sister. Why I don't know. But rumor is they got into a fight where your mom beat your sister to death and she died. Yep, your mother is a murderer. But that ain't the worst of it. Your mama ain't exactly been honest with you as far as your daddy. Your daddy is the pimp named Black. That Mexican ain't your daddy and all these years your mom got the nerve to pass him off as your poppy when she know damn well he ain't. That pimp is your daddy."

I closed my eyes as tears fell. I was reeling from the things my aunt was telling me. My mother was a walking lie. I mean lie after lie after lie was told to me and the truth just unfolded in front of me. I didn't know that woman. And now I really didn't want to. The confirmation I needed was right in front of me: my aunt. My daddy wasn't Demarco. Although this sounded weird, instantly I was hit with a wave of hope. Maybe if I could find my real father he could love me. Love me in way that Demarco never did if only I could find him.

"Where is my father?"

"In the slammer."

"Can you take me to him please?"

"I don't know where he is. And if I did I wouldn't cause one thing I don't do is go around no coppers 'less I have to. You go into an institution you might not come up out of it."

I thought back to the lady in the fish market: *"Black asks about you all the time."*

I stood to my feet, still reeling from her words. "Thank you, Auntie."

She said nothing just watched me walk out.

I sat on her porch for a minute and hid my face in my knees and broke down crying. I felt lost. My feelings were hurt and the last person in the whole world that I expected to hurt them had. My mom.

When I heard a sound I looked up and saw my great-aunt standing in the doorway. I thought she was going to come outside and hug me but she didn't.

I got off her steps and walked to the fish market, all my aunt's words weighing heavily on me. Once I got to the fish market I walked up to the lady Meka and said, " I need you to take me to my father: Black Mitchell."

When I came home that day after everything I had learned I looked at my mother so differently. For as long as I could remember I looked up to my mother. She was my hero. Now I didn't. Our interaction wasn't much anyhow since she walked around the house like a zombie and spent most of the time in her room. She only said two sentences to me. One: "Heat up a frozen pizza if you hungry." Or two: "If anyone calls I'm not here except for Demarco." So it was very easy to maneuver around her. When I wasn't there she wasn't answering the door or the phone anyway. Thing was I was 50 percent in love and 50 percent in hate with my mother. I didn't want that. I wanted to 100 percent love my mom like I always had. So one day I figured if I sat her down and talked to her, gave her a chance to explain things, maybe she would tell me the truth and I would 100 percent love her again. There would be no anger. So when Meka texted me and said she could take me to see my father, I ignored the text and went into my mother's room. She was resting in her bed.

I took a deep breath and sat down next to her. "Hey, Mommy."

"Hey, Dom."

"Mom, can I ask you something?"

"What?"

"I don't know, Mom. I know Demarco is gone but something is really bothering me. Is he my daddy? 'Cause I just can't believe he is because of how he treated me and the fact that he is gone but never calls or checks on me." I bit my bottom lip as she kept a poker face on.

I just wanted her to tell me who my real daddy was. I should not have had to hear this from other people. I wanted my mother to tell me and fix this. If he was not and my mom told me the truth I could forgive her, move on, and not even bother to respond to Meka.

But then my mom made that choice for me with her words. "Look, Dom. I have a lot on my mind. I don't know why I have to keep going over this with you. Yes, Demarco is your father. He got me pregnant when I was eighteen years old. I swear on a stack of Bibles that that is your daddy. That's on your life. Don't you think I would tell you if someone else was your daddy?"

And in that moment, that 50 percent love slipped to 20 percent love and 80 percent hate.

In a soft voice, I said, "Okay, Mommy." I stood and walked out of her room and into mine. Once there, I closed and locked the door. I pulled out my phone and texted Meka the words, Yes. Take me to my father.

So now, the next week as I waited with Meka outside the waiting room of Kern Valley State Prison, I thought back to the day I left my aunt's house and paid her a visit at the fish place and her being more than willing to take me to see my daddy. I kept my meetings with my aunt and Meka a secret from my mom and I was going to keep my visit to see my dad a secret as well. Maybe once I got the truth from my father I would confront my mother. I wondered how long he had been locked up and why he never came to claim or see me. He should have since Demarco obviously didn't want any part of me and my mother accepted that. But at the same time, if my father was a pimp he wasn't a saint either. But I didn't want to judge him too harshly until he told me his side of the story. I didn't want to get disappointed like my mother had disappointed me. But I desperately needed to hear what he had to say.

When we were led to one of the tables I took a deep breath as I sat down next to Meka. When I went to the fish shop Meka had confirmed for me that my mother was a former prostitute and that they shared the same pimp: Black. She also confirmed that my mother had in fact gone to prison for killing her sister. Lies, lies, lies my mother told. I couldn't believe that this was really who my mother was. And I wasn't going to ask her nothing; she would lie! The proof was here and my mother was a liar so she couldn't possibly tell me the truth now. I wouldn't believe it at this point. I mean for thirteen years she lied about who my father was and allowed Demarco to mistreat me. She had the chance to tell me the truth and she chose not to! She probably would have always lied to me. Thank God I had met Meka. I remembered her words at the fish market: *"If you mother won't take you to your father I will. And I'm sure he will be very happy to see you."*

"He's coming out, Dominique," she whispered to me.

I stared up in awe as a dark-skinned man came walking toward us. As he came our way my hands covered my cheeks as I hungrily stared at him. He was average height and build with smooth dark chocolate skin. His eyes were as black as his skin and he wore his hair in neat skinny dreads that were pulled back into a ponytail.

His expression was unreadable when he sat across from me.

"Hey, baby," Meka said. "Did you get that money on your books last week?"

"I did. Thank you," he said in an even tone. Then he feasted his eyes on me as I eyed him nervously.

"I don't have to tell you who this is. I mean she looks like you spit her right out."

He threw back his head and laughed, revealing pearly white teeth. Then his eyes scanned me from the top of my head to my feet slowly. Then tears out of nowhere made the corners of his eyes shiny then slid down his face.

"Hi, daughter," he whispered wiping away the tears.

"Hi, Daddy," I said nervously but happiness budded through me.

He turned to Meka. "Leave us for a while, Meka."

"Okay, daddy." She puckered a kiss at him and sa-shayed away. He eyed her for a moment before turning back to me.

"Meka told me about you a couple days ago. It was a big shock. But I wasn't expecting you would be in front of me today so suddenly. How did this come to happen, daughter?"

I blushed when he said that. It felt good. "I found out that you were my real father and the man who my mother said was my dad really wasn't. I asked Meka to take me to you and she said that she would."

"Why did you want to meet me? Wait. Before you answer that, tell me what you know of me."

"I know that you were my mother's pimp is all."

"Yes. I was her pimp. That's all you need to know about that for now. But one thing Cashmere never did was she never told me that I had a child running around. You have to know that if I did know I would go out of my way to facilitate a relationship with you, baby. Jail would have not kept me away from you. The only thing that could is death. And both our hearts are beating, pretty baby."

That made me smile and cry at the same time. "All I ever wanted was a father's love. I never got that. I don't care that you're locked up, Daddy. I don't care that you were my mother's pimp. I want to be in your life."

"Pimp. Interesting. I hate that word. Well, Dominique, I must admit that I heard those same words before from your mother. And I took her and her sister in and I took care of her more so like a father. They both had nowhere to go. I gave them food, shelter, and a daddy's love. I also schooled them on the streets because, let's face it, at that time I was in my mid-forties. And I'm a black man living in America. I could leave the earth any moment and if I did I wanted them to both know how to fend for themselves. Those are things a daddy is supposed to do. And if that wasn't enough, I was grooming your mother for bigger things because there was always something more special about her just like I see there is something special about you."

I beamed at the compliment.

"After your mother went to jail for murdering your sister and was released I thought she would show some appreciation. But she never came back home. She ran off with another man. She left me after all I did for her. Then I got locked up for a crime I didn't commit." He fought tears.

"What?" I asked with wide eyes.

"A murder, baby. But I was set up. That's on Allah. You have to believe me. I'm fighting the case as we speak."

I believed him. Why would he lie to me? What did he gain from that? Nothing. So I had to ask him one more question. "Did you hurt my mother? Force her—"

"Listen to me carefully because I will not say this again. Your mother chose to stay with me. She could have left at any moment. She could have gone to the police or even social services. But she never did. That should tell you something."

That made me feel so much better.

"She did betray me though I must say, Dominique. She left me when I needed her the most."

"I'll never leave you, Daddy. I promise."

"Thank you, sweetheart. So now I need you. Get with Meka and let her groom you into a cash cow. The money will go toward me getting a lawyer and fighting my case."

"I want to help you in any way I can."

"And you have no problem taking my instruction?" he asked.

"No, Daddy. Just will you . . . will you love me like most fathers love their daughters? I know I'm not perfect. But I don't know it, a daddy's love. It's supreme love to me. More important than anyone else loving me. Without it I feel dead inside. I don't want to feel dead anymore. But will you love me?"

"I already do." Tears dropped from his eyes and soon I was bawling and he held me, stroked my hair, and whispered, "It's okay. Daddy's here."

"I'm hurting so much." I sobbed.

He continued to comfort me. In that moment, my love dropped down to 0 percent and was now 100 percent hate for my mother.

Chapter 15

Dominique

I took a deep breath and knocked on Meka's door. I thought back to all the things my father had told me. The rules were simple. My father had told me over our visit. He was going to groom me to be exactly what my mother wasn't. He told me for the time being I had to lay low with my mother and not let on that I knew her secrets. I had to wait to get my first letter from my daddy to know what my next step was, which arrived three days after our visit.

Before I read the letter, I tore the envelope up and threw it in the trash so there was no way it could be traced back to Meka. I was told to do this to every letter. And I had read the letter over and over again.

Dear Dominique,
I'm so grateful for you coming to me. Allah has blessed me with a beautiful princess. I am honored that you want to be there for your father and that you also want to build a relationship with me. Just remember your mother has no real bearing over your life anymore. However, until I am released I would like you to stay with her and do not tell her that we have spoken. You need to continue following her rules like nothing in your life has changed. In life it is always best to move in silence. However, you are never to go with her law over mine. I am

older and seasoned so I know what's better for your life. Now that I have you in my life I will make sure no one hurts you again and I won't put anyone in front of you. That was your mother's mistake. She allowed her husband to continue to hurt you so she could keep him around not worrying what the repercussions would be. She was living a lie, a fake identity. I won't let her do this to you, Dominique. But as a father, there is only so much I am able to do for you being locked up. So I have to get out of here. That's why I need your help. You have my blood running through your veins so you will be the most solidified moneymaker out there. No one will be able to touch you. Just like your mother is. But you needed to be groomed. I mean there are rules to this. I'm trying to get a lawyer to get out of here and we can establish a relationship. If you can start working for Sunshine that will help me greatly.

I knew Sunshine was code for Meka. Black said in case anyone ever saw these letters they wouldn't get traced back to her.

Sunshine can show you how to make a lot of paper. You better listen to her. She knows what she is talking about and if you don't follow what she says it will get back to me and I will be very disappointed in you. You don't want that do you?

"No, Daddy, I don't," I said out loud as I read the letter. My eyes scanned over all the rules to the game. Then when I heard a knock on my bedroom door I quickly hid the letter under my pillow. My mother poked her head in my bedroom. I had my back turned to her.

"Has Demarco called?" she asked pathetically.

"No, Mom. I would have told you if he did."

I heard her sigh before closing my door and trudging back into her room.

I walked out of the house with my backpack pretending I was going to school when really I was going to Meka's house. But like I said, my mother didn't answer the phone so she really had no real way of knowing. I always forged my mother's signature when I missed a day. But Meka told me I couldn't miss too much school. We could get caught up.

When I got to Meka's apartment, there were four boys who looked to be around my age sitting on the couch while Meka sat in a chair across from them sipping from a glass cup.

"Hi," I said nervously to both.

She tossed me another letter from my daddy. "You can read that later. You got work to do. Strip down."

"Huh?" I asked confused.

"These little brothers are from down the street. They don't have any money, but you are going to pretend that they are paying customers. Don't tell me you a virgin, Dominique. You look like a virgin. But your dad ordered this initiation tonight. All four of them."

My heart thudded in my chest. I had only had sex with Mr. Douglas. And he had taken my virginity. But I felt safe with him. I didn't feel safe here. But still I said, "No, and if my father wants me to do this then I will."

"Good 'cause it's no time to turn back now. I'm going to coach you through this. By the time you leave my crib there won't be anything innocent about you. Now let's go strip down."

I closed my eyes and proceeded to get naked.

"Open your eyes! You in control when it comes to servicing men. Don't ever forget that you hold the power. Not the men."

I nodded and kept my eyes open and I stripped down to nothing while all four of the boys who looked like they were also in their teens eyed me in disbelief almost.

Then I looked at her.

She smirked and said, "You say you not a virgin so go on and handle it, sweetie."

"Okay." And that's what I did.

Chapter 16

Cashmere

"No, Mama, I don't want to go with you. I appreciate you offering but I don't want to."

I didn't bother making eye contact with my mother as she stared down at me disapprovingly as I lay under the covers of my bed in my bedroom in the middle of the day. But I really didn't care what she thought. Just a week before my world was turned upside down.

Man. Every time I thought about the situation I was in nonstop tears. Demarco had finally decided to leave me. To sum up the feeling I felt, it hurt like pure hell. There were times when my fingers itched to scratch my skin. And there were times where my body craved something stronger than alcohol to dull the pain. I guess old habits die hard. But I continued to struggle on and deal with what I had to deal with: losing my better half. He had finally gone ahead and done it. Demarco had left me and was going to file for divorce. I was so glad that Dominique wasn't there and hadn't heard what he had said: the secret that I had been keeping from her since she was born. That Demarco was not her father; Black, my old pimp, was. When Demarco and I moved in together to start a life as young lovers the last thing I thought I'd find out was that I was pregnant at eighteen. Initially although I was young, the thought of it made me so happy. I would have a baby. With all the things that my young body had endured when Black had me out there on the streets from all the men, getting raped to all the STDs I had gotten, I didn't think I would ever be able to conceive. And then to have the love of my life profess his love to me forever, it was a dream come true. But then that was when I was hit like a bag of rocks because I remembered I was also raped by Black in front of Demarco and he could also very well be the father. There was no real way to estimate because shortly after the incident Demarco and I resumed having sex and we didn't wear condoms so while it could very well be his baby or Black's, I was most assured that it was Demarco's because the incident with Black happened only once whereas Demarco and I were having sex on the regular. So we both just hoped and prayed that it was his. Demarco told me one day early on, "Why don't we not chance it, baby, and you go ahead and get an abortion?" At the time I was three months. I closed my eyes to those words.

"I mean, you're a spring chicken now. We can get you pregnant again."

I couldn't imagine terminating something growing inside of me. So I assured him, "Come on now. As much as we mess around you gotta know that this is your baby. What are the chances that it will be Black's?"

He smiled, rubbed his hand around my newly formed bump, and said, "Yeah, you're right, baby."

And he was very supportive of me during the pregnancy doing all the things a soon-to-be father is supposed to do. Rubbing cocoa butter on my tummy. Massaging my feet and being so gentle and careful of hurting the baby when we made love. When Dominique was born, she was very pale and she had my eyes. So initially we thought she was very well his. As Dominique got older she darkened, which was still no sign because I was dark skinned and she looked so much like me. Then one day Demarco came to me and said, "I love her but I don't love her. I'm afraid of completely giving my heart to her unless I know for sure she is mine."

So I told him, "Baby, Dom is yours."

"You think so, baby?"

"Yes."

But when he looked away I saw he still had a little doubt. I mean I did as well but every day and night I prayed that the baby was Demarco's. So we did it. Although I didn't want to because I feared what the results would be. And sure enough our biggest fears came true when the results came back that Demarco wasn't the father of Dominique. It was the worst devastation ever. And things just weren't the same, period. At first he tried, even after he found out she wasn't his. For days he wouldn't even talk. But like a man of his word he married me like he had promised me we would. But it never made things better; things only went downhill from there and never came back up. As Dominique grew, we grew further and further apart, until the gap between us was so wide I just couldn't close it by myself. And a baby would have but I couldn't get pregnant.

And, thus, here I was.

"Cash!"

I slowly turned and looked at my mother as she stood in front of me shaking her head in disapproval.

With this shit eating at me I couldn't work so I called my scheduled clients and told them that I wouldn't be in all that week. I just couldn't fathom working and feeling the way I did. I mean sometimes I struggled getting out of bed; and with something as simple as going to the bathroom I just wanted to drop on the floor and break down. I didn't bother talking to my mother because I didn't want to hear her self-absorbed ass speak on how she didn't need a man to define her because she knew her worth and apparently I didn't know mine. Yeah, whatever, maybe I didn't. And yes, I needed him, not any man, but I needed Demarco. *Does the fact that this man has been the love on my life since I was eighteen make it more understandable?* I wanted to ask her as she rumbled on about how she wanted me to go on a vacation with her.

"A change in scenery is what you need, Cash. You never know. You might find you another husband. Girl, you only thirty-two with one kid. Hell when I met Hank I was well older then you and a little too old to be popping out no more babies but it didn't stop him from loving me and putting a ring on it."

I shook my head at her. "I'm not going to Aruba with you, Mom. No, thanks."

She sucked her teeth at me. "So what? You just gonna sit in this room and waste your life away over a nigga who don't want you?"

I almost lunged toward her from the bed then stopped myself. I closed my eyes briefly and took a deep breath. "Mom," I said carefully, "if you start that shit again I'm throwing you out."

"Okay. Okay, Cash, damn! You know it's fucked up how you talk to your mother."

I shook my head at her. The supposed Christian.

"But I'll chalk it up to you going through some shit right?" She walked toward me and cupped my face between her hands. It brought me back to that day at the shop when she tried to come back into my life when I was eighteen. It made me sad all over again 'cause back then Demarco wanted me so bad.

"I just wish you could see that this shit is not about you. You didn't do anything wrong. Demarco is having problems with Demarco and he is taking that shit out on you. The sooner you realize this, the better off your ass will be and you will realize that you can do better. And you will find someone to treat you better. Maybe Demarco just ain't the one. I mean how in the fuck is it you fault that Dominique is not his baby? You didn't ask for that bastard to rape you. And maybe if Demarco had stepped up sooner when the shit went down it wouldn't have ever happened! But to turn around and to pull the shit that he been pulling and blame it on that shit? Come on. If you couldn't accept her then you should have kicked rocks a long time ago. Why wait until now?"

Tears poured from eyes. My mother wasn't helping; she was making me feel a whole lot worse. "Mom, stop please."

"Okay. I'm just saying this is not your fault, Cashmere."

Whether it was my fault didn't stop me from feeling as horrible as I felt. Didn't matter who was wrong who was right, none of that. All that mattered is that I wanted my family restored.

Just then there was a knock on my bedroom door and Dom poked her head in. "Hi, Mom." She gave me a quick smile. Then she said to my mother, "Hey, Grandma."

"Hey, pretty girl. Come and give your granny a hug." She walked into the room and my mom pulled her in her arms, kissing her on her cheek.

When Dom pulled away my mother said, "Are you okay? You look like you're in a little pain. Why you limping, baby?"

She stuttered. "Ah. I was rushing to my next class and twisted my ankle is all."

"Are you okay?" I asked her.

She looked away but said, "Yes."

"Well I'm going to get going. I need to start getting my things together. Cash, I can't believe you won't come with me but oh well. I'm telling you it is just what you need to clear your mind then you'll come your ass back and say, 'Demarco who?'"

I didn't respond. She blew us both kisses and walked out.

"Where is Nanna going?"

"She said Aruba."

"Oh. You didn't want to go, Mom?"

"No, Dom." I rubbed my weary, red eyes. "I wouldn't enjoy myself. Not with your daddy leaving."

"I'm sorry, Mom. Do you need anything?"

"No. Thanks for being concerned about me. I know the past couple days I haven't really been spending time with—"

"Mom, you don't have to explain yourself; it is what it is and I understand. I'm just sorry you're hurting."

"Thanks for understanding. I know I may seem useless to you right now but give me a little time and I will snap out of this I promise." It was hard for me to look at my daughter because I felt so guilty. I was being so weak and so emotional but the way I felt it was just too hard to smile and act like everything was okay.

"Well, Mom, I have a thousand-word paper I have to start on. I'm going to be really busy so get some rest." She kissed me on my right cheek and left my room.

I looked away. Normally I was all up in Dominique's room, helping her with her homework or we were watching a movie together. It was always some type of bonding. But I couldn't do it today. I was too, too down. I knew she would be okay; she was a good kid.

All I did was drop back a capful of Nyquil so I could rest my pain away. Before I dozed off I called Demarco's phone but he wouldn't answer.

Chapter 17

Dominique

I was so relieved that mother didn't catch on to any changes in me. She was too occupied with Demarco and where he was that she didn't notice that I had, number one, drifted apart from her and, number two, now had a great deal going on. I didn't trip and twist my ankle. I was sore from what I had done at Meka's house. She would never know. And she would never know that I had talked to my daddy. And lastly, my mom would never know that I now had resentment toward her for her never telling me the truth about who my real father was. But like my daddy said, I'd have to go along with my mother's normal program so she was not alerted. Because now that I had met my father, I wanted to continue to have him in my life and judging by my mother, I was sure she would shut it down because she didn't want all the secrets of the past to come out. Since my mom never checked on me, she stayed in her room, I planned on sneaking out. Meka told me she was going to pick me up at the corner.

So I waited until my mother was asleep and snuck out of the house. I knew she would never know I was gone. Also I played the role like everything was okay and I didn't know the truth. She was too preoccupied with Demarco anyway to care.

I hopped into Meka's Honda Accord. "Hi," I said shyly.

"Hey. Now you sure you ready for your next excursion?"

"Where are we going?"

"You ever head of a strip club name Starz? You gonna be working there on the second floor."

I gasped. I didn't think I would be comfortable working in a strip club and taking off my clothes.

"I don't—"

She cut me off. "I told your daddy and he is all for it."

If it was what my daddy felt that I should do, then I would have to.

"Don't worry, honey. By the time you get up there you going to be feeling just fucking fine. I'm going to school you. Just remember the basics; look each man in the eye like I taught you the other night. Remember, you are in control but you act like they are. Don't concern yourself with how fine, ugly, or fat or in shape these niggas are. The only attraction you have is to the money. If you follow those rules you make some major paper up in here and your daddy will be so proud of you. "

I smiled and sat back in my seat. That's all I wanted was for him to be proud of me. Now that I had my father in my life, that's all I wanted was his approval.

When we got to the strip club Meka had already prepped me and gave me a fake ID. I was no longer thirteen but instead twenty-three. We sat in her car and she gave me something to drink and a pill. Meka didn't let me get out of her car until I had drunk the whole concoction she gave me that had a bitter taste and burned going down my throat. I had to take small sips of it to get it down.

She then told me to get with Honey inside and she would put me on. "Here. When you get inside hand this to Honey." It was a bottle of prescription pills. I tucked them in the left front pocket of my jeans.

"Aren't you coming?"

"Girl, no. So they could say I was pimping you? You'll be fine."

I didn't want her to leave me on my own but I had no choice so I nodded and walked into the club in search of Honey.

As I walked around a tall, older man like my mother's age walked past me. As he did he continued to stare at me like he wanted to say something. I blushed and looked away. I asked the bartender who Honey was and he pointed at a woman who was walking toward the stage. I made my way over to her.

She was an older woman who was pretty with blond hair, contacts, and a huge butt.

"Hi, Honey. I'm Dominique. Meka—"

She cut me off. "You on your own, little girl. I'm not here to babysit no bitch. Now don't you got something for me?" She held out an anxious hand to me."

"Oh." I handed her the pill bottle and she tucked it away in her left jean pocket.

"Tell Meka I'll do her rounds tonight and tonight only. Let's go to the second floor to get started."

I nodded.

She showed me where it was and I walked up the stairs. As I did I noticed a man seated at the bar continued to stare at me. He was older like my mother's age, handsome, brown skinned. I shyly looked away then looked back his way again. He continued to watch me.

Once I was on the second floor I could hear Jay-Z and Kanye West's "Niggas in Paris" blasted in the club. The beat that boomed out of their speakers matched the rate of my heart that seemed to pound louder. I struggled to keep myself from crying. I didn't want to be there.

"The fuck you standing there for? Get the fuck up on the stage. And I'm telling you now you gotta get buck-naked. And up here at Starz, anything goes. I'll beat your ass for wasting anybody time. Meka gave me permission."

I nodded fearfully. I didn't want that. I hoped my last butt whipping was Jada and her mother. Thing was I didn't think I could do the dancing let alone what they were doing on this floor. I was scared. But looking at the lady in front of me with her arms crossed under her chest and her head cocked to the side at this point I didn't think I had a choice. So I stood and watched women who were completely naked twirling on the poles and dancing naked on the stage. There were also women around me on the floor in front of men nude. Some were positioned in front of the men, dancing, while some others were on their laps and in corners of the room I could see that some of the women were servicing the men. *Oh, God, please don't make me have to.*

"Why you looking like that? Anything goes in here. That girl over there is only fifteen and she doing it like a pro." She was pointing at a girl who was hanging from the pole. She did it so good and gracefully. "Can you dance?"

"Not that—"

"Well keep your ass off the pole; we don't want you to break your neck tonight."

I nodded. But I was afraid. I couldn't do what she was doing. The girl looked so relaxed and at ease. Someone slapped my butt. I jumped, and turned around with wide eyes as a man who looked super old winked at me and went to one of the tables to sit down. I was embarrassed out of my mind that he touched me like that in public. It reminded me of the many times in elementary school that boys would do it. Embarrassed, it always made me cry. But I had to be a big girl now.

"Get used to that. You are property of all these men in here for the duration of their stay."

I nodded. But did I really want to be anyone's property? I turned my focus back to the girl on stage.

"I'm sure Meka gave you *something*. She popped what you popped; that's why she looks like that, boo. She's feeling good up there."

"She is?" I didn't think I could or would with all these man looking at me and trying to touch me. The only man I had let touch me was Mr. Douglas and I trusted him.

In a few moments, the pills and drink started seeping in altering the way I felt. The moment my head nodded, Honey yanked my clothes off of me and shoved me on the stage. I was out of my mind and, sweating. Only I wasn't sweating on no pole or having men stick money in my garters. I didn't have on any garters. I was now completely nude. *The floor where anything goes.*

"And if a man wants to get fucked you have to fuck them." Those weren't my words; those were the words of Honey. And she was right because as I completely nude gave a man a lap dance, high out of my mind, he had his way with me. I looked across from me ashamed but the girl across from me was preoccupied with the dude she was entertaining and another in another part on the room doing the same.

I saw things I'd never forget in that room.

Honey was right; anything goes. And that anything went on and on and on.

Fluid was running down my legs. Didn't stop another guy from leading me to a corner.

And what he said, what he asked for, I did it.

I hated the hands that caressed my body, some gentle, some rough. I didn't enjoy any of it. I felt like I was cattle. I was slapped, prodded, drinks poured on me while the song "No Worries" by Lil Wayne rang out in the club. But I had tons. Would I get over this? Would what I did fill me with shame for days to come? Would I be able to do this again? And if I couldn't would it make my father hate me or still love me? What percent would it be?

My vision was no longer right; it was blurred and the room started spinning. Still I felt hot breath on my back and the sound of grunting. I felt my flesh being sucked on and a stinky smoke being blown in my face. And this all went on for what seemed like forever. Before it was finally over, I had several bills clutched in my hands.

Feeling woozy, I stood and fell down. Then I had no further strength to stand again. So I sagged in that corner and stayed for fear that if I got up I would just fall again. I rested there a few minutes; my heart was beating real slow and I kept my eyes closed. Fluid continued to leak and run down my inner thighs.

Honey found me there and started laughing. "Girl. Put your clothes on."

"I don't think I can," I moaned. I could barely hold my head up.

She helped me slide into my dress and shoes saying, "A mess straight up." She slid my feet into the wedge heels Meka had me wear. She helped me walk toward the stairs and down them. I fell once and she had to lift me back up.

"Girl, you better pull it together!" She yanked me into the bathroom where she helped me clean myself up.

"Thank you," I told her.

"You welcome." She left the bathroom.

A few minutes later, I was able to stand on my own. I went to the sink to wash my face.

Once the water hit my face I started to feel better. I sat down on the toilet and kept a wet paper towel on my face for safe measures.

I got a text from Meka: More men are coming in! Go to the first floor and offer lap dances.

I groaned inwardly. All I wanted to do at this point was go home and get in my bed. I wasn't a fan of this place. I wished I could run to my father and cry about what I had just done. But the only way to get it like that, to be able to run to him, was to stay. I wanted to make him proud and sex was his business. If I could perform and do the things the other girls in here did he would have to be proud of me and want to embrace me in a way that Demarco never did. I knew I had to do what he said and thus what Meka said because she was in charge of me. So I took a deep breath, stood, and went back to the first floor.

Once my feet were planted on the first floor, a guy beckoned me over. I took a deep breath and copied every move that another girl across from me did. I knew my body was stiff unlike the girl who was really flexible and had such a good rhythm.

"Relax, baby, and smile. Don't look so scared," the man said to me winking.

I offered a small smile.

The guy from earlier suddenly reappeared and walked in my direction. He paused behind me and whispered in my ear, "Meet me in room seven when you're done. I'll pay more than what he's giving you."

I nodded. *The more money I make the better,* I thought.

A few minutes later I was finished with the lap dance. I collected the twenty dollars. Meka had prepped me before and told me how much lap dances cost and if they wanted more it would be extra. To tell the truth I was so out of it upstairs I knew I was shorted by several of the men up there so maybe if this guy gave me more it would make up for how short I was.

I asked a girl who was walking by where the private rooms were and she directed me to them. I quickly located room seven.

For a second I paused outside the door. Thing was, I didn't want to be in the room with him at all. At least out in the club there were people around so I was somewhat safe. I mean he didn't seem all that bad so maybe he'd be nice to me. I hoped. But people changed behind closed doors. Mr. Douglas had shown me that. I hoped he wouldn't hurt me or be rough like some of the other guys. What made it a tiny bit bearable was the alcohol and the pill Meka had given me but I still was uncomfortable with what they were doing and inside I was screaming for them to stop. It wasn't like Mr. Douglas. I knew and had love for him. Those men were strangers just like this man was. And also I was no longer feeling warm and fuzzy. I was now 100 percent alert. So no matter what he asked me to do to him I had to find a way to distract myself. I focused on a happy time. A time that I laughed. I thought back to our school trip to Magic Mountain and laughing on the Apocalypse ride with Jada, back when we were super close. It was funny because I was also the quiet, scared, shy one in my classes but I was the only one on the ride who could handle it and enjoyed it. All my classmates who got on were screaming, including Jada, and one even threw up. I chuckled, relaxed a little bit, and took a deep breath.

I opened the door and slid inside.

I walked over and stood in front of him as he sat quietly in a chair. His hands were between his legs and he was staring down at the floor. Even as I stood there in front of him he still stared at the floor.

"I called you into this room because I ain't going up there to that cesspool and see that sick, twisted shit because if I can't handle what is going on the first floor I certainly can't handle what is happening on the second floor. At the end of the day, those pretty girls dancing and smiling, in my eyes, are being victimized. I'd go crazy and hurt someone and lose my badge if I were to go up there and see those sick bastards having sex with those girls." He paused. "Are you twenty one?"

Was he a cop? My heart started thudding in my chest. He said badge so he had to be. I stuttered. "This is only my second time here. I'm twenty-one," I lied. "Here's my ID." I pulled it out of my bra and handed it to him.

He looked at it, looked me in my eyes, and frowned. "Right," he said dryly, like he didn't believe me. "What is your name?"

"Dominique Pena."

"Where do you live?"

"Inglewood." He was making me real nervous. His eyes continued to pierce me. Like either he didn't believe me or he wanted to know more information. Maybe both.

"Relax. I'm not going to arrest you. I'm not here to arrest little girls who aren't old enough to consent to what is going on up there. I'm here on police business."

I nodded, my eyes wide. So he was a cop!

"How long have you been working here?"

"I promise I just started today."

"So you don't know anyone named Patrice Wilson?"

I racked my brain and came up blank. "No. I swear, sir."

He nodded like he believed me. "Yes, you look young but a lot of girls in here do. And well they actually are young. To me twenty-one is still a baby in my eyes and I'm thirty-seven and I couldn't touch one of these girls in here. I wish I could shut this bitch down and other places like it." He paused and had a sad look in his eyes before continuing. "Anyhow your age is not the only concern. And your ID I can prove is fake. You look like someone I used to know a long time ago. Pretty often in my line of work I see many faces but there is a face." He looked down and chuckled.

I narrowed my eyes confused.

"The face you favor is a face I can't even begin to forget even if I wanted to."

"Who?"

Chapter 18

Dominique

I stood nervously at my door with the detective standing next to me. I didn't know what my mother was going to say once he told her where he found me. Thing was the person he said he couldn't forget about was my mother. And once he found out Cashmere was my mom he told me to meet him at his car. "Meet me at the black Tahoe. You better meet me out here or I will come looking for you," he threatened in a stern voice.

I nodded nervously. On the way to the car, I texted Meka and told her a cop had caught me and she needed to get out of there. She never responded but on the way out I looked for her car and I didn't see it. So I assumed she had left.

Once I came back outside and I got in his car I asked him, "Why are you doing this? Why didn't you just arrest me?" I almost believed that maybe he was going to have sex with me. Why else would he not arrest me?

He calmly turned on his car and said, "I don't want my cover blown and if I arrest you then it will be and I'd have to take you in. But I won't. Instead I'm taking you home. Now where do you live?"

And thus we were standing outside my house. The officer rang the doorbell. I held my head down in shame as the door unlocked and we came face to face with my mother.

She took one look at me then looked at the cop, gasped, and said, "Caesar?"

Chapter 19

Cashmere

I had been asleep for the whole day due to my Nyquil shots. That was the best way for me to deal with what I was going through. The sound of the doorbell woke me out of my sleep. I sat up in my bed and rubbed my eyes. I got out of my bed wondering who it was and rushed out of my room and down the stairs.

I opened the door and gasped. Caesar was standing on my doorsteps next to my child. The last time I saw him I was only thirteen and he had betrayed me, stomped on my heart when I saw my sister on top of him at the hotel we were staying at. It had hurt me so bad because he was my first love. *Shit that was years ago. What the hell is he doing here with my child?* I thought.

His eyes locked with mine and he had a soft smile on his lips as he stared me up and down. I was already in a bad mood and so frustrated by the fact that I continued and continued to call Demarco and he wouldn't pick up. After my series of calls it seemed that he turned off his phone completely. Then I was hit with all these images in my head of him making love to another woman, being hugged up with one at night while I spent my nights alone. With tears in my eyes I dialed his number again and it went straight to voicemail. I was so frustrated to the point that I beat the phone into my dresser so hard the screen cracked, then in rage I screamed and threw the phone into the wall. The shit split in two pieces.

The last thing I expected today was to find Caesar at my doorstep. Not in a million years. And why was he here with my daughter? I knew she told me that she was going to the basketball game at her school with a new friend she had just made and would get a ride home with her. I was happy, for one because she was making new friends, and for two it meant I could sleep all day long. Although some days I did it even with her home and felt like crap about it. At least today I could do it and not feel bad.

I ignored his eyes as they continued to look me up and down. "Can I come inside?"

I narrowed my eyes at him and slid back, opening my door wider for them to both step inside.

As he walked inside, I said quickly, "Haven't seen you in a while."

"I've been in Shreveport, Louisiana. I came back home a few months ago. I transferred to the LAPD."

I said nothing else. I wanted to keep the conversation light. No need to rehash shit.

Once they both stepped inside we walked into the living room. We all stood and my eyes locked with my daughter's. "Okay," I said evenly, swallowing. "Tell me. Since obviously she won't."

He flashed a police shield toward me. "I'm a detective. And I found your daughter somewhere that she had no business being."

"Where, Dominique?"

She looked down and had her lips pulled in.

Caesar cleared his throat. "She was at a strip club named Starz."

All of a sudden my heart thudded in my chest and my eyes widened. "You lying!" I fired at him. My child wouldn't be in a damn strip club. Caesar obviously came here to start some shit. With his tacky ass. I had other shit on my mind to deal with to entertain this bullshit.

"Tell your mother where you were," Caesar said.

She hesitated.

"Tell your mother," he said sternly. His face remained calm.

"I was there," she whispered.

"Are you serious? Dominique! What in the hell were you doing in a strip club?

"I, ah—"

"You only thirteen! And you said you were going to a game." I was outraged as I stared at my daughter struggle over her words. That shit didn't even sound like my child. "Who did you go there with?" I demanded.

"My friend from school Tish?"

"So is Tish the one you were supposed to go to the game with?" I pressed.

"Yes."

"Well how the fuck did y'all end up at a strip club? I don't even get why you would even be around somebody who would go to a place like that. What are you thinking?"

"Well since Jada and I aren't friends anymore, I just started hanging out with Tish."

Now it made sense. She was lonely and hanging with the wrong crowd. Still I pressed her so she didn't think something like this was acceptable. "For what?"

"Just to see what it was like. Mom, that's all I swear. It was Tish's idea. And I don't know. I just wanted a friend."

"Look. I know you upset that you and Jada aren't friends anymore but obviously this girl is not a good replacement if she hangs in places like a damn strip club."

"She was willing to give me a lap dance. Now I don't know exactly what she was doing but she also went to the floor where anything goes."

My eyes were wide as golf balls.

"That was just a dare!" she protested. "Tish dared me! And I was only on the second floor for a second."

What in the fuck was going on with Dominique! "You at a strip club willing to give lap dances? You only thirteen, shit! I got enough on my mind. I don't need this. You know what I'm dealing with."

But inside I felt partly responsible. I was so caught up with Demarco I wasn't keeping my mind on my child completely. But that still gave her no right to go to a damn strip club. What was she thinking going somewhere like that? Maybe it was because of me and lately how I hadn't really been active in her life since Demarco had left. I couldn't bear for her to tell me that's what it was in that moment. I knew I was being weak. I knew that at the moment I sucked as a parent. But damn I was human and with Demarco being gone I couldn't properly function like I used to. I knew it was fucked up because I had a child I needed to put first and set the example for. But it seemed like the only thing that could restore me was getting him back. I shook my head as guilt and shame washed over me for how weak I was being. Was this how my mother felt?

I gave her a murderous look and said, "Get your ass in the room!"

"Okay." She looked like she wanted to say more to me but she didn't. She did as I told her to.

Once Caesar and I were left alone, I demanded, "And just how did you manage to be the one bringing my child home from a strip club? I see sleazes always were your type. I see it never changed that you don't like good girls. Let me find out from my daughter that you pushed up on her and I'll have you *killed*."

"Look. You have things so wrong. You did then and you do now. But I'm not going to go into the past right now. Just know I could have taken your child in as well as close the strip club down. But I'm working on a case and a patron of the club is involved. I didn't take your child in because I didn't want my cover blown, and also, the moment I laid eyes on her, I knew she was yours. You were all I saw in her face. From the way she walked to the sound of her voice." He shook his head and chuckled. "It's crazy. After all these years your face has always been a permanent imprint in my mind, Cashmere. Probably always will be. That's why I got her out of there. She didn't belong in a strip club. And years ago neither did you. So you should be thanking me."

I started to ask him what he meant by I had things wrong years ago. But really would it matter? That day I caught him with my sister was years ago. Couldn't anything change what transpired after that. So why even bother to ask him to expand on the comment? Even if a part of me wanted to know. It was best to leave it alone. So I did.

So I stared Caesar up and down with an attitude letting him know with my expression that he was not welcome at my home.

"Well I'll get going. If you need help you let me know. My cell is on here and my office line." He held out a card for me. When I didn't reach for it, he laid it on my coffee table.

He walked toward the door. Once he reached it he turned back to me and said, "It was really nice seeing you. You look the same just prettier."

I rolled my eyes and smirked. "Get the fuck out of here, Caesar."

He looked away at my rejection and walked out the door.

I shook any thoughts of Caesar out of my head, but still kept tripping off the fact that I just saw him. I never ever thought I'd see his ass again. Crazy.

I walked to Dominique's room, opened the door without knocking, and found her laid on her bed on her back looking sad at the ceiling.

I stood in front of her and rehearsed in my head what I was going to say to her and the proper punishment I should give her, like maybe grounding her, beating her ass, or both. I was at a loss because I never had to punish her before and shit I was lost. What is the right sanction for your daughter going to a strip club? Yes, I went when I was thirteen but I was trying to survive. Dominique didn't have those issues. When I looked at her sweet, innocent face it was still hard to believe she actually went there. My Dominique? But she admitted it so I had to accept it.

I took a deep breath, about to speak when I heard the doorbell ring. *Gotdamn it!* Who was it now?

"I'm sorry, Mom," she whispered.

"Save that apology 'cause I'm not done with you," I said sternly.

She looked like she wanted to say something but she stopped herself.

I knew my face held disappointment. But I couldn't hide it. This was the first time my daughter had actually disappointed me. And today was the first day I had actually yelled at her. I wondered if my anger was just because she was caught in a strip club or also because I was stressed behind Demarco. Yet I also felt responsible for her being at that damn club. Because my attention wasn't on her like it normally was. I knew it. I knew it was wrong as a mother. It didn't mean I didn't care about my child, or that I didn't love her and wasn't concerned for her; I was just devastated over my husband.

I walked out of Dominique's room and ran down the steps. When I got closer to the door I could hear my mother's voice. "Cash? Dominique? Y'all here?"

"Shit." I didn't want to be bothered with her ass right now.

I opened the door, stepped back, and she walked inside. "What's up, Cash?" She walked past me and sat down on the living room couch. "Come and sit next to me, my child."

"Not now, Mom. I've got some stuff to do."

"What?"

"Why?" I snapped.

"Well damn! I was just coming by to see if you want to go to the spa."

"No. Like I told you I have things to do. I'm not leaving this house."

Then she gave me a look. "You ain't got shit to do. You probably ain't left the house since *he* left. Hibernating like a damn animal is not going to make that fucking man do right and come home, Cash! You sound crazy, baby. Don't give yourself false hope. He is not—"

"Mom! I don't want to hear your shit right now! Why don't you go check on your grandchild and ask her what she has been up to instead of talking shit about my husband?"

She looked alarmed. "What?"

"Ask her!" I snapped.

She put her purse down and walked up the stairs toward Dominique's room in a quick pace.

Relieved she got off my husband, I turned to head back up the stairs when I heard the doorbell again. "Goddamn, who is it now?" I said out loud.

"What you yelling for?" I heard my mom ask. I ignored her and walked to the door.

As soon as I opened the door, I came face to face with a chest. I backed up and my heart thudded so hard in my chest that it felt like I had been punched when I saw yellow reflective tabard. I almost wanted to close the door in his face. But instead, I took a deep breath and came face to face with a police officer.

"Hi, ma'am. My name is Russell Thompson. I'm a police family liaison officer for Inglewood PD. Does Demarco Pena live here?"

"Yes, why?" I demanded in a panicky voice. And already I was shaking not knowing what he was going to tell me.

"Ma'am, there really is no easy way to say this. He was killed in a collision on the 405 freeway and . . ."

Okay. That's when my world just seemed to stop. I mean literally.

I wanted to misunderstand him as he spoke. And although I tried to pretend that I didn't, I heard him well. He said my husband was killed. And, at that point, my ears were ringing, my breathing was coming out in pants, and all the energy within me was abruptly zapped. I lost my balance, right in the doorway. The guy was unable to stop me as I hit the floor in front of him.

Chapter 20

Cashmere

I could feel his arms wrapped around me. But it didn't stop me from passing out.

I felt a cold rag on my face and heard someone call my name. I blinked rapidly and slowly opened my eyes to see three faces in front of me: my mother, my daughter, and an officer.

As soon as I saw him I remembered his words. But that shit . . . I mean it just couldn't be true. Demarco wasn't dead.

I sat up quickly and threw the washcloth off of my face. "Why the fuck are you in my house?" I demanded of the officer.

"Cashmere," my mother said gently.

"Shut the fuck up, Mom." Tears formed in the corner of my eyes. I wiped them away quickly. 'Cause if I let them motherfuckers fall then basically I was telling myself that the bullshit he said was true. That my husband and the love of my life was dead. This could be a crazy motherfucker playing a prank on my family.

"Ma'am," he began gently. "As I told you before you collapsed your—"

"Oh so you are going to continue with that bullshit." I jumped up off the couch, marched up to him and got all up in his face. "So you are going to continue with this bullshit!" Without warning, I took a swing at his face. I started hitting him repeatedly. I had to do something to stop him from saying that shit again, that Demarco was dead. I couldn't bear to hear that again! Tears streamed from my eyes as I punched on the officer.

"Cashmere!"

I felt my mother's strong arms around me as she restrained me.

"Get the fuck off of me!" I shouted. But she was stronger and held on to me.

"Gotdamn it stop this bullshit." My mother spun me around and started shaking me. "Listen for a motherfucking minute 'cause beating that officer's ass is not going to change reality." She looked me in my eyes frantically. "That officer is telling you that Demarco is dead. Baby, he is dead. I'm not going to let you sit here in denial. Demarco was killed! He ain't coming back!"

He ain't coming back. He ain't coming back. He ain't coming back. He ain't coming back. Those four words kept percolating in my head.

I glanced over at Dominique who had her legs curled into her chest on the couch and was crying silently. It was all I could take before I was on the floor beating the ground with closed fists and screaming my lungs out as I looked up toward the ceiling as if asking God why.

Chapter 21

3 Months Later

Dominique

"'Make it rain, trick. Make it, make it rain, trick!'" was sung as I danced seductively in front of three male college students. Travis Porter was playing. And I knew all about that. Nowadays, I making it rain all the time. I had landed this date on my own. I had propositioned one of the guys while I was with Meka at Trade Tec College. He called two of his friends over and I was entertaining all three of them. Meka said she wanted to test me and based on my response, I was becoming a seasoned wifey. I had countlessly been working for her and going on so many dates it made me better and better at this.

"Get naked," one of the guys said as I danced around them. I stripped down until all I had on was my bra and panties. The reason that I didn't care much about what I was doing was because I was always faded and feeling good. In order for me to get through a partner I had to be under the influence. When I was high, I felt invincible. I felt pretty, fine, sexy, charming, mature, and a good dancer all at the same time. There was no way I could do this sober.

"Twerk it, baby," one of them said.

I placed my hands on my knees and rotated my hips so my butt flapped up and down. All they kept saying was how pretty I was. How good I danced. I didn't even care that my underwear was down to my knees, my bra was now off, and one of the guys was filming me with his cell phone. And the more I danced the more excited they got until all three of them were naked and took turns . . . with me. Although after the third guy I was tired they gave me more to drink and they invited some more guys over. It was about thirteen guys in the room and I had some sort of intimate relations with all of them. At one point, because of all the alcohol I had consumed, I was going in and out and every time I came to I was either on my back with a guy on top of me or they were on their back and I was on top of them. But each time the guy from that point on was a different guy. I counted that I had blacked out about six times. Then after that I remember going out and never coming back to again.

"Bitch, wake up." Splash.

I blinked rapidly as cold water was thrown in my face. I coughed, wiped my face, and opened my eyes. I sat up and looked around me as loud music played. I saw a bunch of guys and even girls hanging out. Some were seated on the couch and others stood around. Some danced and held cups in their hands while some stood around and looked at me and laughed. I knew I was sobering up.

I looked down and saw I was naked. I gasped and covered my breasts and vagina with my hands. I was the only one in the room with no clothes on.

"Just ratched," one of the girls said, looking at me in disgust.

My dress was callously flung at me by one of the guys: the one I had propositioned. The same one who had thrown the water in my face. Grateful I pulled it on. My flip-flops were also near me so I pulled them on as well. I couldn't find my underwear or my bra.

"Go on and get the fuck out. You ain't staying for the kickback," he said.

The girls continued to look my way and laugh. In that moment I no longer felt so invincible. I no longer felt pretty, fine, sexy, charming, mature, and a good dancer all at the same time; it all faded with the high. That was normal for me. And then I would feel bad. Even a little ashamed. When I would tell Meka this she would remind me that I was doing this for a greater cause: for my father. She reminded me that he needed the money. That he was trying to get a lawyer to fight his case so he could get out and be there for me. So that always wiped the shame and bad feelings away.

Moments like these were pretty often, where I felt gross. Because that was the way they were now all looking at me. I attempted to run out of the living room, my destination the door but I was tripped and fell to the floor.

Then the guy came yet again: "Man, do you know how to get the fuck out? I'll help you."

I screamed in pain when he pulled me by my hair and dragged me toward the door. He opened it and pushed me out so hard I fell from the steps into some rosebushes.

He turned and walked back into his apartment. I started crying tears of humiliation as the thorns from roses poked me. I crawled out as best I could and continued to get poked in the process. I walked over to Meka's car. She was waiting outside for me, parked on the street.

I hopped in and wiped my tears away.

"Damn I didn't know this was going to take you this long! Shit I went and got something to eat, shopping and all that."

I ignored her. "Please don't make me have to work out of their houses again," I pleaded. I cried again thinking how humiliating that was. Those guys said it would only be them. They never said they were going to invite other people. I felt humiliated. Even though I shouldn't have cared what they all thought of me, I should have only cared what my dad thought, but still. It was embarrassing and I hated how the guy had treated me. I didn't deserve that. But I was in their home so obviously at their mercy.

I wiped the thoughts of what happened the night before out of my head as we waited for my father to come out for our visit. As Meka rattled on, I pondered over my situation. It was crazy to still think about the fact that Demarco was dead. Although he wasn't my real father, it did hurt me that Demarco was dead. Yes, he always treated me like I meant nothing to him. But he always meant something to me. I loved him.

But after I found out he wasn't my daddy, this may sound crazy, but I felt relief just as much as I felt pain. It's obvious why I felt pain. But not so obvious why I felt relief. I realized I felt relief because if he wasn't my father that meant there was a chance that the love and attention Demarco was never able to give me if I could find my daddy he could. And Black, that was what he did.

Truth was, I would never like who I was and what I did but I accepted it. He said what I was wasn't a bad thing. That in life once you accept your role it all makes sense. And he accepted me for who I was. He accepted me as his daughter, something Demarco never did when I was always doing well: making straight As and whatnot, making honor roll, performing in ballet recitals, looking all adorable. I played the cello, and even played basketball. I excelled at everything and still it got not a single response from Demarco. He never cared. And he was in my face daily. Crazy that even though Black was locked up he showed me more attention, affection, and love than Demarco ever did. So what does that tell you? Should I have gone by the fact that Black was locked up and label him a bad guy, or by what he shows me?

My mom wasn't locked up but she had been lying to me all my life. Telling me that a man who wasn't really my daddy was and never telling me about Black. And allowing Demarco to treat me with hatred. She belonged in jail for that. And Demarco hating me because of who my daddy was? Why did I have to be hurt? Like I had something to do with who created me. I wanted to feel like I mattered to not just my mom but to my daddy as well. And finally I had that. I wasn't going to do anything to mess it up. Black would smile at me, hug me, kiss me, say he missed me and he was proud of the money I made for him. He even wrote me! Therefore, no matter how hard it was or how horrible it made me feel, I would continue working for my daddy. I would do anything for him. I already loved him. And he said he always loved me. How crazy was that? I couldn't thank Meka and my aunt enough for taking me to my father. Sometimes I even serviced some of Meka's clients for free when she was too tired just to pay her back.

But crazy part was, it would always just be one parent I had active in my life. Because now I no longer mattered to my mother because she was so sad about Demarco, first being gone and now being dead. And now my mother was on her depression because Demarco was no longer with us. She wasn't going to work, cleaning, or cooking. His death made her even worse. I thought back to the night of the funeral.

I couldn't leave to go with Meka because there were far too many people at the house paying their condolences. And Bev and my grandparents wanted to stay forever and a day. So I went to my room pretending I was just too upset to be around anyone. When Meka texted me at midnight I thought surely everyone would be gone by then and I could sneak out. To be on the safe side I

*changed into my pajamas and tiptoed past my mother's
room to make sure she was asleep. If she was I planned on
racing back to my room, changing, and leaving. But as I
brushed past her room, like I was going to the bathroom,
the image I saw before my made me jump. My mom was
seated on the edge of her bed with a gun pressed against
her temple.*

*When my mother saw me she jumped and hid the gun
behind her back. "Dominique, why you not 'sleep?" Her
eyes were wide like she was asking herself if I had seen
her.*

*But I rubbed my eyes and pretended I didn't see what
I saw. "Mom, what are you doing up?"*

*"Nothing." She stood and rushed toward me wiping
her tear-soaked face. She wouldn't even look in my eyes
just slammed the door in my face. It was better that
way. That way I didn't have to be fake and hug on her
when I was really mad at my mother. I'm not saying
I wanted my mother to kill herself but right now she
wasn't exactly my favorite person in the world. When
I crept back toward her room an hour later, I opened
her door and saw her sprawled across her bed with a
Grey Goose bottle and knocked out asleep. I shook my
head, removed the gun from her bed, and put it back in
Demarco's office.*

*Then I went back to my room to throw my clothes on
and leave.*

After that my mother and I never even talked about
that night and what I saw. She continued to mope like her
life was over and I supposed it was for her. That, that's
how she really felt. It enabled me to do what I wanted.
Matter of fact, every night I would sneak out of the house
and she had no idea.

I was going with Meka to see my dad every weekend.
When school was out all my free time was reserved for

working. There were clients I had accumulated on my own, and some I got from Meka. Meka said Black refused to have me working on street corners. I was glad of that. I would be so afraid out there. What if someone picked me up and stabbed me to death?

"Are you listening to me little girl?" Meka demanded snapping me out of my thoughts.

"Sorry what?"

"Your daddy said for you to keep your focus that's what!"

"I am."

"Hey. I'm just curious. Do you even like having sex?"

Good question, I thought as I nodded absently. I never really gave much thought to whether I liked sex or would ever like it. From the moment I first started having sex it was for the exchange for something not solely for the act. From Mr. Douglas to now. The exchange always went back to the same thing: love. But say I met a nice guy one day, you know, fell in love. I wondered would I want to have sex with him and if I did would I enjoy sex with him after all the partners I'd had? I never gave much thought to the way it made me feel. I guess I just thought it was my duty to do it. It was for the better good of my daddy. A man who obviously cared about me. So, no, I didn't enjoy it. Some of the men were disgusting. Old, fat, and some ugly. Even the handsome ones managed to make my skin crawl. Meka told me it would feel like that. She was right. This was the reason I became acquainted with using something.

"Now when you just feel like you can't hang with a nigga, like you just too through, pop a molly." Now the molly thing . . . Initially, the only time I had done that was that day at Starz and after that, when Meka would offer it to me I would tell her no. I didn't want to get hooked like Meka had revealed that my mother was hooked on

Ecstasy. But one time I had a client who was hurting me so bad I needed a way out. I remember the day. He was older like in his fifties. He was six foot four, really husky with a gigantic thing.

I was in the shower soaping myself down. I had worked all day and I was so sore. As I soaped my body I suddenly saw the bathroom door open. "Meka?" I called.

"No. Not Meka." Before I could say anything else, the shower curtain was slid back and the huge guy, naked, stepped in the tub. I instantly knew he was one of Meka's regulars. He snatched me up.

Alarmed, I protested, "Wait! What are you doing?"

"Meka said it was cool. I seen you here a couple times."

"But. But. But. I'm tired. No!"

He didn't take that for an answer. "I already paid for you shit so it ain't no, no."

I cried out in pain from the impact of what he was doing to me.

I couldn't take it. And this man was showing me no mercy. So I started crying like a baby and continued to yell out, "Meka! Meka!"

She came in the bathroom quickly and said, "I told him it was okay, Dominique."

"But he's hurting me," I said with sobs in my voice.

"I got you." Her head disappeared. And seconds later she came back with a pill. She dropped it on my tongue and left the bathroom. I swallowed it eager for this pain to stop. Within fifteen minutes I could feel the effects of the molly because he still was not done with me.

But I never got a chance to answer her question because my daddy was walking our way. As soon as he did I smiled and stood to my feet. I hugged him.

"Dominique," he whispered in my ear. "You get more prettier each time I lay eyes on you."

I blushed. "Thanks, Daddy."

He released me and turned to Meka. She giggled and hugged him. "Hey, daddy," she purred in his ear.

"How is business going?" he asked her once he pulled away.

"It's going, daddy. Your little princess here is making her rounds at Starz and at the pad."

He eyed me proudly as he sat down. Meka sat down as well. "I tell you, baby, I couldn't be prouder of you," my dad said zapping me out of my thoughts. "Meka said you out here really handling things."

I looked down shyly. "Thank you, D—"

"No!" he said sharply. "Never put your head down when I give you a compliment. Own that shit."

I kept my head up and eyed him nervously. "Okay."

"So how are things at home?"

"Well Mom is still upset about Demarco's death."

My dad showed no emotion at that. I couldn't expect him to. But he did ask me, "You never told me how you feel about that?"

"I don't know. For forever I thought he was my daddy. And he's not. And he never treated me with love. So it's hard to describe how I feel." But I did feel some sadness; it hurt. I had shed tears because although he had treated me the way he did, I loved Demarco. And although angry I felt bad for my mom because she loved him. But my father's next choice of words caused me to reevaluate the way I thought about them both.

"A life lost is never good. But don't expect sympathy or a hug from me for that shit! That motherfucker was given a gift." He placed his palm up. "And he rejected you! Treated you like you were shit lying in the street. I will never forgive that! He had my baby girl and he denied you what a man never should. So you gonna look like a fool and anger me if you sit here in my face and tell me you feel anything besides triumph." His fist hit the table making me jump.

He was right. Demarco had rejected me my whole life so I shouldn't feel bad he was no longer here. And I had every right in the world to be upset with my mother. The only one I could actually trust was my dad.

"How is your mother?"

"She is really sad, Daddy."

He smiled and looked into my eyes. "You know in all my years, I only been in love twice. Cashmere is the second one I ever came to love. And trust me I been around so many women in my lifetime. But no one could ever hold a candle to that woman. She had something special. That no other women, hoe, or bitch could compare to. You just have that in the world. Some women have a special quality and some are just generic. Someday a man is going to feel that way about you. And you better trick him for all he's worth." He cracked up laughing at that.

I glanced at Meka and she had a hurt look on her face.

"Now daddy may be having some good news to tell you soon."

"What?" I asked eagerly.

"Now it's a surprise, baby girl. You'll know soon enough. I don't want to say nothing until I know for sure dealing with this expensive-ass lawyer. But just know that if it rings out to be true you won't be working for much longer."

That made me happy because I hated what I was doing and was only doing it for him.

"Now let me talk to Meka. For a minute."

"Okay."

Meka quickly turned her frown upside down and they moved to another table. I placed on my ear buds and listened to the new J. Kole CD. My dad always had me do this when he handled business with Meka. He said it wasn't for my ears to hear. I was curious as to what they were talking about but I didn't want to be nosy.

On the way out to the car, I noticed Meka was visibly quiet. "What's wrong?" I asked her.

"Don't motherfucking worry about it!" she snapped. And she usually never snapped at me.

I had a sharp intake of breath at her snapping at me. But I kept quiet and when she unlocked the door to her Regal I as quietly as possible slid inside. I didn't want to make her angrier. I wondered what she was so mad about. But I thought twice about asking.

Once she got inside the car and closed the door, Meka turned to me and out of nowhere she punched me in my face so hard I cried out in pain.

I held my face confused. But she continued her assault on me. Her hits were harder than Mrs. Douglas's and Jada's. I continued to cry as she hit me. I knew my mother has always raised me to fight back but I had always been scared to actually fight back. I was weak and I knew it and accepted it.

"I'm out here grinding for his motherfucking ass since I been twelve. Working at a nasty fish place putting every single paycheck I get from there on that nigga books, and what's left of the money I make selling my pussy after paying all my bills. I'm driving a fucked-up car, live in a fucked-up building, and can't even take a day off! And on top of all of this, I'm putting up with your weird ass"—punch—"and that motherfucker"—punch—"got the nerve to say he still love your mama? What the fuck." Another punch. "It's enough I gotta look at you every day and you look like that gray-eyed bitch. But I still gotta hear him talk about her! Hell the fuck no." She held my chin in a death grip and slapped me upside my face.

I cried out loudly.

"Shut the fuck up, bitch."

She gripped my hair in between her hands and delivered more blows to my body. I continue to bawl. Finally when she started breathing hard she shoved me away roughly.

"I wish they had never let that bitch out of jail."

She tried to catch her breath. All the while I curled up in a ball and cried as quietly as I could. She did this because she hated my mother. How could I look at Meka the same? I thought I could trust her. She had hurt me all because of my mother.

She then pulled out of the parking structure and drove down the street. When she got to a red light, she grabbed me by my hair again and pulled me toward her. "Listen and listen well," she hissed. "You better not tell Black that I attacked you. Or I will get in Black's head and make him hate you forever! Trust me I've done it before. You got it?"

"Yes!"

She shoved me away again. "Fuck you and your mom, Dominique. Don't ever think I like you and I definitely don't like your bitch-ass mother."

I nodded through my tears and stared out the window.

Chapter 22

Cashmere

Dead.

Just as Demarco was dead all my days, hell, my body seemed to be the same. It was crazy. How I was supposed to go on without that man when I loved him so much? Each night, I went to sleep and each day I woke up there was a constant ache in my chest and a lump in my throat. It never seemed to go away. It traveled with me throughout my days.

It had been over three months that had passed since he had died. The burial was so hard for me to get through even though I got drunk right before and even that didn't help me. It was still hard. I wished to God that my father was there. He didn't have the power to bring him back but he would have been more welcomed than my fucking self-righteous mother. My daughter had grown so distant from me. The only one I could really count on for support was Bev. In fact, she was the one who got me out of my bed and had me working again. I mean it wasn't like I had any choice in the matter at all. For the past month, every Tuesday through Saturday she would come and pick me up. The first couple times I refused and talked shit, saying, "I'm grown, Bev. I don't need to go to the fucking shop."

"Well if you fucking grown act like it and get out of this fucking bed!" she had yelled back at me. Unlike my mother I wouldn't even dream of yelling back at Bev because she had been more of a mother to me than my own mama.

"Hell, Cashmere. You thinking staying in this bed is going to make your situation better it's not. You'll never be able to heal from this shit if you don't go back to your normal life. And now we short at the Compton shop so bring your ass. You got five minutes to come out here."

And so I did, talking shit all the way.

I mean it did keep me busy. And if in moments I needed to break down I could go in Bev's office and do just that. It was kind of hard being at the shop in Compton with her because there were so many memories of Demarco there because that was the place where I met him. So no matter what I did it always brought me back to him. But I figured it couldn't be worse than the house. His smell still lingered there. And I suppose since he has been to all the shops working at one verses the other wouldn't make me hurt less. But what I had at the Compton shop versus the Inglewood shop was the support of Bev. And I needed her support now more than ever.

And this morning was no different. Bev was in my driveway. Despite the fact that my stomach was cramping like crazy from the night before and carried over to today she still pressed the issue that I go. And since it was keeping me busy I went. I knew I couldn't wither away and die. Although most of the time I wanted to.

I remembered Mrs. Hope had always told me to not run from the pain; run toward it. I was struggling to do that these past few months but by me going back to work I was making a small effort. The next thing for me was to have reunification with my child. I thanked God that the worse thing she did was going to that strip club. But it was right before Demarco had died so I didn't fully discipline her like I normally would have. Normally would have?

What was I talking about? I never really had to punish my child because she had always been a good kid. But I knew she must have gone on a dare with her friend and it was probably because mentally and emotionally I had checked out with my chasing after Demarco and then grieving over his death. And I didn't feel good about it. I prayed my daughter didn't grow to hate me like I grew to hate my mom. I mean I never abandoned Dominique, all her basic needs were met; I just wasn't involved like I normally was. But if I could pull out of this I knew I would revert to the mother I used to be just a few short months ago.

I sighed and continued to sew the hair into the hair net of the client I was working on. Eric Roberson was blasting through the speakers in the shop.

"How's your stomach feeling?" Bev yelled out of her office.

"Still cramping," I said.

I figured my period was probably coming. I knew I was stressing super hard since Demarco had left and it hadn't come the previous month. And it was probably going to be really heavy. But Bev always told me it was better to stay active on your menstruation.

When I finished the client I went into Bev's office and sat down. She was writing something but looked up and said, "What's up, Cash?"

"Do you have an aspirin?"

She pulled a bottle out of one of her desk drawers and handed it to me. They were Motrin. I grabbed two out and poured some water from her Arrowhead dispenser. I dropped the two pills down my throat and washed them down with the cold water.

"Still cramping?"

"Shit yes."

"You think maybe it's not your period? When you finish do you want to go to the docs?"

"No. I think my period is coming; you know I always had that problem of being irregular when I'm under stress. My doctors have told me time and time again not to stress. I never listen. But I'm so glad you forced me out of bed and to work. I'm not saying my life is great; it hasn't been great in a long time even when Demarco was alive. But I, honestly since he left, couldn't imagine another day let alone future without him and for the past few months I have been living in misery. I really wanted to die. I almost started cutting again. I'm so glad I didn't. And while my days right now aren't all sunny, since I've been getting my ass up and coming to work they ain't been as dark as they have been. Thanks, Bev. For the first time in a long time I actually have hope that I can heal from this."

"No problem, honey. I know and that's why I'm so glad that you're back to working even if I gotta drag you out of bed and bring your behind here. I know that Cash is unbreakable but you just needed to be reminded."

I chuckled.

"And you smiling again?"

"What can I say? Crazy Bev has always had that affect on me."

She chuckled. "So in all of this that has been going on, how is Dom?"

"In all actuality, you know what's so crazy and disappointing to me? What I learned about myself. Bev, I as a parent have been fucking up. I was so hell-bent on chasing after Demarco when he left that I put that in front of Dominique. I started to feel like I'm not all that different from my mother. I haven't been cooking and really checking on her like I normally do as a parent. And I want to fix that. I plan on going home and making her favorite meal and sitting her down to talk."

"Dominique is a good kid so I'm sure she is fine and will understand."

I took a deep breath and admitted to Bev how I had found out that Dominique was in a strip club.

"No, she shouldn't have had her behind in there. But Dom is a good kid. You don't see no crazy videos of her twerking, smoking drugs, having sex and doing crazier stuff. Now when you see shit like that then you know it's time to worry. But she has never been a bad kid. She probably was just curious is all. That just means you have to buckle down and stay on her. But, Cash, don't be so hard yourself. We all make mistakes. You been through a lot in your life and you still managed to be a good wife and a good mother. In my opinion, you will get over this in its entirety when you realize that you are not to blame for Demarco leaving or his death.

"I can't put my finger on it but I wholeheartedly feel that Dominique not being his was not why he acted like he hated you or even why he left. What I believe is that it had more to do with him than you or Dominique. Thing is you can't give up on your life because he left.

"And yes, you neglected Dom lately but it's understandably so. But you didn't do the shit your mother did. You have always been stronger than her. So don't even begin to compare yourself to that woman ever. I know she has come a long way, Cashmere, but I can't help but feel that a lot of shit you had to deal with you wouldn't have to had she stood up as a woman and as a mother. But I'm not telling you this so you can get angry at your mom or throw blame her way. Who has times for grudges anyway? I'm telling you that so you can see you need to not beat yourself up. Makes sense?"

"Yeah. You always do. If it wasn't for you I don't know how I would have gotten through then and how I could get through now. So I thank you for that."

"What are second moms for? I'm always here for you."

I gave another smile. "Okay. I'm feeling okay right now but be aware that come midnight, when I roll over and the chest I've rested my face on since I was eighteen is not there I may call you whooping and hollering. I mean I'm not saying that the pain is not lessening with each day. But even when I have my okay moments the pain sometimes has a way to creeping back in and being so fucking intense."

"If you need to call me, call me. I don't care what time it is."

She walked over to me and gave me a hug.

I hugged her back.

Chapter 23

Dominique

"You tested positive for syphilis."

I gasped at the nurse practitioner in front of me who said that. Even though Meka told me STDs were nothing to worry about and that she said she had all of them before except for herpes, genital warts, and AIDS, I didn't care. Syphilis was serious and scary to me. I remember in my health class, my teacher said it can make you blind, paralyzed, and even crazy. I didn't want that. To not be able to see again made my heart skip a beat just the thought of it. I wasn't strong enough to live my life blind. I normally used a condom with the men I had sex with. But a couple times I knew the condom ended up breaking, and a couple times men like Meka's client forced me to have sex with them without one. And the whole time I was doing it with Mr. Douglas he never used a condom.

If my mother only knew. But luckily I went to the free clinic that Meka told me about called Curtis R. Tucker Health Care Center on Manchester. So my mother would not know about this! At the clinic you could get birth control and STD testing and it was free. I was glad she gave me the information about the clinic but ever since Meka had attacked me and made me do something I regretted I didn't think I could ever look at her the same. I could never warm back up to her. I had lied to my mom that the busted lip Meka had given me was a result of getting hit in the face with a basketball. She had bought it or maybe she plain out didn't care. But since my mom was the type who at the drop of a hat was willing to fight I figured she believed my story. And she looked really concerned when she saw it. Lately my mother seemed a little more attentive to me. But it changed nothing about how I felt about her and how I saw her.

The nurse handed me a paper cup and some pills. "Take these. They should cure you and do not have sex for seven days."

"Okay," I said quietly.

"Are you on a birth control?"

"Yes," I lied. I just wanted to get out of there.

The lady gave me a doubtful look. I gave a small smile and looked away.

"Okay. You're done." She handed me some pamphlets. "Here is some information on safe sex. Make sure you read it because the next time it might not be an STD. You may end up contracting HIV, in the world we live in, young lady. So be careful."

"I will. Thanks."

She grunted and started writing something down in a file. I left and quickly walked to the parking structure and got in Meka's car.

She dropped me off at the corner of my house and I walked the rest of the way so it didn't look like I was with her. When I got home, I was surprised to smell food cooking and it smelled really good. My first reaction was that my grandma was probably there. But when I walked into the kitchen, I was surprised to see that it was my mom standing behind the stove. She was bent over it and, with mittens on, was lifting a pan out of the oven. When she felt my presence she turned around.

She smiled when she saw me. "Hey, baby," she said. She looked happier and more upbeat. I remembered how in the past, when my mom smiled at me, it always made my day. She always had this way of making me feel loved and like I was the most important thing in her world. Now to know what I knew about her, to know how she had been lying to me all of my life, now when she smiled at me I felt nothing. Funny. I didn't even know if I loved my mom anymore. Sounds crazy but I'd have rather it be her locked up than my daddy. At least he was always honest with me. My mother allowed me to love a man I didn't belong to and a man who hated me and all along she knew. I wanted to say, "Screw you, Mom," when she said, "Hey, baby." But instead I just gave her a fake smile and said, "Hey, Mom."

"How was school, baby?"

I couldn't think of the last time she had asked me that. School meant nothing to me anymore because it had meant nothing to her anymore. I went and performed like a robot. Did my work and went to work with Meka.

I watched her grimace. I started to ask her if she was okay. But I didn't really care at this point.

"Man, these cramps are killing me."

"Oh really?" I secretly prayed my period would come soon. The pregnancy test I took at the clinic came up negative. But still. They were not 100 percent accurate.

"Listen, I know it's been crazy lately. And I've been completely out of character, with Demarco leaving and then passing away. It's . . ." Her eyes got watery. "It's been hard. But I'm slowly trying to get things back in order. I want you to know that I'm really sorry for neglecting you and your needs. No one is more important to me than you are, Dominique." She searched my eyes I guess to see if what she was saying was registering. It was but I found it hard to believe that I was ever first in her life. Demarco was. But still, I went along with what she was saying.

"I understand, Mom. It's okay."

My mom looked satisfied at my words that we could rebuild our relationship. She walked around the table and gave me a hug. She then gently turned my face toward hers so she could study my mouth. "Is it still hurting?"

"No, it's fine."

"Now you sure it was a basketball? 'Cause if someone is messing with my child you already know."

I gave a fake laugh and my mother chuckled. "I promise, Mom, it was a basketball."

"Okay." She went back to what she was doing.

A few minutes later, we ate dinner and my mom tried to engage me in a conversation. I participated though, pretended it was like old times. A couple times, I saw her glance at where Demarco normally sat. Sadness washed over her eyes. Then she shook her head and gave a smile like she was redirecting her thoughts.

"Hey. I made a lemon cake, too. Want me to cut us both pieces and we can watch a scary movie?"

I really didn't want to but I agreed because my mom looked really pitiful. "Okay, Mom."

"Okay. Why don't you throw a DVD in while I cut the cake?"

"Okay." I jumped up and went into the living room. I shoved *The Amityville Horror* into the DVD player. My mom came back with two pieces of lemon cake.

"I gave you a big hunk," she said chuckling and handing me a plate with a tall glass of milk.

"Thanks, Mom," I said with my pasted smile.

She then sat down next to me with hers in hand. I saw her grimace in pain and assumed it was from the cramps. "My period will probably be here tomorrow; that's probably why I'm craving something sweet." I watched her dip into her cake and I dipped into mine. I played my mother's game but it really changed nothing. Meka was going to pick me up tonight to work and I was still anxiously awaiting another letter from my father.

Chapter 24

Cashmere

The next morning, I had a cramp so sharp I screamed. My body felt really weird. I sat up in the bed and pulled the covers back. I saw blotches of a brownish-like fluid on the sheets. I instantly had the urge to poop. I stood from the bed and headed toward my bathroom. But before I could get there, a cramp hit me that had me doubling over in pain. I struggled taking another step. Something was not right. I felt like something was pushing out of me. "Dominique!" I called. But when I looked at my clock on the wall I saw it was after seven and she was gone to school. I had to get to the hospital.

I needed to call Bev.

I grabbed the home phone off the nightstand. I moaned low in my throat as the pain continued to pulsate through me. I dialed Bev's number. She answered on the third ring.

"Hey, when you come to pick me up I need you to take me to the hospital. Something is not right."

"I'll be there in a couple minutes!" she said.

As I waited for Bev, the urge to go was still there. I struggled to get to the bathroom as the feeling of having to poop got more drastic by the minute. I sat on the toilet and pushed down, but the harder I pushed the harder it was to have a bowel movement; instead, I felt my vaginal walls stretching then something slipping out of me. I gasped and looked in the toilet bowl! I screamed and my eyes were wide. It was an embryo! As the remains of it slid out of me I felt heat rush my entire body, and became so lightheaded I collapsed right there on the toilet.

I woke up to an IV in my arm and the sound of beeping. My eyes fluttered open and once my eyes focused I saw I was in a hospital room.

What the hell?

I heard feet shift. I saw Bev and my mother were seated in the hospital room, near my bed. I sighed and memories of what happened to me flooded my head. I remember waking up and being in pain, and seeing a dead embryo in the toilet. Man, that shit was so crazy. It had to be a fucking nightmare. That shit could not be real and I was going to find out now.

"Hey, baby," my mom said with a smile.

I ignored her. Her smiled dropped at my disdain.

"How you feeling, Cash?" Bev asked.

"Not too good." I tried to stretch and was hit with sharp pains in my abdomen. I winced from the pain.

"Okay," I said evenly. "Tell me something: was what slid out of me a baby?"

They both looked perplexed. Like they both didn't know what to say.

"Yes, baby. You had a miscarriage. And you hemorrhaged. The baby was seventeen weeks."

I closed my eyes and a rush of pain hit me. I couldn't even move as tears seemed to flood my face. I could not describe the pain that I felt. Here all I ever needed to save my fucking marriage was all this time living inside of me? And I didn't know it! My husband had left me and was now dead. And the baby! The last piece of him was dead as well. I didn't know what else to do so I snatched the IV out of me and got out of the bed. "I'm so fucking tired of this shit!"

Both Bev and my mother rushed toward me. "I know you're upset. But calm down, Cashmere, and get back in the bed," Bev said.

"Come on, Bev, how much fucking more am I supposed to take? My husband leaves me; then he is killed. I have a miscarriage! I'm so tired of this shit!" I shoved my sleeve up took one of my fingernails and prepared to dig it into my right forearm. I wanted my skin to tear so bad.

I heard my mother and Bev scream, "No!" at the same time. They both grabbed me before I could get a chance to dig in and for the pain I was feeling I was really going to dig in. So I didn't feel so fucking dead inside!

I snatched away from my mother who looked lost. "Let me guide you back to the bed, Cashmere."

I allowed her to put me back in the bed. "Neither one of you understands how I feel. How bad this shit feels. How much it hurts. Neither of you do!" I started sobbing loudly.

Bev came over to me and started hugging me and saying, "Let it out, Cashmere; that's the only way you going to heal from this."

I continued to sob in her arms while she held on to me. When my crying calmed down Bev helped me get comfortable in the bed. The nurse came back in the room and reattached the IV into my arm. Once the nurse left, I asked, "What was it?"

"It was a boy," my mom said.

I shook my head bitterly. I was so mad at myself for not even thinking that I could be pregnant. I guessed after so many false alarms a part of me felt like I couldn't conceive. That it would never happen. Who was to say that the night Demarco had left if I had told him I was pregnant that he wouldn't have stayed? He wanted nothing more than a child. It would have improved his temperament and made him a better husband to me and even a better stepfather to Dominique. I felt so, so stupid. If he hadn't left he probably would be alive right now as well.

"I know you pretty much hate me. And you sure as hell don't respect me or want to hear what I have to say. But, Cashmere, I don't want you to sit in that bed and beat yourself up more for this. I know what you thinking. If you had known you were pregnant things would be different. Cashmere, don't even begin to do that shit to yourself, baby. I can't stand to see you punish yourself anymore. I love you. And if you let me I can help you get through this."

I saw my mom start to sob. It made me soften toward her. She loved me, I knew. Yes, she had fucked up but she loved me and she was showing it now by being there after all the shit I had been talking to her. And I had no energy to attack her right now. What purpose would it serve? It wouldn't change the shape of things. It couldn't reverse shit.

"Thanks, Mom. But you can't fix this and you can't take away the pain. I appreciate you trying and I appreciate you caring. But you can't."

"That's fine and all, Cashmere, but I'm here. And I'm not leaving you."

I nodded and looked away. I felt irreparably broken. Like nothing could ever fix me and like nothing could ever make me feel good or whole again. That's truly how I felt.

I closed my eyes and pretended this shit was one big dream.

They performed a D and C that would have kept me in the hospital for three days. Then because my fucking mother said I was feeling depressed, they kept me for a fucking seventy-two-hour hold because they feared I was going to kill myself. Once I was evaluated the doctor extended the time and diagnosed me with severe depression. So I was forced to stay in their psych ward. Four days later I was reevaluated again, prescribed some Abilify, and released. My mother stayed at my house and looked after Dom during my hospital stay. A couple times, Dominique had come up with my mother to see me. Shit was so embarrassing.

The last thing I wanted my child to think was that I was incapable of taking care of myself. I just wanted to get home, be with my baby, and keep busy to get my mind off of this. The morning they finally released me, Dominique was in school; my mother came to get me alone. All I needed to do was wait for my prescription and I was free from that bullshit hospital. As we walked over to the pharmacy, my mother asked me, "You feeling better, Cash?"

"Yeah," I said. I was certainly better than when I had first gotten there. But there was still an ache in my heart that's for sure. I shook my head as my eyes got watery again. My mother rubbed my back to comfort me.

Once we made it to the pharmacy, my mother sat down and pulled out her phone. I walked up to the window and I gave them my prescription.

"Give us fifteen minutes," the pharmacist told me.

I nodded. I turned to walk over to where my mother sat and collided with a chest. "I'm sorry," I said without looking up.

"Cashmere?"

My eyes narrowed and I looked up at Caesar.

"How are you?" He looked concerned when he saw my appearance. "Are you all right?"

"No, not really," I said truthfully despite who it was I was talking to.

"Is there anything I can do? Assist you with? Cashmere, the last time I saw you, I meant what I said when I told you if you needed anything you could call me."

I shook my head at him. "Caesar, you are the last person I would ever come to for help. Believe that. You seem to forget—"

"Maybe if we talked you'd feel different."

"Oh I doubt that, Caesar. I'd probably hate your ass more."

"No. You'd actually have clarity."

I gave him a crazy look. "At this point in my life clarity won't do shit for me."

"What's taking so long?" My mother, with her nosy ass, came and stood next to me. Her eyes locked with Caesar's and she looked him up and down.

"Who is this, Cash?"

"No one important," I bit out hatefully.

"Damn like that, Cash?" she asked stifling a giggle before turning serious and mean mugging Caesar. "Now if you a stranger trying to get at my fine child, you have to excuse my daughter. She is going through a lot. She lost her husband and just recently had a—"

"Mom, shut up!"

She ignored me and her voice got louder. "Had a miscarriage. Now if you some no-good nigga from her past you best get the fuck on, 'cause my daughter don't look too happy to see you and I'll have my *commissioner husband* pay your ass a visit," she threatened. She took a fighting stance like she was ready for war.

"Calm down. I'm definitely not a stranger, ma'am; and, Cashmere, like I said, I'm—"

I sucked my teeth and said, "I'm done talking to you, Caesar." I grabbed my mother by her arm and we walked away to the pickup side. Caesar just stood there and watched me. Then a few minutes after I pretended to ignore him, he left.

Chapter 25

Dominique

I was seeing stars and I was feeling good as Tyga's "Bubble Butt" blasted in the club. Meka said we couldn't go back to Starz so she had me working strictly for Barbary Coast. She said the place was known for players and pimps. I was winding and twirling on a random guy in the lap dance room.

Lots of thoughts went through my head as I danced. My mother was finally home from being in the hospital for almost two weeks. It was crazy. I mean for one thing she was pregnant and lost the baby. I wondered if she had known she was pregnant and had Demarco would things have been different. I didn't think he would have treated me any different because I was never his. In my opinion the baby wouldn't have done anything but put a Band-Aid on their messed-up, miserable marriage. But I probably wouldn't even have gotten a Band-Aid for my messed-up relationship with him. While I knew my mom was in pain from the reality of what she was dealing with, I couldn't focus on her. I was dealing with my own stuff. I mean, for so long and no one wanted to tackle or assist me with my pain. So why should I have cared about hers? Chasing after a man was far more important to my mom so I would keep focusing on my dad: the man who really cared about me.

The fact that he was my mother's pimp and the fact that he was in jail meant nothing to me. Like Black had told me, if my mother hated him and working for him so much why didn't she leave? She could have gone to the police or social services and she never did.

Since my mom had told my grandmother about me going out and being in a strip club she watched me like a hawk. Meka was pissed. I couldn't even get out to see my father. I only snuck out a couple times while she was asleep. It was crazy to me because she seemed like she would be cool. Nope. I thought back to how she sat me down for a talk while my mother was in the hospital.

"Now your mother told me all about where she found you. Dominique, what's wrong with you? I'm not here to judge you but being in a female strip is hella ratched, little girl." Then without blinking she asked, *"Are you fucking?"*

"No, Grandma."

"Girl, you better be telling the truth. Because I done seen all and done all. I could have self-destructed but I have been lucky enough to have been with good men. First Cashmere's father and now my commissioner."

My grandmother thought she was such hot stuff because she was married to a police commissioner. But he was retired so she really should have gotten over herself. But her next comment surprised me.

"He is fucking around on me though. I don't know who it is but I can feel it. Everything is so different now. Simple things: the way he calls my name; the way that he kisses me. It is all so very different. Crazy part is that I've never been faithful to any man I've ever been with. But the one I am faithful to is not to me. Don't tell your mom because I been talking so much shit about your daddy your mom won't let me live the shit down. It's different though. But your stubborn-ass mama just

won't get it. Some men cheat because they just ain't shit and some cheat because they feel neglected in some way. They don't feel needed. See Hank thinks I'm still in love with Desmond. But your mama, she did everything right by Demarco so that motherfucker don't have the right."

Grandpa Hank always seemed to dote on my grandmother and be so enamored by how pretty she was. But I did notice that on her last couple visits he wasn't with her, which was new.

I saw a tear slide down her cheek. She wiped it away quickly. "If I find out he is fucking around on me I'm—"

"Let me guess. You're going to divorce him and take him for all he has, Grandma?"

She paused. "For the first time I don't know what I'll do. For all the years of wrong I've done maybe, just maybe now, it's catching up with me."

"Do you ever miss your other husband? My real grandfather?"

"Oh just about each and every day, girlie." She chuckled. "I have dreams about that man. What I wouldn't have done for fate to be different and he be the one striding through my door every day. Now don't get me wrong; I love your smooth and fine grand pappy. And he puts it on me just right in the bedroom. But that true mind-blowing, nipples hard, pulse-racing love I only experienced with Desmond. And even still, when I had it, I fucked it up with bad choices. Sometimes I ain't shit."

"What about your other daughter. Do you miss her?" I asked in a soft voice.

"I mean she was my firstborn. So I can't say that I didn't love her. But you want me to be honest with you. To keep it trill. No, not really. She was the devil's spawn. Hell, I almost died giving birth to her so I should have seen it as a sign of what was to come. But I didn't. I love her because she was my baby. But I honestly don't think

she would have amounted to shit. She is in a different bucket than your mother bottom line. God bless her though."

Wow. How can anyone say those types of things about their flesh and blood? *My grandmother was really mean.*

"Now while we're on that, let's get on you and your babysitter's club adventures at the strip club."

"Huh?"

"The point is, Dom, you don't have any business being in there. Bottom line. You need to behave yourself, be a role model, go to school, and keep your focus where it belongs: not on ding-a-lings but the books. At your age sex is overrated unless these little bastards know what a Hermes bag is and for a nut they gifting you with one. And if they don't you don't need to be opening up your mouth or your vajayjay to them got it?"

I nodded.

"And, little hooker, don't think you going to run amuck on me. I know all the tricks of the trade," she said sternly. "Try to sneak out while I'm here. I ain't your pussy-ass mama. God bless her. I love her but I ain't. And I will fuck you up." She blew me a kiss and said, *"Now be a sweetie and get your glammommy something cold to drink and some snacks."*

"Yes, ma'am," I said. I ran into the kitchen. When I came back out I brought her some cold lemonade, hot Cheetos, and some Pecan Sandies cookies. I set them in front of her.

"Here." She handed me her iPhone. *"Put it on the Mary Jane Girls, put it on your mother's dock, and take your little behind to sleep. When you get out of school tomorrow, I'll take you to the MAC counter okay?"*

"Okay." I put the music on for her.

"Don't even think of trying to sneak out. Now give me a kiss, baby."

I pecked her on the cheek.

"Sleep tight," she said.

"Thanks." I went up the stairs to my room.

But by ten o'clock I smelled marijuana and saw my grandmother in the middle of the floor, puffing away and dancing to the Mary Jane Girls and giggling to herself. Then as the last Mary Jane Girls song played, she was sprawled across the floor sobbing and saying, "I miss you so much, Des."

By eleven-thirty she was out and so was I. It was crazy to me that my grandmother was always talking about God and being a Christian woman yet she smoked weed and I always wondered if she slept with other men.

As I finished up one dance I was told to do another. Only I gasped when I walked into the room. I was shocked to see Uncle Dame seated in the chair I was just a few seconds from straddling. He was rubbing his crotch with a smile and looked up just as the door closed behind me. He met my shocked gaze and surprise glazed over his.

"What in the fuck are you doing here?" he demanded.

I was busted.

I tried to make a run for the door but Dame was on me and grabbed me by one of my arms. "Sit your sneaky ass down."

I nodded and sat in the chair he had vacated to get me. I kept my eyes downcast as he stood over me.

"Now tell me what the fuck you doing wrapped up in this cesspool of bullshit?"

"I, ah—"

"The fuck you stuttering for?" he shouted.

I started crying as he continued yelling at me.

"This is a fucking disgrace. You being here! You only thirteen fucking years old! This is not a place for you. You should be at home studying or some shit like that. Man, if Demarco was alive to see this crazy shit!"

I continued to nod my head as he lectured me. Then he paused for a minute to catch his breath. This mess was going to be over for me real soon because I knew he was going to tell my mother, that's for sure, and she was going to kill me!

"Now get up."

I stood to my feet. And as I did he moaned low in his throat. He sat back in the chair.

His next words surprised me. "Come here. Stand in front of me." I did, confused, and he ended my confusion when he said, "You look just like your mom."

His eyes traveled down my body and he licked his lips. Then he wiped the wetness away with the palm of his hand. "Now, sexy. Do what I'm paying your little ass to do. Yes, I knew who I requested."

"But, but . . . you're my uncle."

"I ain't your motherfucking uncle. I'm not blood, Demarco dead, so that shit frees me by default," he said and chuckled. Then he slapped me hard on my butt. "Now make that ass clap."

I couldn't believe Dame was making me do this for him. I mean he had been around since I was little and had always been like a father figure to me. Thing was, I guess you never really knew a person. My mother had proved that to me. And damn, Uncle Dame had confirmed it.

When I stood there with my mouth wide open, he reached over and slapped me on my butt again. I wanted to run out of the room but he stopped that by saying, "Don't even try it. You not my niece today. You just a regular trick. Matter fact. Fuck a lap dance. Get on your knees, little Dom."

I gasped. "No, Uncle."

"What?" He grabbed me by my ponytail and yanked me until I tumbled forward in front of him. The pain was killing and shooting through the roots of my hair. Dame held on to my head with one hand and with the other he unbuttoned his jeans and shoved them to his feet.

He pulled my face down and said. "I seen how you get down. Open your motherfucking mouth."

He yanked my hair super hard. I cried out from the pain and from the shock of what he was making me do. I wouldn't perform so he gave a chop to the back of my neck. I had never been exposed to this type of treatment from Uncle Dame. It hurt to know he would treat me this way. He shoved my head into his crotch.

I resisted the urge to regurgitate. Thing was he showed me no mercy as he held on to my head with my hair. I couldn't bring myself to do it. I just couldn't! I gagged and vomited all over him.

"Shit." He shoved me away. I fell like a heap on the floor and continued coughing and wiped my nose and mouth with the back of one of my hands.

He stood over me and yanked my shirt off of me. He used it to wipe the vomit off of himself. He then threw it back at me. I breathed a sigh of relief that he was done. Well, I thought he was. But I heard his pants drop entirely and he grabbed me from behind. "Come on!"

"No, Uncle."

He ignored my protests and positioned me on my knees. He covered my mouth with one of his hands and held my ponytail to roughly force himself on me. I whimpered.

"I guess you think I should feel bad but you shouldn't be in this bitch anyway. And as for your bitch-ass daddy, I never liked that nigga anyway. He was too fucking emotional and too pussy whipped by your mama," he said between pants.

He was breathing harshly. And I continued to cry. He covered my mouth with a hand so no one could hear me.

And no one did.

I was screaming inside.

Chapter 26

Cashmere

Bev. She was what kept me going in the midst of all I was dealing with. Like clockwork, she resumed driving to my house, and getting me out of bed and back to work. In fact she didn't even give me a chance to go back to my not getting out of bed ritual.

When I would be at the shop, I told her to give me all the clients who needed sewn-in weaves. I knew eventually I'd have to go back to the shop in Inglewood. But I didn't want to. I didn't need anyone in my face asking me if I was okay or feeling bad for me. That would bring me right back to my husband. Here no one really knew me except for Bev because I never came there too often. All the old heads had been long gone. And plus, I still needed to be close to Bev because if ever I was having a moment where thoughts of Demarco or thoughts of the miscarriage came, I could just slip away and she would finish up the client. Or no matter how many times I whined about Demarco being dead and how fucked up it was Bev never got tired of lending an ear. She never rolled her eyes or snapped like my mother did.

While I worked I listened to music. And other times I listened to Bev's clients. They told me all about what was going on in their social life, with their kids and husband. A lot of times they wanted my advice on what to do about

their husband cheating and whatnot. It was funny; when
I gave them my advice they always seemed to respect it.
Whereas I didn't because of all the stupid choices I had
made in my life. Another thing I was glad of was the fact
that my aunt didn't bring her fat ass in here. Since her
cancer she didn't have any hair. If she ever came her
ass to the shop, I wasn't going to do that "turn the other
cheek" shit like I had done when I was younger. The way
I felt, I was looking to vent some frustration and her ass,
trust me, she could get it.

"So what do you think I should do?" the young client in
my chair asked zapping me out of my thoughts.

"Run that by me again?"

The client gave me a gentle shove. "You weren't listening," she said laughing.

"I heard the beginning then I zoned off. Start from him
calling you."

The last time the client was here she told me that her
fiancé had caught her cheating. "Well my boo took me
back. We been back together since the last time I was
here."

"Oh good." I attached the closure hairpiece to the top of
her tracks. "How has it been?"

"Well thing is he said the wedding is still on but my
baby, he is not being the same toward me."

"How is he being different?"

"It's just not the same. When I'm around him sometimes he snaps at me out of nowhere. He never did that
to me before. And when we're in bed, even after sex, he
scoots away from me. It's like he hates me sometimes.
Why do you think he is acting that way?"

"Because you fucked someone else," I said bluntly.

"But he took me back. He forgave me."

"Doesn't matter and no, he didn't. Obviously he is not over the fact that you slept with another man. He may have told you that he is but he's not."

"Well what should I do about it? You know that's my boo."

"Well in all actuality, if he continues this way, angry, I wouldn't go forward with a marriage that's for sure. Because the husband you just might get is more than likely not the man you fell in love with but the man you see right now. Would you want to be married to that person?"

She looked sad. "No. Can this be fixed?"

"Maybe. You can sit him down and have a talk with him and even go to therapy. But what you have to understand is that he may never be able to get over you cheating and things may never go back to the way they were. If you choose to stay with him you'd have to accept what he becomes. Or if he continues to make you unhappy you can leave. He just might straighten up if he sees you are not going to put up with his bullshit because you made a mistake." I stitched the last inch of her closure.

"What would you do?"

Her situation and her question brought me back to how it was with Demarco. I wondered if I had left Demarco if he would have hung. And if I left and he didn't change or fight for me back what other man did God have in store for me? Looking back, I also asked myself would I have done things differently. I couldn't say that I would have although I knew that deep down I should have. I should have left.

"Why don't you—"

"Hey, Caesar!"

I looked up surprised as Bev walked toward Caesar who was standing in the front of the shop and gave him a kiss on his cheek. They then embraced. When they separated I saw he had three young teenage girls with him.

"So you brought three clients. Okay." Bev looked around while saying, "Let me see who is available." She spied me standing there frozen wondering why Caesar was in this bitch and how he knew Bev.

"Cash. How much longer do you got on that weave, baby?"

Surprised when my name was called Caesar looked my way. He gave me a nod but I ignored him and responded to Bev. "I'm going to put some layers in, flatiron it, and I'm done; why?"

"I have a client for you. I'll do the other girl and whichever one of us is done can do the last girl. Is that all right with you?"

I nodded wanting to ask a ton of questions but said nothing.

Then suddenly there was a twinkle in Bev's eye. "Matter fact. Let me introduce you two." She guided Caesar forward by one of his hands until he was standing in front of me. "This is my goddaughter, Cashmere. Cash, this is Caesar."

"I know who he is, Bev. I just don't understand why the nigga here," I said hoping the client didn't hear, but by the smile that cracked on her face, I saw she did.

"Oh you two know each other?"

I ignored her comment. So she went on.

"Cash, Caesar started the nonprofit out here that helps young girls stop prostituting. When he gets new girls they come here to get their hair done and he buys them a new wardrobe. The program helps them get drug treatment, their GED, and even a job. God bless this man! 'Cause Lord knows we need this out here. One drive down Compton Boulevard will shell shock someone who is not from around these parts. And it is hard as hell to get those girls to leave their pimps. Did I mention he is single?"

I rolled my eyes at her. Although I had to admit that I was surprised and impressed with what he was doing. Who knew?

"That's good what you're doing, Caesar," I said without looking up. I grabbed my scissors. "Bev, give me ten minutes and I'll start on her."

"Okay, babe." But as she smiled, her eyes bored into me like she was trying to figure out where the negative energy was coming from. I knew Bev. She read for sure.

She walked away toward her station and said, "Come on, baby. I'll get you now."

Caesar remained standing near me. "So how have you been?"

"Fine," I said dryly. I cut some layers in Jeanette's weave. "What side you want your bang on?"

"The left," Jeanette said.

I cut a swoop bang smoothly.

"I didn't know you worked here," Caesar said.

"I don't. I'm just helping Bev out. Not that's it's any of your business."

Jeanette chuckled. So did Caesar.

"Her hair looks really nice."

"Thank you. Now you are going to have to move so I can finish what I'm doing."

"Right." He walked back over to the chairs and sat down.

"How you want it styled?" I asked Jeanette.

"Can I get Shirley Temples? Roy likes those."

"Shirley Temples it is."

"Damn how do you know him? 'Cause dude is"—she snickered—"on you. You gave him the panties and he sprung? Keep it trill?"

"I ain't gave him shit."

She busted up laughing at this point. "Now back to me. You didn't tell me. What do you think I should do?"

"Talk to him. Go to therapy. Give it six months after that. That's enough time to see if he is going to get over it. Is he doesn't, leave him and don't look back."

I started curling her hair. When I looked at her face her eyes got watery. Probably how mine would have gotten if someone had told me that about Demarco when he was alive. But it was the best thing to do for her and would have been best for me. Sometimes what's best hurts to hear.

"But I don't think I can do that even if he doesn't change."

Damn she sounded like me. But it was the best thing to do if a person couldn't get over their pain or anger and love you like they did before.

"Do you really think the therapy will work?"

Truth was I doubted it would. Her man would probably always hold the cheating over her head but I told her, "If it doesn't you have to be strong enough to walk away. Give it a shot though; if you love him try. Anything is possible right?"

She smiled at my words and seemed more confident about her situation. I was sure she ignored the first part of my sentence about walking away if it didn't work.

"Cashmere, you give such bomb advice. I bet you have a perfect marriage."

"How do you know I'm married?"

"You rocking a big rock that's why."

I looked down at my hand and thought, *if she only knew how bad things were in my household.* I finished one last curl, sprayed her hair with oil sheen, and took off her cape. "Your hair looks cute. Take a look at it."

As she looked at herself in the handheld mirror, I glanced up and caught Caesar watching me. I looked away.

"Thank you, girl." She gave me a hug. "For my hair and the advice."

"You're welcome. You can pay up front."

"Okay." She walked off.

I turned my attention to my next customer, the young girl who had arrived with Caesar. "Come on, sweetie," I said to the young girl sitting next to Caesar. When she came to sit in my chair. I asked her, "How old are you?"

"Fifteen."

"How long you been in the game?"

"Two years."

That meant she started when she was thirteen. Which was not surprising at all to me since I started when I was only thirteen. That was the average age when most got started. And the men out there, although they acted like they didn't know, they knew they were having sex with young underaged girls. The police knew as well. But still, the Johns all got slaps on the wrist. And the pimps rarely got caught. It was crazy. Back then, I was doing something against my will. And I was at more of a risk of getting locked up than the one forcing me to do it and the one benefiting from it. Crazy.

Them motherfuckas knew.

"Are you done?"

"Yes, ma'am. I'm tired of this shit."

God I wanted to ask her more. Tell her my story. But with Caesar there all up in my mouth and seeming to hear every word that came out of my mouth I kept the conversation to a minimum. "You can do it. Trust me."

"Thank you."

"Now how do you want your hair done?"

"Can you take out this weave? I hate it. My daddy forced me to put it in. I have black hair underneath it."

When she said daddy I knew she was referring to her pimp and the hair she said she hated was a twenty-two-inch blond weave and made the girl look way older than she really was.

"I can do that. Let's give you you back and a new start."

By the time I took the weave out, washed and put a deep conditioner on her hair, flat-ironed it, and trimmed her edges she looked more like the fifteen-year-old girl she really was. But still, there was something old about her eyes. Probably how my eyes looked at that age and would probably always would look. I mean that's what that life will do to you. And if it didn't change you on the outside it for sure changed you on the inside. That person you were before. Man, that person dies and not enough therapy or prayer could get it back. You are forever changed. For me I knew that my past would always and forever haunt me.

By the time I finished with her hair, Bev had done the other two girls hair because the work on theirs was less complicated.

"I love it," she said looking in the mirror. I had flat-ironed her own long hair bone straight and gave her Chinese bangs.

"Reminds me of how I used to look before . . ." She shook her head and looked down.

"I understand more than you think I do," I told her. Her eyes narrowed at me and I thought she got it. And the fact that I was standing there in front of her at a shop as opposed to being on the track with her said it all. It said she could be done too. That it didn't have to be just words.

She gave me a smile. "Thanks again."

She went off to where the other two girls were standing and Caesar approached me again. I cleaned off my station not giving him eye contact.

"Her hair looks really nice. The other young lady's hair looked good too. You really are talented, Cashmere."

"Thanks," I bit out.

"You know, I probably won't give up until you have at least one final conversation with me. I'm a cop. I know where you live. I can show up there. Pop up at your job."

"That's stalking, motherfucker. Cop or no cop I'll have your ass thrown in jail," I said in a quiet yet threatening tone.

He chuckled. "Same ol' Cashmere. I was just messing around."

That comment made me crack a partial smile. Because it brought me back to us being young and me being so in love with him. But shit, I was only thirteen back then what the fuck did I know about that? It probably wasn't even real love.

"But seriously can you give me fifteen to twenty minutes of your time?"

"Why, Caesar? What is so damn important?"

"If you give me just that time, I'll tell you, Cashmere," he said calmly.

"If I agree to meet you just this one time and entertain your bullshit conversation will you then leave me the fuck alone?"

"Once you hear what I have to say, Cashmere, you won't want to leave me alone."

I grimaced at that comment. "Okay! I'll meet you on Friday at Sweet Tooth Café."

"You still remember that place?" he asked.

"Yes. It's down the street from here. I see your boogie-ass mom sold it to some Koreans."

"Yes. Yes, she did. She sold it not long after I went away to college. I've never been back there so it would be nice to see how it . . ." His voice trailed off when I looked away. "What time, Cashmere?" he pressed calmly.

"Noon."

"Okay. Well I'll get going. I'm going to go buy them some clothes. I'll see you then."

I ignored him and went back to straightening up my counter.

By Friday, the day I was to meet with Caesar, I had gone into the shop to work with Bev for a few hours. At noon, like I promised, I walked down the street to the café. In all actuality, nothing had changed about it other that the owners were no longer black. When I got there, Caesar was already seated and waiting for me. I had to admit to myself that my reason for going was to really find out what he meant when he said that if we talked I would feel different. I chuckled to myself, thinking of all the moments we had shared there. It didn't seem that long ago at all. But it was. Back then I was a young, innocent girl. Not long after meeting Caesar, my innocence was destroyed.

His head was down when I approached him. But when he saw me he stood, smiled, and pulled my chair out for me. I let him and sat down facing him. He sat back down as well.

"So how are you feeling?"

"I'm all right."

"You sure?"

"What did I say?" I snapped.

"You hate me, Cashmere. Still. After all these years."

"Should I not? Time doesn't take away the wrong a person does you know. I don't care how long it's been."

"I know it doesn't if they've actually done wrong. But just maybe, just maybe . . ." He paused. "You know what? More importantly, I'm concerned about you. I mean you were in a hospital. And your mother said you had a miscarriage..."

I looked away. I was trying to block that shit out. But before I could stop myself, tears started spilling from my eyes and down my cheeks. Why the fuck did he have to bring that up? Those past two weeks were weeks I wanted to forget in their entirety and he just had brought them all back to me. Without a moment's hesitation, Caesar grabbed a hold of my chair pulled it closer to his and pulled me out of it with a strong grip on me. Then he placed me on his lap and wrapped his arms around my upper body like I was a baby. And, yes, I hated him. But in that moment he provided the comfort I needed to where I wasn't looking at eighteen-year-old Caesar and what he had done. I was looking into the eyes of a thirty-seven-year-old man. And his eyes offered so much damn comfort.

I'd never forget the words he continued to say to me while I sobbed. He said, "It's okay, Cashmere. You're safe. You're safe." I mean he said it over and over again and I cried my eyes out. After a couple minutes, once I gained my composure, I got out of his lap and sat back in my chair.

"I honestly feel so stupid for letting you hold me. I mean you fucked my sister when you knew I—" I paused.

"When I knew what, Cashmere?"

"You knew back then that although I was young, I was in love with you. That was fucked up!" I frowned and looked away.

"Hey. Look at me." Once I did his eyes locked with mine. "What if I told you that I couldn't have willingly had sex with your sister? What if I tell you that we never, ever had sex?"

"I'd tell you that you're a motherfucking liar. I saw both of y'all naked and her on top of you."

"Did you actually see intercourse? Or did you just see her on top of me? If you were in court you would lose."

"Stop playing, Caesar. You're a cop. I know how you crooked-ass motherfuckers try to twist shit." I thought about the white cop who had forced me to have sex with him when I was only thirteen and in the streets.

"Listen!" he said firmly. "That day, I came over there to see you. Excuse my language, baby, but I never gave a fuck about your sister. I was up late the night before because my mother continued to drill me on you. Saying that I had better leave you alone, that she would not stand for me seeing you. Cashmere, back then you meant more to me than my family and even my dreams. You were sweet, you were special, and you were someone I was never gonna come across again. I can say that now at the age of thirty-five because I never did. Anyway, I told my mom that night that I didn't need my family. I told her I wasn't going to Grambling. I was going to move out and just go to a local school. Cashmere, I couldn't leave you out here like that. I wanted to take care of you. Make sure no harm came your way. And I couldn't do that being thousands of miles away. So I decided to give up on that dream of going to Grambling. Anyway, I came to see you and like I said my head was killing me as I drove over there from all the arguing from the previous night. When I got there your sister told me you would be right back, that you ran to the market up the street. She saw how upset I looked; she acted concerned, so I told your sister thinking I could trust her. She gave me an aspirin and a glass of water, or so I thought. When I did wake up, I woke up naked and disoriented. And no one was there."

"What are you saying?"

"I'm saying that I was drugged by your sister and made to look like I had slept with you to get you out of my life. I'm saying that I was set up. My mother paid your sister to do it. And she willingly did it. After that day, I never saw you again. Lord knows I looked for you. But I'm not from Compton, didn't have an ounce of streets smarts. I used the only resources I knew. I went to your school but you never came back there. I went to your aunt and she wouldn't help me. She gave me some weird speech about not fucking with your fate. Then something horrible happened: my father was murdered."

I gasped.

"It was crazy because it was in our neighborhood. It was a carjacking. My mother thought we were so much better because of what we had and where we lived. It was so ironic to me." He chuckled bitterly. "I always told her it was her punishment for tearing you and me apart. For being so foul. So anyway, just to get away from her and the pain of losing my dad and you, I decided to go to Grambling after all.

"And after all these years, I never really repaired my relationship with my mother. It's just not the same. I have never learned to trust her again. But I never slept with your sister. She faked the whole thing, Cashmere, I swear to you. I would have never done something like that to you. I never wanted her. I always wanted you."

My eyes were wide. It made sense. In the back of my mind at that time I had always wondered why Caesar never got up and chased after me even after I had vandalized his car.

"How did you find out that it was a setup?"

"My piece of shit brother told me. I decided to do something with my life. He didn't. He dropped out of three colleges, ran up all his credit cards, and the last straw was when he totaled his Benz. Well my mom got tired of all his recklessness and cancelled his credit cards. They had a screaming match and he blurted it out in front of her and me. Crazy part was when I confronted her she didn't deny it. Her belief that you weren't for me was so strong she didn't deny it. Because in her mind she thought she was doing what was best. If you don't believe me trust and believe that my mother will admit what she did to you. We have been strained for so many years trust me she will be more than willing to make it right between us by making it right with you. So, Cashmere, just say the word. I will call her bougie ass right now and she will rush over here to talk to you. To confess the dirt she did years ago."

"That's not necessary." *Wow*. I was blown away from what he had just said. All this time I had hated Caesar and he had never betrayed me. *Wow, Desiree*. I loved my sister but she was just such a fucked-up person. And his mother was worse.

Then suddenly his eyes got watery. "You'll hate me for saying this but, Cashmere, I know what happened. Years ago, I looked you up in our system. I know you were convicted of murdering your sister. There was a case with a pimp named Black Mitchell. But, baby, how did it get to that point?"

I took a deep breath and told him everything. From my aunt throwing me out to Black taking my virginity, to the drugs and the prostitution. I left nothing out. I even told him about how I was forced to have sex with his bitch-ass brother. Through the entire speech Caesar had his hands over his face. That didn't hide his trembling lips or stop the tears that ran down his face at all I had been through. His shoulders at one point started to shake uncontrollably. Shit made me start crying as well.

He continued to cry even when the last of my tears dried up. After a few minutes of silence he said, "Things would have been different if I had been able to save you, Cashmere. You didn't deserve to endure any of that shit."

Any hatred I ever had for Caesar was gone. I believed him. No one could ever tell me different that's for sure. There's no way after all these years he would be lying; for what? What did he have to gain? And I believed his mother was up to it as well as my sister.

"I knew you were married with a child so I stayed away. But the day at the hospital, your mother said . . ." He shook his head. "So where are you now, Cashmere? Are you happy?"

"Hell the fuck no. I'm miserable. I fucked up my life worse than anyone ever could."

"Why do you say that, Cashmere?"

I swallowed hard. "Years ago I was raped by Black after I got out of juvenile hall. I found out I was pregnant but I didn't know if it was Black's or my husband's baby. He was worried that it was Black's and it was. Ever since we took the paternity test he was never the same. He married me despite not wanting to, hoping I could give him a child. I was never able to. Well I was but by that time he was long gone. Anyhow while we were married, I allowed him to be mean to Dominique and I can't forgive myself for it. He treated her like she wasn't there after we got the paternity results. And I allowed it because I loved him so much and didn't want to lose him. I just kept thinking that once I got pregnant things would be better! But I was never able to. Well, sort of. He was unhappy with me, with our family for such a long time and he left me. Not long after he left, he was killed in an accident. Crazy part was that I was over four months pregnant. I believe that if he had known I was pregnant he wouldn't have left. But it's too late now isn't it?"

"Well, Cashmere, I'm sorry for all that you have had to go through. Losing someone you love is hard to recover from. I know because my dad's death really affected me. But, you can't beat yourself up for mistakes you've made. You can't change the past even if you wanted to. And I'm sorry you lost your husband. I'm sorry you had a miscarriage as well, baby."

"Sometimes I hate myself because I feel like I'm no different than my mother. I have made so many damn mistakes." There was silence as I looked down at my feet.

Caesar slid a hand across the table and covered mine with his. I smiled at him.

"With everything you are dealing with, Cashmere, what can I do to make things better for you?"

I shook my head. "Stop it."

"No. I'm serious. Let me be there for you."

"I—"

"Let me."

"Okay. I really need to be held. Can you do that for me, Caesar?"

"All night if you want. And I won't let you go until you tell me to."

So how crazy was it that I found myself wrapped in the arms of a man I hadn't seen since I was thirteen?

And he did exactly what he promised. He held me in his arms in a bed at a local Motel 6. And as I shed nothing but tears about my situation, what I was going through, he continued to hold me and say the same exact thing he said at the café: "It's okay, baby. You're safe. You're safe. I'm here now."

It felt really good to be comforted and to have someone tell me that they would be there for me..I just in a million years never thought that that person would be Caesar. I didn't think I'd ever come across him again.

I turned in his arms and faced him. "Come on, Caesar. It's been years. What do you want with me now even after all the crazy shit I told you?"

"Well for one I'm concerned about your well-being right now, Cashmere. And second, part of me feels responsible for the way your life turned out."

"So you saying you feel sorry for me?"

"No, baby. When you love someone you naturally care. You're naturally concerned."

"You can't love me after all this time, Caesar. Come on. I know you are messing with someone. You a cop and you're fine as hell. Stop it with that. We never even had sex before. Matter fact, after all these years why haven't you married and had some kids?"

"I'm a man, baby. I'd be a liar if I said that I haven't had sex with other women or been in relationships. But something . . . I don't know how to say it but I'll try my best to properly articulate it. There has always been something that made me unable to form a strong connection with any of them. In addition, someway, somehow I was always comparing them to a thirteen-year-old girl named Cashmere. I mean you were my first love, Cashmere. Sometimes a man always craves that person, the one who got away. No other women can really measure up to them. Somehow, someway they always seemed to come up short. Almost like never being fulfilled by any of them. I always wanted to know if what happened between us had never happened, if I was able to get you away from your sister what our life would be like now."

Wow. That is some powerful shit, I thought. In my own way I had always loved Caesar. He and Demarco were the only men besides my dad in my life. It was crazy that after all these years Caesar still thought about me, wanted me.

"And even now that you know what you know about me, about the things I've done? Come on, Caesar. You're from the upper crust. I used to sell my body. I abused drugs, committed murder. And look, I used to cut on myself." I showed him one of my arms. Those scars were still there. They probably always would be. I gasped and watched in shock as Caesar's eyes watered from what he saw. All those long and ugly scars crisscrossed up and down my wrists. He shook his head quickly and started gently kissing each and every scar tenderly. I closed my eyes as some of my shame eased with each kiss. And maybe I shouldn't have but I lifted his face between my hands and started kissing him on his lips.

He returned the kiss gently. First they were soft pecks. Then he opened my lips with his tongue and invaded the inside of my mouth. Despite everything that was going on and in spite of everything that was going on I needed it because as he laid me down and started rubbing all over my body, Caesar's hands were making me feel alive, whole again. That shit was real crazy to me!

"I want us to pretend that this is the first time, Cashmere. Pretend we are young all over again. You are thirteen and I'm eighteen. Forget about all that shit that happened to you."

"Caesar, that sounds crazy how—"

"Just do it, baby. It will be like leaving all that shit behind you and starting again."

A look at his face showed me he was serious. "Just close your eyes, baby, and try. Let me make you feel good. Don't worry about anything else. What happened to you then, the past, none of that. Don't even worry about the bullshit you dealing with today 'cause that will be over soon anyway. Just focus on my voice and how I make you feel."

I took a deep breath and closed my eyes. I could feel Caesar's gentle hands move over mine and tremble almost like he was nervous. He started kissing me all over. Then his tongue followed. As he placed kisses on my neck and collarbone his hands went to massage my breasts and rubbed on my nipples. I moaned as sensations engulfed me. More kisses followed until he was gently pulling, and nipping at my nipples. I moaned as sensations engulfed me and fueled me up with desire. Then he traveled lower, until his upper body was centered between my legs. He kissed me all over my belly and placed kisses on my hips and thighs. I hadn't had a man take his time with me

like this in a long time so I didn't focus on whether I was
wrong for doing it. I simply enjoyed it because I knew I
needed this! He fingered me between my legs making me
moan and twist my lower body. He then started licking
at the folds of my flesh. I bit my bottom lip as he expertly
sucked on me and reached his hands up and caressed my
breasts. I moaned loudly. He stroked and sucked, driving
me insane. I felt my knees shaking and writhed in agony.

I continued to enjoy all the sensations with my eyes
closed feeling like I was back there that day where I
almost gave Caesar my virginity but was afraid to.

When I felt his body rise and him spread my legs apart
I held my breath as he was about to enter me. Once he
did and I felt the pressure inside of me, I screamed in
pleasure and pain. I felt his lips on mine. "Let it out," he
told me. He continued to thrust inside of me, completely
filling me up. And he was really gentle. More gentle than I
had felt since forever. I continued to keep my eyes closed
but rose to meet his thrusts. He started groaning low in
his throat. I felt myself climaxing and my eyes rolling into
the back of my head. He let out a scream that was so loud
he became hoarse. Then he collapsed on my chest.

Shit was crazy. Almost like a dream. Everything I was
going through seemed unreal but all of it was true.

Afterward, we just lay in each other's arms. *Unbelievable,* I thought. "Whew," I said.

"What?" he asked.

"This shit is just crazy. You come back into my life after
all these years and you still wanted to hit this."

He laughed. "You still a young tenda. And you were
feeling just right and screaming just right."

"Well thank you. I guess."

"But that's not all I want. I hope you know."

I pulled out of his arms and sat up in the bed. "What do
you want?"

"Listen. I don't want you to think I'm insensitive to your pain. What you're going through, with you losing your husband and your baby. But I have always dreamed of having the opportunity to make you mine again, Cashmere. At the risk of sounding like a stalker, I've driven by your home a few times. You were never out of my sight or mind. The work I do in my spare time is all because of you. Because I couldn't save you. Cashmere, I—"

I refused to even entertain the thought that this man wanted any aspect of me. "Oh God you are creeping me out. You can't possibly still want . . ." I paused. "What are you saying? What do you want?"

"What I am saying is that I want the opportunity to make you mine. What I want, all I want, is you. Cashmere, I just want that chance you gave me years ago. And now there is no threat that anyone can come in and screw things up for us."

I swallowed hard. "Look, Caesar. Your words are sweet. All of this was sweet and what I needed for the moment. But I have so much shit I'm dealing with right now. Yes, things are getting better for me. But just two weeks ago I cracked and could not get released from a damn hospital and I'm a grown-ass woman. I was unstable as I was trying to recover from my husband's death; and then losing this baby sent me into a downward spiral. I've been there before and all this pain opened up a lot of old wounds. I almost started cutting on myself again. And with all the crap I have been dealing with I have been to a huge degree neglecting my child. I feel like when I try to get on track something sets me back. I have enough common sense to know when someone is gone they are gone. Three months ago I told myself that me moping around the house, wanting to end my life, pretending my child didn't exist wouldn't bring my husband back and if he were alive he might not want me because when he was alive he didn't want me. So I needed to engage in something to take my mind off of it if I were ever to heal 'cause if I didn't heal I was either going to go insane like in my juvenile days or take my life.

"Then one early morning, my friend Bev popped up and got me out of the bed and forced me to go to the shop. That shit was working; pouring myself into work gave me something to focus on besides my sad, sad life. I even talked to my daughter and promised her that she would have her old mommy back. And then what happens? The same day I find out I was pregnant was the same day I lose it? Come on. How the fuck can the gods be this cruel to me? But even still, I knew I had a reason to stay on this earth. That's Dominique. So I have no choice but to try to pull it together. I'm going to pray, have faith, throw these bullshit depression pills in the trash, and get it together.

"Caesar, what you are asking for, I don't know if I can give you. I will need some time to get right with my child. I know she probably thinks I'm weak as hell. And I have the best daughter ever. A sign that I have been neglecting her is the fact that she was in that strip club. But I felt like I couldn't really get on her too hard about it because if I was doing what I was supposed to be doing I highly doubt she would have been there."

I chuckled and shook my head. "I mean I have to admit this shit is really crazy. Us running into each other, years later. And to know that you never . . ." I smiled. "I want you to know that I believe you, Caesar. Regardless of whatever happens between us."

"I'm glad you do, Cashmere. And I want you to know that this has always meant more to me than some teenage crush. And I'll give you all the time you need to deal with what you're dealing with. But I'm here. Just know that. And for whatever you need from this day forward, no matter what it is, you can count on me, Cashmere. So take your time. I'll wait for you. You're worth it."

I smiled at that, leaned forward, and kissed him. His hands reached up and grabbed me around my waist as the kiss became more passionate. Before things went too far, I pulled away. "I need to go, Caesar."

"Can I get a little more time with you?" he asked.

I laughed. "You can take me to Verizon. I need to finally go get another damn phone and that's it. I have to get home to my baby."

Chapter 27

Cashmere

I came back from Verizon with a new phone, some groceries, and a plan: to get my life back on track. I went into the kitchen and started cooking. I was going to do a baked ziti with a salad and even make a homemade strawberry cheesecake for dessert. I put the Italian sausage along with onion and bell peppers in a frying pan to cook and put on the boiling water for the ziti noodles. Dominique would be on her way home and I hoped to have the baked ziti in the oven by the time she got there.

It was crazy that after all these years Caesar and I had reunited! I felt like a teenager all over again being with him. Having sex with him made me feel like I was making love for the first time. The other thing that Caesar did for me was take my mind off of Demarco. I didn't think any man could do that again but he did. I grabbed my phone out of the box and turned it on. I took a deep breath as I did this. Getting another phone meant that I had to completely go back to my normal life. One thing I also did when I was at Verizon was Caesar's suggestion: that I put GPS on Dominique's phone. Yes, some time had passed since she was caught in the strip club and I doubted it was a reoccurring thing for my daughter but better safe than sorry.

Soon my phone started buzzing telling me all the voicemails and texts my phone had picked up in the past few months. I knew I needed to resume my customers at the shop in Inglewood. Now I felt more confident in going back.

As I scrolled through my voicemails, I saw there was a voicemail from Demarco. I gasped. *Should I listen to it?* I was curious as to what he had to say although he was dead. Suddenly the doorbell rang. I ignored it. I didn't want whatever the message said to bring me back down. I was making progress. I couldn't let myself get depressed again. What if I wasn't strong enough to pull myself back out now? And the message could be merely about our divorce. What did I need to hear that for?

The doorbell rang again. Maybe it was Caesar. I set the phone down. Picked it back up again, took a deep breath, and set the phone down. I went to see who it was. It was a good diversion from listening to the message. I again asked myself as I walked toward the door, would listening to the message drag me back and I lose the progress I made?

I looked into the peephole and saw it was Dame. I hadn't seen him since the funeral. And of course it felt awkward as I opened the door for him.

"What do you want?" I thought back to the last time I saw this bitch: at Demarco's funeral. At the wake the bastard had the nerve to proposition me. He watched me the whole time.

When I got up to go into the bathroom I saw him waiting for me outside the door. I rolled my eyes at him and tried to walk away when he grabbed one of my arms stopping me. He said, "How you holding up?"

I looked away. Memories of all the cruel words he called me came back to me. I wished that I hadn't agreed to let him come but he apologized to me and begged to come lay his friend to rest. So I allowed him to.

"Look I know things were crazy the last time I came over but like I said, I didn't mean those things. I just had to cover up how I really felt. How I always felt about you."

"The fuck you talking about?" I demanded.

He chuckled. "You know you got a smart-ass mouth. But I can handle it. Look, Cashmere, I want you to know that I meant everything I said as far as how I feel about you. I always wanted you and you know it was a sticky situation with you belonging to my homeboy and my boss. But he's out the picture now. Cashmere, I still want you. I can accept you and Dominique. You need a man around here to take care of things and Dominique needs a father." He wrapped an arm around my waist. "I know you're upset about Demarco but shit those emotions and feelings will pass."

"Look, motherfucker, and hear me well. There will never be a day when anything happens between me and you. Are you insane? The day I lay my husband to rest? You are a horrible human and truly a piece of shit. Fuck no. I want no part of you!" I snatched away from him and walked back into the living room.

He followed me, grabbed one of my arms again, and spun me around. "Look. I'm telling you that I am in love with you, Cashmere, and all these years I had to hide that shit from him. Now I don't have to. Just give me a chance to show you that I can make you forget all about him. Yes, he was my friend but I'd be a liar if I said I'm not relived he passed so I'd have the—"

"Get . . ." I paused, took a deep breath, and looked around quickly, hoping no one heard me. My mother shot up from her seat and slowly crept our way, telling me that she did if anyone else hadn't. I lowered my voice. "Get the fuck out my house," I whispered to Dame.

My mother came to stand next to me. "Everything okay, Cash?"

"Yes," I said still eyeing Dame. "Now leave."

"You don't even want—"

"If my daughter told you to leave then that's what your punk ass needs to do," my mother whispered through clenched teeth.

"Mom, stop," I snapped.

He shook his head and turned and walked toward the door.

I just hoped he got the fuck out. I could not believe he had propositioned me at my husband's funeral.

But in Dame fashion, he couldn't just get out! He had to talk shit. "You sitting in this motherfucking house acting all high and mighty and you wasn't a fucking whore, man! You the motherfucking reason why my friend is dead, bitch!"

My mom ran toward the door. "You betta get the fuck out of here before you end up in jail!"

Hank came to stand beside my mother. "You need to leave," Hank said sharply.

"Fuck all you mothafuckas! Demarco should have left you so he could still have his life, you worthless tramp!"

He slammed out of the house.

Dame's voice snapped me out of my thoughts. "Well can I come in? It's important. About Dominique." His eyes were wide and there was urgency in his voice.

Alarmed, I stepped aside and let him come in. "What is it? Is she okay?"

"Sit down."

I walked over to the couch and Dame sat down next to me. He then pulled out his phone. It was a Galaxy Note and had a huge screen. "I'm logging on to WorldStarHiphop.com."

"Okay what's that? And what does it have to do with Dominique?"

"Shut the fuck up and look!"

He pulled up a video and placed the phone in front of me. "Look at this. *Your baby girl.*"

My eyes shot to the ceiling when I saw my child ass buck-naked and having sex with random boys on the screen of his phone!

"What the fuck it this?" I exclaimed as angry tears at them violating my daughter flew from my eyes.

"What it is, is your baby girl slutting. I said I didn't want to be a part of this but shit. It's quite embarrassing. So as a man, I came to tell you because I care about Dominique. I know she's not Demarco's baby but still . . ."

Just then they did some disgusting shit to my baby. I shoved the phone away and started screaming in outrage. I shoved the lamp off my end table in a rage.

Why is she allowing them to do this to her? I asked myself silently. What was wrong with my baby? Was what I was doing that bad? All the years of love I had showed her was not enough to know better than to do some shit like that?

"You need a man around here to keep her in line. That man can easily be me."

I shook my head and tuned him out as he talked. I had to get this shit off of the Web.

I didn't know what to do so I knew I needed assistance in dealing with this shit. "Naw, fuck this shit!" I snatched up my phone, exited out of my voicemail, and pressed the middle button for Siri.

"Call Caesar!" I commanded.

When the phone started ringing Caesar picked up on the second ring. "Hey, baby."

"I need your help. Please get over here now!" I then tossed my phone back on the couch. I sat with my head between my legs and covered my face with my hands, crying. I tried to block the horrible-ass images that I just saw. But I couldn't.

"Do you want to see the rest of it?" Dame asked.

I ignored him. My shoulders shook and I cried silently. I grabbed my phone and then called Dominique's phone. It went to voicemail. I sent her a text telling her to get her ass home.

Chapter 28

Dominique

I stood on my doorstep as I got a text message from my mother demanding that I come home. I wondered what this was about because she hadn't been this sharp with me since she found out I was at the strip club. Part of me wanted to ignore the text and not even come home but I couldn't do that. I had to keep cool until I could leave my mother's house and be done with her forever.

The door was unlocked do I stepped inside and walked from the foyer to the living room. I almost gasped when I saw her and Dame sitting on the couch. Memories of what he had done to me at the strip club the week before came back. I looked away disgusted. I hated his guts more than the man who forced himself on me in Meka's shower. He was a stranger looking for sex, whereas Dame had pretty much watched me grow up.

He was there when I was snaggletoothed with pigtails. Acting like he really cared about me, like we were blood. And he forced himself on me when I begged him to stop? What kind of man was he? I remembered what he said that day he raped me.

I was lying there crying and he asked, "How much do you usually charge for these niggas to have some of your honey pot?"

I didn't respond so he yanked me by my ponytail again. "Answer me, you little bitch. Acting just like your mama."

"One hundred for sex and fifty for head."

"Well I ain't paying you shit." He chuckled. *"I'm like family so since we keeping it in the family I get my services for free."* He kicked me in my back roughly. *"Understand?"*

I nodded through my tears.

"Aye, we gotta do this again. Next time I'll get us a room with a Jacuzzi, bring a molly and a couple lines of coke so you can really get wild." He chuckled. *"I'll be back the day after tomorrow and you best be prepared to leave with me. I wouldn't bother running to your mammy; she won't believe you if you did, and even if she did believe you her ass won't care."* He chuckled.

But later, when Meka demanded what took so long and where the money was I told Meka what happened and she said, "Oh hell naw. Y'all was in there for a minute; that's money wasted. He wants to fuck for free? You know what your daddy would do to you if he knew you gave up pussy and dome for free? He would disown you. And he would have personally stomped him in the head. You are not fucking with that low-budget nigga again. We can have that nigga banned from the club. Matter fact, I'm gonna tell security to never let that bastard in again. We about making money and if you ain't got no money you ain't making sense and if you got no money, then your ass don't belong in here!"

"But what if he tells my mom?"

"Nigga implicates himself if he tells."

"He said my mom won't believe me."

"Girl, if he snitches on you then you snitch on him bottom line 'cause what you got to lose at that point?"

"Okay." But I still was worried.

Meka saw it. "But he ain't so let it go."

So the next time he came back to the club he was not allowed inside.

"Hey, Dominique," he said snapping my out my thoughts.

I didn't respond. I knew my mother was confused as to why I didn't hug or kiss Dame but I didn't care. "Hi, Mom."

She reacted quickly, jumped up, and roughly grabbed me by one of my arms. "Sit the fuck down." She flung me on the couch. "And tell me why in the fuck you are on a goddamn video having sex with some nothing-ass niggas who are obviously gay to be naked in a room full of other niggas!" she screamed at the top of her lungs as tears continued to still slide out of her eyes.

I gasped and looked at my uncle. It was unclear what video she was talking about. But one thing was clear. He was trying to get me in trouble. But I wondered if he told that he had forced himself on me.

"Dame. Show her the video."

He aimed his phone in my face. I refused to look and kept my head down and my eyes closed. My mother gripped my face in her hands and said, "Open your motherfucking eyes, Dom!"

I did and saw myself performing the day I went to those college guys' house. But I really wasn't focusing on this because all I saw was red.

"I seen how you get down."

I guessed when he said that he wasn't just talking about Starz.

"Dominique, I'm really concerned about you. What you are doing is not healthy."

Was he serious after the way he had treated me?

"Fuck you, Dame!" I fired. My mom had never ever heard me curse before so I knew she was shocked.

"Shut the fuck up!" my mom said.

"What you did on this tape is disgusting," Dame said not touched by me yelling at him.

I lost it. I didn't care. Since the truth was out let all the truth be out. "Tell her what you did to me too since you want to tell the truth."

"Now, Dominique, it's not nice to make accusations."

"Did you seriously think I would keep your secret since you trying to get me in trouble with my mom?"

My mother paused and looked at Dame suspiciously and then back at me. "What are you talking about? Dom, spit the shit out 'cause I'm pissed and—"

"Dame raped me, Mama. That's what!"

My mother released my face and slowly stood to her feet.

"Shut the fuck up, lying little girl," Dame fired looking nervous. He couldn't hide his nervousness.

"I'm not. I'm not lying about anything." I turned to my mama. "Mom, that's me on the video. That was me in the strip club and that was me that *Uncle* Dame raped. I swear on one hundred Bibles that he forced me to go down on him and he forced me to sleep with him. Take me to the doctor, Mom! Get me examined and you'll find his semen in me because he didn't wear a condom! He didn't want to."

The look on my mother's face told me that she believed what was coming out of my mouth. I wanted to tell my mom that Meka was my witness but I didn't want to expose her. But by the looks of my mother I didn't think I needed to. I didn't need a witness.

There was a beeping sound coming from the kitchen. I knew it was the timer of the stove. My mom must have been baking something.

"I don't believe you, Dom. Hold on; let me turn off this oven." My mom walked into the kitchen.

Dame looked satisfied that my mother busted me out. He stood near the door and said, "Told you."

My eyes burned into Dame's. I hated Dame. I 100 percent hated him. There was no fifty-fifty, no eighty-twenty, no nothing. "I hope you die," I snarled. I had never said that before but I meant it.

He matched my look. "You little bitch. I'll have you and your mammy right now if I want. You both are sluts. Like mother like—"

My mom came back into the living room with a butcher's knife in her hand. Without a moment's hesitation she rushed up to Dame and tried to slam that knife into his chest. She looked possessed like in that old horror movie *Carrie* after they poured the pig blood on her.

He backed up and said, "Bitch, are you crazy?" They battled over the knife. "Bitch, let the knife go!" He tried to take it from my mother but she wouldn't let it go. She struggled against him. Dame pulled the knife out of her hand.

"You must be a dumb motherfucka if you think I'm going to believe a sorry-ass nigga like you over my child! I don't care how many niggas she sleeps with I'll always believe her over you."

My mother threw the lamp on the end table at him. It missed him. My eyes grew wide as she pulled another knife out of her pocket and went after Dame again. He ran around the living room to avoid getting stabbed by my mother because I knew that was her intent! Her eyes were now dead, wasn't no life in them.

Then like a new thought just came to her she said, "Matter fact. Dom! Get one of your daddy's gun! I'm gonna kill this motherfucker right now."

With wide eyes I shook my head. I didn't want to do that and the perfect stop to this was the doorbell. I ran to it and opened it, instantly recognizing the officer who had taken me to my mother that night at the strip club. I heard a scuffle and turned around to see Dame now on top of my mother.

"You bitch-ass nigga, you better kill me now, mother-fucker, 'cause if you don't I'm going to kill you."

Caesar pushed me aside and stepped in the living room with his gun drawn. Dame was on top of my mother and straddling her with his hand over my mother's, the one that held the knife.

"Drop the knife!" Caesar commanded with his gun pointed at Dame.

"I'm trying to stop this crazy bitch from stabbing me."

"Drop the fucking knife!"

Dame snatched the knife from my mother and tossed it.

"Now slowly rise to your feet with your hands up."

"Man, this bitch tried to attack me and you treating me like I'm the criminal?"

"Just do it!"

Dame huffed out an impatient breath, and rose to his feet as instructed, with his hands up. My mother stood to her feet and started attacking Dame with balled fists. "You fucking piece of shit!"

"Fuck you, bitch. You and your daughter are tramps. Your daughter giving up the ass at the fucking Barbary Coast. She is the ho of the club. Yes, you did well for yourself. You raised a slut."

I watched my mother's horrified face as she watched me, her attack on pause.

"Hey, man. Watch your mouth," Caesar warned.

"Fuck you. You ain't shit without that shit and badge, my nigga. None of your fucking buddies here. Nothing." Dame got in his face and sized Caesar up. Caesar was silent as Dame remained in his face.

"This what's up, motherfucker. I'll beat your ass."

That's when Caesar grabbed him and slammed Dame on his back. Dame tried to fight Caesar on the ground. But Caesar managed to get him in handcuffs.

"I want him arrested. He raped my daughter!" my mom yelled.

Caesar looked up surprised but regained his composure.

"No, I didn't. That bitch liked it. And she wanted it," Dame yelled. "Just like your ho ass. Had Demarco never walked in that day I could have had you too. I told him time and time again not to marry you! Now look where it landed him."

"I'm taking you in for threatening a police officer and suspicion penal code 261," Caesar said.

"Man, fuck you!" Dame said. But it didn't stop Caesar from dragging him out of the house.

My mother forced me to give the cop a statement about what Dame had done. And I told him exactly how he had treated me. The whole time I did my mom sat there rocking back and forth and crying.

"I'll call you once I get him booked," Caesar promised her.

Then it was just me and my mother left in the house. After minutes of silence my mother spoke. "Dominique, I don't know where to start. You are not the child I thought you were. You doing shit I never thought you would. You look like a tramp on that video. I'm disgusted with what I saw." Her eyes got watery.

So am I, I wanted to say. *I'm disgusted with who you are, Mom.*

"Your whole program is about to be shut down. I'm taking and picking you up from school. And I'm going to find a therapist for you to talk to. Point blank. You not allowed to watch TV, talk on the phone. Nothing. Matter fact, give me your phone. I don't know what's going through your fucking head but maybe a doctor can tell me because I raised you better than this! To be letting men abuse your body like that." She punched a fist into the palm of her other hand. "You let your uncle rape you and you didn't even tell me. But then again I told you to stay out of strip clubs! So had you not been in that bitch the shit wouldn't have happened."

I nodded my head to all she was saying like a song was playing. I handed my mother the phone and she set it down on the couch.

"I mean I don't even know what to say to you. I can't even . . ." She broke down crying on the couch, to where her whole body was racked with sobs. "I can't even look at you. I can't even look at my own baby."

I tried to play it off and look sad. "Mom. I'm sorry. I've only—"

"Go in your room!" she yelled.

I nodded and as I walked up the stairs she continued to cry and say, "Not my baby," over and over again.

I knew she would watch me like a dog so I didn't even bother sneaking out. I would just have to make up for the money lost by working harder tomorrow.

The next day my mom kept her word and got up super early to take me to school. When I got out of school I saw my mother's truck parked out front. I thought smarter and snuck back inside and went to the administration office and asked the secretary. "Can I please use the phone?"

"Sure, honey."

I dialed Meka's number. When she picked up, I whispered, "It's Dominique. Don't come where you usually go to pick me up. Drive around to the back parking lot where the football field is and I'll meet you out there."

"Okay."

I met Meka out there and jumped in the passenger side of her car quickly.

"What's going on?" she asked suspiciously.

"My mother came to pick me up is all." I didn't want to go into the rest. I just wanted to make up for the money I lost the day before to give to my father. I didn't want to think of all the chaos that happened the day before. I wanted to get drunk, pop a Molly, and drown in customers.

Chapter 29

Cashmere

I sat outside Dominique's school for damn near an hour. Normally her school was out at three-thirty. After thirty minutes of waiting for her, I called the school office to see if her last period class had been dismissed. The school secretary said that it had.

"Well did Dominique Pina check in?" I asked.

"Yes. She attended the whole day," she informed me.

"Then why can't I find her?" I asked.

"You may want to walk around the campus. You know how these teenagers are," she joked.

But I was too stressed to laugh. "Thank you." I ended the call. Where the hell was she? I even got out of my car to walk around the campus as different sports practices commenced in the gym and on their football field. But Dominique's ass was nowhere to be seen. I even looked in the library that had an afterschool study hall. She wasn't there either.

I dialed her number but when the phone started ringing in my car I remembered I had her cell in my purse. "Shit." I tried to give her the benefit of the doubt and assume she walked home but that was still the wrong fucking thing to do when I specifically told her little ass not to leave the school and that I would pick her up. I walked back to my car. It was now four-thirty. I got in my truck and headed home to see if she was there. On the way, Caesar called me.

"Hey," I said in a distracted tone.

"How are you? I just checking to see if you were all right."

"No. I'm not. I can't find Dominique and I'm on my way home to see if she is there."

"Okay. Has she ever run away before?"

"No, never. But I don't know. Her behavior is so erratic nowadays. I really wouldn't put it past her."

"Well check to see if she is home and if she is not, text me a picture of her and I'll have a patrol car go out and look for her. I got a crack in a case so I can't leave right now. But when I can get away I'll also go out with you and look." He added, "And I won't stop looking until we find her."

Something about that "looking until we find her" scared me. Made my heartbeat speed up. I couldn't believe we were talking about my daughter who had always been such an angel. So sweet and innocent. I swear I used to think she had an invisible halo on her head. And then those images of her on that video sexing all those bastards made me see her in a different light. She was no longer innocent to me. They weren't forcing her on the video. She was willingly doing it. But why? I rubbed my temples distressed at the images in my head. I had to fix this shit. Right the wrong and save my child from this self-destructive path she was on. To do this, I could no longer look at her as an angel but a girl I couldn't put anything past.

"Well let's just hope her ass is home. I'm still going to fuck her up. But at least I know she is safe."

"Okay. Let me know."

"Bye."

I pulled into my driveway, put the car in park, and hopped out. The front door was locked. I hoped it meant that she came home and locked the door.

I unlocked the door and went inside, "Dominique!" I called. No response. I looked in the kitchen and the bathroom downstairs and went upstairs to her bedroom. "Dominique!" I called again. I still heard no response.

"Fuck! Where the hell is she?"

I went back out to my car and grabbed my cell phone. Since it was a new phone it didn't have any pics of Dominique. They were all in my old phone, which was destroyed. I went back into my living room and snapped a picture of Dominique taken in the fall that sat on the glass picture stand in the living room. I then texted it to Caesar.

As I prepared to step back outside I saw a hole in the wall where I had thrown a knife at the motherfucker Dame. I wished to God that I had killed him. Then I thought back to what he said about some strip club called the Barbary Coast. Maybe that's where her ass was!

I ran outside to my truck, jumped inside, and punched the name into my GPS. Once the GPS started up, I backed out of my driveway.

By the time I made it to the club over on Western, in the city of Gardena, it was almost six o'clock. And even though it was fairly early I knew from my old days of stripping that it could be a morning, noon, and night type of job. My sister and I never worked at the Barbary Coast because it was too fucking hood in there. But most strip clubs operated the same way.

I wasn't surprised when I walked inside there were girls working the poles. And at this point, sadly, I could say I wasn't surprised to see my daughter's little body twirling on one of them with her eyes wide and clearly high as a fucking kite!

My eyes teared up instantly and my shoulders shook with sobs.

"Aye. If you ain't buying a drink get the fuck out," the bartender shouted at me as I stood there near the bar.

I ignored him and walked toward the stage. Without a moment's hesitation, I walked up the five steps to the stage as my daughter's back was to me as she popped her booty in a way I had never seen her do and didn't know her ass knew how to do. I took a deep breath and brought my left arm around her collarbone hooking it like a V, knocking her off balance. Then as she rested her body on mine backward and screamed, I dragged her little ass off the stage.

The DJ stopped the music and yelled, "Bitch, get the fuck off the stage."

I ignored him too and heard Dom yell, "Mom, get off of me!"

"Shut the fuck up," I whispered in her ear.

I pushed past patrons and staff and walked toward the exit. The bouncer tried to block my way. "What the fuck you doing?" he demanded.

I got directly in his face and said through clenched teeth, "I shitted her out. And I'm taking her home. You got a problem with that then I'll just call the police and have them escort us out this bitch 'cause she only thirteen!"

He took in my words and stepped aside.

Chapter 30

Dominique

I struggled against my mother as she continued to drag me until we got to the car. Once we got there, I pulled away from her. I was so embarrassed that she came here and snatched me out of there like that like I was a little girl. I wasn't a baby anymore! I was a woman now. And I needed the money to give to my daddy.

My mother hemmed me up against the truck and slapped me. I winced at the pain and scowled at her silently. She then pulled off her belt and started whipping me with it all over my body. I wanted to scream from the pain but my pride wouldn't let me do it. She raged at me at the top of her lungs.

"What the fuck is wrong with you? In that piece of shit place? Half naked." She yanked at the flimsy bra and thong I was wearing almost making me lose my balance. "You can barely stand in those heels! You're thirteen fucking years old!' She beat on her chest in anger all while tears flowed down her face. "Is this the life you want for yourself? You look like a tramp and all of those perverted, sick men want to do is have sex with you. That's it. They don't give a shit about your ass! They will use you up until you got nothing else to give and you walking around here crazy and strung out on dope. Dominique! That's what this life will do to you. I didn't raise you like this! I've been a good mom to you. I instilled enough in you for you to do better. You see what the fuck I'm going through; why are you stressing me out more?"

As she continued to rant, I thought, *Good mom? You've been lying to me my whole life. And now you want to fuss at me?* I could take it no longer. I spoke up and my next five words had her as quiet as a church mouse. "Like you did better, Mom?"

She took a sharp intake of breath. Then it was like she was nervous about something, like maybe for a split second she silently questioned whether I knew more than she assumed I knew. Then she wiped that look off her face and replaced it with a more self-righteous one. "What?"

I wasn't going to keep my mouth closed any longer. I was tired of keeping quiet. For what? To spare someone else. They never spared me. "You heard me."

She gritted her teeth and said, "Since when did you grow such a smart-ass mouth?" she barked furiously. "I asked you a question. Why in the fuck don't you repeat what you said?" She got all up in my face and grabbed my face in the palms of her hands. "Now what did you say, little girl?"

"I said like you did better."

"And what the fuck is that supposed to mean?"

"What the fuck it means is—"

Her eyes widened and she grabbed my face. "Shut up! Shut up! Cursing at me."

I ignored her. "Is I know all about you, Mom, and all about your secrets!"

That got my mom to finally shut up. But then she put her self-righteous act back on and said, "What are you talking about?"

"Maybe the apple doesn't fall too far from the tree, Mom. The life I'm living now is the life you lived. The things I'm doing are the things you did. Yes! I know everything, Mom! I know what I am. I know you were a prostitute. I know you stripped, did drugs. I know you killed your sister. And I know that Demarco is not my father! You knew all along and you kept it from me. How could you, Mom? And all my life he hated me because he knew I wasn't his. How could you just sit by and allow him to treat me that way? He hated me and it made me hate myself. And now I know the truth!"

My mother was in complete shock from what I obviously knew. I kept out that I knew who my real father was because I didn't want to let on and she find some kind of way to stop me from seeing him. Tears flowed like water from her eyes and her shoulders started shaking rapidly and she shook her head saying, "Dominique, no." She continued to cry. "No, baby. That's not the truth."

"I know Demarco is not my father. There is no need to lie at this point. Tell me for once in your dishonest fucking life who my father is!"

She slid to the ground with her back against the car and cried pitifully like a child. "Dominique, baby. Don't hate me. I—"

"You know what, Mom? You are so self-centered. Always making everything about you. You lied to me my whole life. I have hated who I am for so long. I had no purpose and was afraid of my own shadow. But not anymore. I know who I am. I know what I am. And I no longer hate myself. Mom, I hate you."

She bawled loudly at those words, "I hate you." It was like she was in so much pain from what I was saying. Like each word was a jab to her chest with a knife. That's the best way to describe how distressed my mother looked and sounded.

"Your tears affect me no longer, Mom. I think you're pathetic. I hate Demarco, too, Mom. I'm glad he died! I wish you would have died in that accident with Demarco. I wish you would have both perished! For the life you gave me. You think because you and Demarco had money and businesses and the fact that I had the best of clothes and schools made everything okay? Well it didn't. I would have willingly lived in a box if I had a real father like Jada had to love me. You pretended you didn't see your child suffering and longing for something! You did this shit for thirteen almost fourteen years. And when you did pay attention, when your head wasn't up Demarco's butt, it really didn't matter anyway because all you did was put a Band- Aid over my pain. You never really addressed it. *But you say you love me.*"

"I do love you, baby. More than anything on this earth. I would die for you! Take a bullet for you, Dom! I love you more than I love myself."

"Mom. You don't love yourself. You don't love yourself any more than I loved myself, prior to finding out the truth that is."

"I love you more than—"

"More than Demarco?" I countered. "Think wisely before you answer that question, Mom."

She swallowed hard. "Yes, baby. I do. I swear."

"Then why would you let a man who hates my guts stay with us, Mom, and he is not my father!" I raged.

She gasped. "You heard us that night."

"That's not all I heard, Mom. Sad thing is you would have had me go my whole entire miserable life living a lie! That he was my father! Well now the truth about you is out. The truth about how conniving you are for pushing a man who is not my father off on me is out, Mom. The fact that you were a dick-sucking junkie is out; what you did was no better than what I was doing on that video. And guess what? I loved every minute of it and what I do! I will never go back to the life I used to live. It is the truth. Something you are afraid of. Well I'm not. Thank God my aunt was honest enough to tell me the truth."

Her head snapped up like a robot at the mention of my aunt's name. Then her tears were replaced with rage. "Who did you say told you all of that?" she whispered.

I ignored her. She stood to her feet and rushed me gripping my shoulders and roughly squeezing. "Who the fuck told you?"

She continued to apply pressure, hurting me to the point that my hands were on hers and I couldn't breathe. "Was it my bitch aunt? Answer me! Huh?" She continued to apply pressure until I nodded.

She let me go and I weakly sank to the ground, coughing and trying to catch my breath. She opened the passenger door and grabbed me by one arm and tossed me inside. She then got in the driver's side, started the car, and sped off.

Fifteen minutes later we ended up parked outside of my great-aunt's house. She drove erratically the whole way there crying, sniffling, and sobbing.

She got out the truck, left it running, and yanked me out the passenger seat. "Since you like to run, come with me. I hate for you to see me this way but hell you seem to think you know the truth and that truth paints me as horrible, despite the real so fuck it. You seem to have your mind made up about me and I don't think I can do shit about it. And you just don't even understand that I love you to an amount that is immeasurable and I'd take a thousand bullets for you, little girl." She mumbled like a crazy person as she pulled me, forcing me like her to run toward the house. She didn't stop until we got to the door.

She banged and kicked on the door until we heard, "Who in the world is knocking on my door like they the goddamn police?" My aunt opened the door a pinch and said, "Yes?"

My mom wasted no time and burst into the living room causing my aunt to back up, taking steps backward. Them steps didn't matter because my mother was all up on my auntie. She pressed her body completely against her and demanded, "So you want to tell my daughter shit. You fat, black miserable bitch?"

"Cashmere, get the fuck out of my—"

"What you tell my child, bitch?"

My aunt's eyes were wide. "What? Nothing?"

"Bitch! What the fuck did you tell my child?"

My aunt had fear in her eyes. But her pride outshined it. "I told her the truth! It's about time somebody did."

I secretly hoped that my aunt didn't mention what she told me about my daddy.

"The truth huh? Well you know what, let's tell the truth." My mom looked at me. "Baby. I was not totally honest about some things. Yes, I was a prostitute and I was addicted to X. But what your aunt is not telling you is that she had the power to stop all of that shit! Only she chose not to because she was such a miserable, insecure bitch trying to protect her sorry-ass husband. Dominique. She put me out when I was only thirteen. Your age. A baby. Remember that aunt? When I came back here and told you what my sister Desiree did? Remember what you told me? You put your niece out in the streets because you refused to accept the fact that your husband wasn't shit! His not being shit had nothing to do with me. So instead of accepting reality you chose to accept fiction. That he was okay even after he fucked my sister! It was better to get rid of the proof that he wasn't shit than get rid of the shit. Yet that shit still exist and I wish I had a dollar for every time I heard about him fucking other women, strippers, prostitutes, strawberries still to this day!" My mother stomped one of her feet and my aunt's eyes were wide at the admission.

"The sad part about you is that your piece of shit husband tried to rape me and I didn't tell you. My aunt. My flesh and blood because I knew you wouldn't believe me and I was afraid you'd put me out. You were all the family I had left. You pushed me to the streets. From that point forward, everything that happened to me was against my will. I was a victim! I have always been a victim in all of this. And I never, ever set out to kill my sister. Damn you to hell for telling her that! Despite how bad my sister was I loved her! Her death was an accident. So how dare you sit there and judge me and tell my child lies to make her hate me, bitch!"

God the look in my mother's eyes was so hateful I had to look away. "But I'll tell you who I wouldn't mind killing off. You. Forgive me, God, but, Auntie, I should have murdered you the last time I was here."

My aunt backed up some more. My mom came forward some more.

"I'm about to destroy this whole house and you and my mama and your piece of shit husband can't save you this time!" Without reprieve, in a rage, my mom started flipping couches over. She slammed my aunt's flat screen into the wall along with her DVD and surround sound speakers. She knocked over lamps, the pictures on the wall.

All the while my aunt screamed as she rushed over to her phone and called 911. "Yes, I have an intruder in my house. 9533 Butler Avenue. Nooooo!"

My mom paused in front of a huge cabinet with glass china in it. Pretty pieces sparkled behind the glass.

My mother knocked the entire cabinet over.

My aunt covered her face with both her hands in disbelief.

"I'm not done with you, bitch!" Then she went after my aunt. My aunt took off running but she was no match for my mom who grabbed my aunt by her wig and started throwing blows to the back of her head, all while saying, "Bitch, you turned my daughter against me. You didn't have the motherfucking right. After what I been through and you could have stopped all of it. You hateful, miserable bitch. Everything you have done to me I let you get away with. But not this time. *This* time I'm not turning the other cheek."

My aunt spun around and tried to grab my mom. But my mother backed up and squared up. "Bitch, I been waiting for this moment since I was thirteen. I want to kill you I hate you so much!" She started punching my aunt in her mouth and every time my aunt took a swing my mother backed up or ducked like a skilled fighter. My mother gripped my aunt's head in her hands and started kicking her.

My mom continued to kick my aunt in her head like she wanted to kill her. My mother used all her strength to body slam my aunt into the floor. I could still hear my aunt screaming.

Suddenly, I could hear sirens getting closer and closer. But my mom didn't seem to care about them one bit.

My mother stood over her. "Bitch, don't you ever say a word to my daughter or I will come back and kill you."

I could hear feet pounding on the pavement. From one of my aunt's open windows I saw four police run in the yard and up the steps, and they poured into the living room. They had their guns drawn and they all shouted, "Police! Get your hands up!"

I put my hands up and watched as my mother froze over my aunt. One of the officers secured me and placed my hands in cuffs.

"Get your hands up!" one of them repeated to my mother.

My mother took a deep breath and released my auntie. Two of the cops came forward and tackled my mother to the floor. They placed her in handcuffs.

My mother looked my way and her eyes widened.

"Wait!" my mother demanded. "Don't take my daughter to juvenile hall! She had nothing do with this! Call my mother please and have her released to her. Please."

"Yes, she did! She was helping her destroy my house and she participated in assaulting me!" my aunt yelled.

I gasped and looked at my aunt.

"Bitch!" my mother tried to go toward my aunt.

"Hey shut the fuck up!" one of the cops yelled in my mother's ear. They held on to her and she struggled against them.

"My daughter didn't have nothing to do with this shit!" my mother insisted. The cops escorted us outside. My mother continued to struggle the whole way. "Don't take my daughter in!"

I was put in the back of one police car while they cops struggled to put my mother in another one. She fought them the whole time, twisting her body every which way and whatnot.

"Get the fuck in the car!" one of them yelled at my mother. At one point, one of the cops grabbed my mother's hair and had a balled fist ready for her.

"Go ahead beat me up, motherfucker! I'm not making this shit easy. Call my mother! 661-554-2211 and have her pick my daughter up and I'll go easily. If not y'all motherfuckers gonna need some pepper spray 'cause I'm gonna fight all the way. Jail or bullets don't mean shit to me when y'all got my child in those cuffs for some shit she had nothing to do with."

One of the cops, the one who told her to shut the fuck up, took a deep breath and said, "Ma'am. Because your aunt made an allegation against your daughter we have to take her in."

"Y'all don't understand. She didn't do shit. My aunt is lying. My daughter just stood there! Let my child go. Call my mother to pick her up please!"

But they ignored my mother and she continued struggling against them. But they managed to get her in the car
despite her fighting them. At one point she was sprayed
with something and hit several times with their billy
clubs. The car I was in drove behind them; my mother
screamed and cried all the way to the station. And I was
honestly scared because I had never been locked up
before. How would I survive that?

Chapter 31

Cashmere

I slid in the passenger seat of Bev's car, taking a deep breath. She leaned over and hugged me, then demanded, "Girl! What in the world?"

Once I got booked I was allowed a phone call so I called my mother and demanded that she and her husband do something about the predicament I was in.

"Mom, you gotta get Dominique released. She didn't do shit. Your sister is lying."

"Well why were you even over there?"

"'Cause your sister ran her fucking mouth to Dom that's why! She told her stuff that turned Dominique on me and into the hands of leeches that are tricking my daughter off! Look I ain't got the time to go into all of this. Can you have your husband do something and get her out? And then get her, Mom. I don't want her out of your sight. And bail me out if you don't wanna be bothered with her."

"Well, Cash, Hank is retired."

I closed my eyes briefly. I did not want my daughter locked up so she could learn how to be a fucking criminal. Get introduced to some bullshit or even one of the pimps of the girls who's locked up. A lot of networking happened in prison. I didn't want her to have anything on her juvenile record either.

"What! With all the motherfucking bragging—"

"I will see what I can do. Don't worry."

Three hours later I was released. When I called my mother to pick me up she said, "I'll send someone to get you! I'm here with your fast-ass daughter at your house and if she look at me wrong again I'm going to fuck her up! Matter fact! Take your ass in your room! Cash. What happened to my sweet grandbaby?"

"Your piece of shit sister. Now. How am I free?"

"Yes. Because I talked to my sister and she dropped all the charges. And her price was almost as much as the fucking bail to do it. But hey family is family. You know you left your truck over there, girl. I had to pay Bryon to move it back to your house. Cash, you had no business going to her house in the first place! What you did was stupid. You could have killed her. I know you hate her but that's still my sister and your aunt. Blood!"

I stopped listening after "bail." My only concern at this point was my kid. "Mom. Listen to me. Do not let Dominique out of your sight even for a second. "

"I'm not! Relax and get your ass here so you can tend to her ass. 'Cause she burning her bridge with me, honey."

Bev's voice zapped me out of my thoughts. "Girl, how did this happen?" Bev demanded.

I told her everything that happened. Unlike my mother I was more comfortable talking to Bev.

"Ummmph. That miserable bitch."

"I know. But I'm just happy that my child is not locked up and she is home because despite how I feel about the extra shit she been doing lately this really was my fault. I thank God my aunt didn't press charges." I just couldn't reveal to Bev all the shit about Dom from Dame to the disgusting video that I saw. It was too shameful on me as a parent to not know what my child was doing.

"Now something you forgot to mention to me is how you know Caesar?" Bev asked.

"Well do you remember when I told you I had a crush long ago that went away to college?"

"Yeah. The rich boy."

"That's Caesar."

"What?" She busted up laughing. "It's a small-ass world."

Thing was I never told Bev how the relationship ended. I merely told her he went away to college.

"We had sex," I blurted.

We were down the street from my house at this point. Bev's eyes got wide and she pulled over. "Repeat what you just said."

"We had sex."

Bev screamed in laughter.

"I know that's bad huh? Since my husband just passed away a few short months ago."

"No. It's not. You have to move forward. And I'm happy you did. I'm also happy you chose Caesar to move on with. He really seems like a great guy. Funny thing about the entire situation is that he was who I had in mind to set you up with once I saw you were ready. Shit you beat me to it, child."

Just then I got a text on my phone. I glanced down at it. "Speaking of the devil."

"What? Who is it?"

"Caesar."

The text read: You were on my mind. I wanted to make sure you were okay. Call me.

Before I could do or say anything else my phone rang. It was Caesar. "Hello?"

"Hey. I was worried about you. Are you okay?"

Hmmm. Should I tell him that I was arrested? Hell why not. He knew how my aunt was. "Well I got in a little trouble let's just say."

"Ahh yeah," he said in a husky voice. "What kind of trouble?"

"I was arrested."

"What? Why didn't you tell me?"

"Because I'm grown," I snapped.

He chuckled. "The old sassy Cashmere came out. Anyway I'm on my way over your house right now."

"How you just gonna tell me—"

"Babe, be quiet. I've been worried about you. Last thing I thought was that you were locked up. I really wish you would believe in me and let me be there for you. I'll be pulling up in a couple minutes. I don't even need to come inside. But what I need to see with my eyes is that you're okay, baby." Before I could respond he hung up. I kinda liked him telling me what to do.

"Uhh. Well I'll say."

I looked at Bev and giggled. "You know the funny part is that when I'm with him he takes my mind off Demarco. It's crazy to me that after all these years we were able to reconnect. And he said he doesn't care about my past. I mean when I was out there in the streets I had slept with his brother and I told him and he still don't care!"

"Well if he can take your mind off of Demarco and all that pain, Cashmere, I say keep him around. Look, life is just too damn short to dwell on pain and shit you can't change. You deserve happiness, love, and some goddamn peace. And you can give all of this to yourself and quit thinking you don't deserve that shit 'cause of your past. You were the victim, Cashmere, I tell you time and time again. But you don't have to be a victim forever."

"Yeah. Ms. Hope always said not to define yourself by your pain."

"And she was right."

"Bev, I'm going to tell you something I never told a soul."

"Okay."

"Another reason why I stayed with Demarco is because I didn't think another man would want me because of my past."

"That's some bullshit. And someone just showed you that that's not the case."

"Yep. Well if I can get things in order with my child, then maybe just maybe there can be some sort of future with Caesar. But we'd have to take it slow."

Just then some headlights shined behind us and parked on the street adjacent to my house.

Bev busted up laughing. "Ain't that some shit."

With the quickness, I hopped out her truck. "Let me see what he wants." I tried to sound like I didn't care. But I wanted to be in Caesar's arms again. They comforted me and made me feel like everything was going to be okay. I needed that feeling again.

Bev saw right through it and started laughing while saying, "Yeah, Right. Handle your business, baby girl."

"Thanks for being here for me. I'll call you tomorrow."

"Okay, baby. Kiss Dominique for me. Tell her I still love her."

I chuckled and walked to Caesar's squad car. He was getting out of his and I ran up to him and gave him a hug. "Hey, baby."

"Hey," I whispered against his chest. Something about being in his arms . . . I don't know. It made me feel like I could be vulnerable and completely break down. So that's what I did. I let more tears out. "I don't know where to start. Dominique knows the truth about my past. My aunt told her. One thing led to another and I ended up I jail."

"So your aunt's still up to her same trouble? You know what? That is a miserable woman. She is really no better than my mother. Did you bond out?"

"Yeah. And my mom was able to get my aunt to drop the charges."

"Cashmere. Next time something like that happens call me."

"I didn't want to get you caught up in that shit. You're a cop; how embarrassing for you."

He lifted my chin. "Look at me, baby. And listen well. Next time something goes down, I don't care what it is, call me and I will be there for you. Cashmere, stop thinking you can do all on your own; if you need me, it makes you no more weak. I told you I would be there for you and I will. From this point on I always will."

Why did all of what he just said give me butterflies? Like I was that same thirteen-year-old girl all over again. I believed what he said despite my trust issues. Naturally, my reaction to what he said was calm. I felt no need to question it. That was my first instinct. Then when I started to overthink, that's where the doubt came in. But I pushed those thoughts out of my head. Shit I had to trust someone.

"Okay. I have so much going on. I have to get everything settled with Dom. I need to get her in a detox and some counseling because I know she is on something." But the thought of that led to a whole 'notha can of worms.

Thing was if the question came up about who Dominique's father was, what did I do? Did I tell her who her real father was? All the bad things he had subjected me to? *Damn my aunt to hell for speaking on this shit to my baby. And damn myself for never quite coming clean.* But I was trying to protect her and also maybe I didn't want her to see me in a negative light. But the fact of the matter was she did now and she hated my guts. I had to find some way to fix this before my daughter's life was ruined.

"So I know I never ask but how are things with you?"

"Pretty good; thanks for asking, babe. Just working hard. I'm investigating the death of a young girl who died from taking this new form of ecstasy called molly. She was only fourteen. I've been questioning witnesses all day but I think I have a crack in the case. There's a woman who I believe was supplying those girls in Starz with the drug. I'm going to question her tonight. I've been looking for her for the past three days."

I stopped listening after he said "fourteen." It made my heart speed up. Shit that could have been my child. I really had to get a hold on this shit. I had to save my baby before it was too late.

"Well I have to get inside and check on Dominique. When I get things in order I'll give you a call okay?"

"Okay, baby." He kissed me on my lips. It gave me instant butterflies again! I blushed and looked down at my feet.

As I turned to walk away he said, "Hey, Cashmere."

I turned around quickly.

He stared at me and said, "Is it possible to love the same person for all these years?"

I chuckled and looked at him. "I guess anything is possible."

He blew a kiss my way, turned, and got in his car. I walked toward my house.

When I got inside, I saw my mother sitting on my couch and the smell of weed in the air.

"Why are you smoking in my house?" I demanded.

"Because I needed something to take the edge off 'cause that little bitch! Let me tell you, I'm done with her."

"First off, you way out of line. I don't care what she does, Mom, don't call my child a bitch."

"Hell she called me one! I never thought my grandbaby would do that."

"It's the drugs and she knows stuff that makes her hate me, you, the world! Anyway. Where is she?"

"In her room. I been guarding this living room like a damn pit bull to make sure her ass don't get out!"

I took a deep breath and headed up the stairs. When I got to her door, I took a deep breath, not even knowing where I was going to start. But what I did know was that I had to fix this. One thing was that I was going to find out what type of drugs she was using, put her in detox, then go from there.

I knocked on her door. "Dom?" I waited a few seconds for her to answer. I was met with silence.

Maybe she is 'sleep, I thought. I opened the door and stepped inside. Panic hit me. My heart slammed into my chest. Her room was empty. "Shit!" I ran out her room, yelling, "Mom!"

"What?"

I rushed down the stairs. "She is not in her room. Goddamn you, Mama, you were supposed to watch her!"

"I have been! Maybe she's in the bathroom. Calm down!"

I rushed back up the stairs and ran down the hall and burst into the bathroom. It was empty. Anxiety continued to pulse through me until I was sick to my stomach. I became nauseated and wanted to throw up at the thought of my child being missing. I searched the whole house and still did not find her. My mother followed me but she was more helpless than I was.

"I don't know how she could have snuck out. I swear on my dead mother's life I was watching her," my mom said in a distressed voice. Tears started sliding down her face. "I don't want my grandbaby missing I swear to you. I haven't left the house. All I did was use the bathroom. Maybe she snuck out then."

"Fuck! Fuck! Fuck!" I yelled covering my face with my hands. I had to think of something. I knew who could help me. Well I hoped he could! My heart continued to pound. I wished Caesar hadn't left. I pulled out my cell phone and called him. As soon as he answered, I blurted, "I need you now. Please come back to my house!"

Approximately five minutes later I could hear the sirens on his car as they pulled into the driveway. I rushed to the door and opened it as he had a balled hand up to knock.

"Come in!"

He stepped inside quickly. "What's wrong?"

"Dominique is missing." I started sobbing. "I don't know where she is."

"Calm down, baby." He wrapped an arm around my shoulders. "Didn't you put a GPS on her phone? We can easily find her that way."

"Oh yeah." But as soon as that hope hit me it deflated. "I took her phone back."

"Okay. Let me make a few phone calls."

I listened to Caesar call some officer, I assumed, because he told them to put out an APB and he even texted him a picture of Dominique.

"Where do you think she is?"

My mom said, "Maybe the strip club. You found her in the Barbary Coast."

"Come on. Let's go check," Caesar said.

We both rushed outside to his car. Once inside he put on his sirens and we flew down the street.

Chapter 32

Cashmere

We both came back to the house empty-handed and my heart was heavy. Dominique wasn't there. A check with the patrol officer Caesar had contacted revealed she was nowhere to be seen. They continued to look though he had told me.

I walked through the door being supported by Caesar because I was so distressed it seemed that my energy was leaving me.

Once we made it inside the house my mother rushed up to us. "I'm trying to get in contact with Hank so he can help but he not answering. Did you find her?" My mother asked.

"No."

"Show me her room," Caesar said.

We rushed up the stairs and once there he said, "Does she have a diary or anything like that?"

"I don't think so."

"Well start looking. Maybe we can find something."

I started going through my daughter's backpack, her drawers, but found nothing. Caesar was searching in her closet. I went to her laptop and tried to log on to her Facebook but since I didn't know her password I was unable to log on. It was the same for her Twitter and Instagram. In rage I snatched up the laptop and threw it.

Caesar was looking under her bed and turned around when he heard the loud crash of the laptop hitting the wall. He stood to his feet and grabbed me by my arms. "Baby. Calm down."

I shook my head and tried to snatch away, but he wouldn't let me. "Baby, look at me."

I did and tears ran down my face.

"We are going to find her. Something, some type of clue, is in this room. Thing is it is probably going to be in a spot you least expect, baby."

I nodded.

Caesar knocked her blankets and sheets off of her bed. I tossed the teddy bears and throw pillows to the floor. I grabbed the pillow Dominique used to sleep on. It was covered in a silk pink pillowcase. I could see smudges on it. It made me want to cry all over again. I just wanted my baby back. I pressed the pillow to my face and could smell her scent on it. Shit seemed so alive, like she was right here. Crazy part was as alive is it felt she could be lying somewhere dead, murdered or OD on drugs. Something crinkled in the pillowcase. My eyes narrowed and I grabbed the edge of the pillowcase so the pillow and whatever else was in it would fall to the floor.

They were letters wrapped in a rubber band.

My eyes scanned one of the letters quickly.

Lord, when I say my knees got weak and I thought I was going to pass out when I saw two words . . . Black Mitchell.

Caesar was speaking to someone on the phone and I sat on the couch with my hands covering my face in tears. Every time I thought I was done crying the tears came again and again. I could not believe that that motherfucker had been in contact with my daughter. But how? How did he know about her and how in the hell did she find out about him? When I saw his name on those envelopes I seriously thought the room was spinning.

In the letters he basically told my daughter about the ho game. He gave her tips, all the tricks of the trade. He was basically pimping his own daughter out from prison. Man, when I say I hated that man . . . If I could have killed him I really would. No one would be able to stop me from making his heart stop beating if I had the chance. That was the scary part. If I could take his life, first opportunity I got I was going to. He had destroyed my baby. Corrupted her and made her hate me. Made her what I was once. "And she didn't have to. Shit didn't have to be this way," I cried miserably.

"I don't know why the fuck you won't answer your gotdamn phone! My granddaughter is missing! I need you, motherfucker, and you once again are missing in action!" My mother was raging into her cell phone. She ended the call and sat down next to me in frustration. Her eyes were moist with tears. Her tears were a combination of pain from her husband being missing in action again and for Dom. I knew it had to bother her too.

"I'm sorry, Cashmere. I wish I could be more help to you."

I didn't respond. Part of me would always blame my mother for this shit. 'Cause if she hadn't abandoned us after my father's accident maybe just maybe we wouldn't be here, despite my aunt's talk of that shit being my and my sister's destiny. At the moment I honestly had no energy to hate my mother, rage at her, or take it out on her. Because I felt like I was going to collapse, my heart was thudding violently in my chest. I just kept my eyes closed as hot tears continued to pour down my face.

Caesar had two patrol cars out looking. Two of them were off shift and did it just to help him out. He went a step further and called someone he knew was a private investigator and they were talking in the corner of the living room. First thing he wanted to know after reading the letters was did I find any envelopes so he could trace an address on there. But there were none found.

I felt a hand over mine. It was my mother. She was sobbing and whispering, "This is all my fault. I wish I had killed that bastard when I had the chance."

You preaching to the choir, I thought. "I'm going out to look for her. It makes no sense to just sit around." I grabbed my keys and my phone and walked toward the door.

"I'll go look in my car too," my mother suggested.

I didn't respond but I figured her looking too wouldn't hurt.

I ended up driving for hours and hours and no matter how long I was out there, there was no sign of my child and my tears just would not stop pouring down my face. I even went to ho strolls asking if they had seen Dominique. I showed them pictures of her and even offered money. I went back to the strip clubs and even to my neighbors. My tank of gas went out, but still, I kept driving. When my truck threatened to stop I filled it up again and continued to drive around. And still nothing.

I did it all that night. Went home, rested for a couple hours, and then went out looking again. For a total of three days my child was missing. And I had no idea where she was. Caesar and my mother continued to help. And the investigator still had nothing. I stared into space as I sat on the couch. Caesar had met me back at the house and my mother was also there.

Just then my phone chimed telling me I had a text message. I opened the message and my eyes narrowed at a number I didn't recognize.

> It's me, Mom. This text message is to let you know that I'm not coming back. If you don't know by now I know that my dad is Black Mitchell. Shame on you, Mom, for keeping it from me after all these years. Well he is finally free and I'm living with him. Don't bother trying to look for me. You won't find me so it will be a waste of your time. And if by some miracle you were to find me it doesn't matter because I won't go with you willingly. And if you force me I'll run away again and again. I love my father and he loves me right back. I'd rather have this life than the fake one you offered. A home with no love. Yours just wasn't enough for me. I always felt empty inside. And now my daddy makes me whole. You can always have some more kids with that police officer. Bye.

Okay that's when the walls around me appeared to be closing in. I felt weak, hot, clammy. I stood to my feet and my knees wobbled.

"What wrong?" my mother demanded.

My knees gave in and I collapsed to the floor. The last thing I heard was my mom yelling my name at the top of her lungs before everything went black.

I felt something cold on my forehead. When I opened my eyes my mother was standing over me while Caesar was on the phone. I sat up quickly.

"Caesar, she's up," my mother said.

Caesar looked up, put up a finger and continued with his phone call.

Thoughts of the text came back to me making me moan. "Mom, is this shit going on real? Did—"

"Yes and yes. According to Caesar that Black bastard is out of jail. Matter fact, he was released three days ago."

This all seemed like a nightmare. Everything from start to finish. Losing my husband, Dominique stripping and having sex with other boys, and now this. The unbelievable just happened: my child ran off to be with her father, my old pimp. My world was so fucked up right now. If I couldn't make this shit right I was going to kill myself. I might as well be dead if my child was gone. But how did she know about Black being her dad? How in the fuck did she know he was locked up and how to get to him? My aunt couldn't have taken her to see Black and she knew nothing about getting into the lifestyle. Someone else was involved and they helped Dom enter the lifestyle. I put two and two together based off one of the letters; someone named Sunshine was on there. I didn't know who that was but the investigator read the letter and held on to it.

Caesar ended his call and strode over to me. "Okay. Here's what I know. Black Mitchell was released to a half-way house in Oakland two months ago. He was released from the halfway house three days ago. The systems weren't yet updated and the last time I ran his rap sheet it showed he was still incarcerated."

"I told her," my mom said.

"How the fuck?" I demanded.

"He was locked up for thirteen years, he had very minor priors, and he was released for running a good prison program."

I sighed and closed my eyes briefly.

"Question: I traced the number on the text message. I was able to get the name and address of a Meka Stanton.

It's a crazy coincidence because I'm supposed to question her on the case I've been working on with the young girl, Patrice Wilson. She stays in Compton. Do you know her?"

Chapter 33

Cashmere

Compton, CA, eighteen years ago:

After the officer freed me once he got what he wanted he shoved me out of his car on to the pavement, got in his car, and drove off. "Fuck you!" I winced at the pain of my knees slapping against the hard, cold concrete. I was still drunk out of my mind and the X pill was still kicking in. I lay there for a moment and could hear his tires screeching against the ground as he sped away.

A few seconds later I heard, "Cash!"

"Who the fuck is it!" I yelled.

"Your sister, dumbass."

I looked up as Desiree came out of the shadows. She helped me to my feet. "Man, that horny-ass po po did a number on you."

"You mean you saw it?"

"Yeah, I was right there."

"Well why in the fuck didn't you help me, bitch? Do something."

"Was I supposed to go up against a bullet?" But the gleam in her eyes made me feel like she enjoyed the shit. Like she wanted to see me suffer. I just didn't get it.

"If it were you nothing could ever stop me from protecting you. I hate you sometimes I swear," I said miserably. I was angry about the fact that my sister

seemed to want me to suffer when I never ever wanted that for her. Her pain was my pain. But for some reason it just wasn't the same.

"Okay let that shit go. It's over with. He fucked! So what he's a cop? Just add him to the list of all our other men. Now listen I need you to come on and let's make this money."

I stood to my feet and adjusted my clothes. "What?"

'Meka is at the hotel down the street. She got a high roller and nigga is feeling real freaky. He want some more bitches and he paying up, little sister."

I had been working all day and just wanted to go to sleep. "I'm tired. And Black didn't tell me to go there," I protested. My sister was once again getting me involved in some mess.

"Don't matter 'cause he told me to tell you, little sister, so just shut the fuck up. You been on the block all day and he a little pissed with you. So if I were you I'd advise you to make it up to him by making this paper."

"Fuck Black Mitchell!"

She shoved me forward and flinched at me. At the moment I was too weak to fight back. "You know what, I'm not going to let you piss me off. There is too much money to be made so come the fuck on! You're going! You don't want to piss Black off and he beat your ass again."

True enough I didn't because the beating he put on me earlier still had me sore and bruised up. I shook my head at my sister. She was always anxious for a job. She was on drugs so bad that the amount Black supplied her with just wasn't enough for her anymore.

After the short trek, when we got to the hotel room and knocked Meka let us in. She was a year younger than my sister and had been working for Black since she was twelve years old. I was surprised that she hipped us to this since all the time she acted like she hated my guts.

She unlocked the door for us and stepped aside so we could enter. She was ass buck-naked. We slipped in and she locked the door back. There was music playing and a guy was lying on the bed in his boxers.

"Y'all ladies just in time; y'all can join me in an ass-shaking contest. And he tipping," Meka said giggling.

"No problem with me!" Desiree stripped down and joined Meka. They both put their butts in his face and started dropping it low, flapping their asses up and down to the music. The dude loved every minute of it and started slapping them on their asses. Dollars flew everywhere.

"Is this money bonus?" Desiree asked.

"Yes, baby, go ahead and get that. Trust there's more. I'm real paid."

As they giggled and retrieved the money, he got on his knees in the bed and commanded that they both kiss on him.

I looked away in disgust as they did, forgetting I was in the room. I was so tired of this shit. So tired of this life. I wanted out so bad. Maybe killing myself would be the only real way.

I started sliding a finger up and down my arm pushing one of my nails in deeper as I got toward my vein.

A few moments later, I heard him moan. "Get me ready," he ordered. I heard jerking and him moaning again.

"Who you want first, daddy?"

"I want her over there first."

Then as if all of a sudden they remembered I was there, Meka and Desiree looked at me.

Of course Desiree looked mad that he requested me first. And Meka always looked at me like she wanted to fuck me up, which I was cool with 'cause I always knew she didn't want to see me because I would have beat her ass for sure. But I had no energy to do that right now. And I didn't want no part of this man. No matter how handsome he was or how much money he was tossing around I didn't want it and I didn't want him. I didn't want him to touch me period. But hell when did my young ass ever have a choice in this? Us girls, we never did. Why couldn't someone rescue me from this life?

"Come on over here, baby. Take care of me and I'll take care of you."

How old is your disgusting ass? And you can't see I'm underage? I'm the youngest one in this bitch. Man! *I thought. I tried to translate this with my eyes.*

Death had to be better than this.

I thought back to my black history class and the teacher talking about how slaves' lives were so fucked up, losing their kids, being lashed, raped, or watching their wife or daughter be raped, sold or seeing so much death around them that they looked forward to death and viewed death as an escape from that shit they had to endure every day with no recourse. Shit they looked at death like a little kid looked at going to Disneyland. That's how I was starting to feel. Once I got home the first chance I got I was going to end my life. I was tired.

"Come on."

I closed my eyes briefly, and opened them.

"Come on, pretty girl. Put those pretty lips on me."

I took steps forward with the cop's smell still on me. I climbed on the bed. The guy pulled me on top of him. Before he could make another move someone started banging on the hotel door. "Open this mothafucking door!"

I gasped instantly recognizing Black's voice. Desiree jumped off the bed, went to the door, and unlocked and opened it. Black strode inside.

He paused in front of the bed. "Cashmere," *he said* calmly. "Get off the bed."

I did as he ordered.

"What the fuck is this?" the guy demanded.

Black pulled out a gun and said, "Just a minute and you can get back to what the fuck you was doing." Black turned and looked at Meka. "Meka. Get over here." Once she did, he took one look at her and slapped her so hard she flew into the wall.

She screamed as she hit the floor with a thud. The guy jumped from the bed in fear as Desiree scurried to a corner

Black cocked back the gun. "Nigga, I said don't move. Or I'll pump three into you. Come here, Meka."

She got off the floor quickly, crying, and walked back over to Black. He started whipping her ass. I mean busting her in the mouth, cracking her in the face, yanking her around by her hair. Then he tossed her to the floor and started kicking her, the whole while saying, "Bitch, I told you not to take Cashmere." He then lifted her by her neck so her feet dangled in the air. "I bet' not in my fucking life find you anywhere near her or I will kill you got it?"

"Yes, daddy!"

He slung her into the wall. He then turned to me and grabbed me by my arm yanking me outside. He slammed the door shut and hemmed me up against the wall. With his eyes wide he blasted, "Listen and listen to me well. You are not to go nowhere near Meka and you ain't to service no clients she services. You don't fuck the clients she fucks I don't care what he offering. She has the virus got it?"

I gasped when he said that. He opened the hotel door back, stepped in the doorway. I thought he was going to get Desiree as well but he said instead, "I'm sorry about the inconvenience. You can continue on—"

"Naw. I'm cool. She all beat up. I just wanna go, man."

Black aimed his pistol at him. "You asked for my girls; you better use them and pay up. Or I will kill you from this door to that bed. Now what's it going to be?"

The guy lay back down in fear.

"Bitches, get on that bed. And if you don't pay up we are gonna have problems."

They did.

Black then closed the door and grabbed me. "Black, what about my sister?" I demanded. I couldn't let her sleep with the same man Meka was going to sleep with. She could get AIDS too. But Black pulled me away toward the lobby.

"Wait! What about my sister?" I struggled against him as he continued to pull me. "What about my sister? Let me tell my sister!" I screamed. But he wouldn't let me. He dragged me away.

"Cashmere?" Caesar called my name and snapped me back into my thoughts.

"Yes, I know who the bitch is. But what I don't know is how and why she was with my child," I fired.

"I plan on going over there now and questioning her about Dominique's whereabouts. I need to go now."

"Well if you going I'm going with you. Mom, stay here and call me if you hear anything."

He turned around and said, "Take your car in case I have to take her to the station for further questioning. And, Cashmere, I'm warning you now: no matter what she says to you don't do anything crazy. With your daughter being gone you can't do anything for her if you get locked up. You can't worry about revenge right now. The most important thing is to get information, all the information we can to get your daughter back. And since she was with her she more than likely knows where she is. So you have to stay calm. Got it?"

I didn't respond.

"Got it?"

"Yes," I bit off. "I got it."

Twenty minutes later, we pulled up to some apartments. After we got out of our vehicles, Caesar walked toward me, pulled out his gun, and said, "Cashmere, remember what I said."

I nodded.

We walked into the building to Meka's apartment. Nothing but rage was inside of me and the closer we got the more I ached to get my hands around her neck and snap it.

Once we made it to the apartment Caesar knocked.

We heard a female say, "Oh that's probably the pizza, baby," she said. Without asking, she flung her door opened.

Her eyes widened when she saw me and Caesar. She made a move to close the door but Caesar put his foot in. I stepped forward and shoved the door open with all my might. Both of us stepped in and Caesar closed it behind us.

"What the fuck y'all thinking y'all doing busting in my apartment?" she demanded.

Before I could say anything I looked at who was sitting on the couch and gasped. "Hank!"

"Who is he?"

"My mother's motherfucking husband!" I shots hateful looks his way.

He stood with his hands in the air. "Cashmere, it's not what you think. I didn't—"

"But, nigga, you sure was about to!" Meka fired. "Had him and this bitch not come in here you'd be all up in these walls. Ain't that what you said you wanted to do when you got my number off of Craigslist? You knew what the fuck this was, nigga."

I breathed a sigh of relief that Hank hadn't been fucking her and hadn't got the chance to fuck her today because she was infected.

"We have some question to ask you, miss. So, sir, it's best you leave so we can do so."

He stood and started for the door.

"Uh-uh!" Meka ran after him and blocked him from exiting out the door. "Put the money in my hand! Or else!"

He pulled two one hundred dollar bills out and placed them in her hand. She then stepped aside shaking her head.

Once it was just us three she turned back around to face us.

"So you hand delivered my baby to Black?"

"Go on with that shit, Cashmere. You hand delivered your baby to Black by making her feel unloved and unwanted by your nigga. Yes, I know all about it. And so does Black and he is pissed. You ain't gonna never see that little girl again. Trust!"

That's when I rushed her. And Caesar wasn't fast enough to stop me from slamming her on the floor by her neck.

She struggled against my weight on top of her. "Get the fuck off of me, bitch!"

I spat in her face and started choking her. "Bitch, I'm gonna murder you right here," I said through clenched teeth. That's when Caesar lifted me off of her.

She took her time standing back to her feet. "Bitch, you'd never get the chance to kill me. And pigs ain't the only ones with guns."

I snatched away from Caesar. "Your gunplay can never scare me, bitch. I'm right here and I'm not pulling out shit. We can go right now."

She stood with her arms crossed under her chest. Fear glistened in her eyes despite the talk she talked.

"Right. You talk that shit but don't want to pop off at all. All I want to know is my daughter texted me from your phone today. So that means you were with her today. Where the fuck is my daughter, bitch?" I demanded.

"I ain't got to tell you shit, Cash. And I won't." She looked at Caesar. "And as for you, copper, unless you got a warrant get the fuck out my house."

"You're on my list to be questioned regarding the death of Patrice Wilson. I don't need a warrant for that. Because witnesses say you were with her the night she died."

Her eyes got wide. But she recovered quickly. "But you ain't coming for that are you? You came to my crib with this bitch who wanna know about her bitch daughter! And like I said, dirty motherfucker, got no warrant get the fuck out."

"Oh I can get one. And if I do be prepared for me to tear this place apart. You know. Since you've got a gun and all. And unless its registered I'd have to take you in and book you." He gestured toward the counter that had several pill bottles on it. "Along with those pill bottles that I'm sure have molly in them. Which is what Patrice died from. But at the moment, I don't care about none of that. Now it's best if you just cooperate with the questions we have for you, ma'am. This is a serious matter. A child is involved."

I glanced at the counter and saw that some of the pills had spilled from the bottle. They were clear capsules with white powder in them.

Meka looked a little shook when he said take her to the station. Then she brushed it off. "Officer, I ain't got nothing to lose. Jail and death don't scare me. I'm so tired of this life any fucking way. But I'll talk only because I want to. I'd love to."

I tossed a hand to her rambling. "Shut the fuck up with all of that! Where is my child?"

"I don't know where the fuck she is. I ain't seen her in three days. I sent that text because Black told me to." She looked at me and snickered. "He wanted you to know the real. Bottom line is this: little girl came to me for the truth so I gave the shit to her. And yep, I been grooming her all this time. Introduced her to the game. I don't like you, Cashmere. Never have. And I don't like your bitch daughter. I have no loyalty to a bitch like you, who always thought she reigned supreme and I been putting it down longer and been loyal to Black from day one. I don't know where the fuck Black lives; all I do know is that I gave her the money for a Greyhound ticket and I dropped her off three days ago at the station and that's it. He wouldn't tell me where. I wasn't invited to tag along. Y'all motherfuckers happy?"

Thing was when I was with Black I never saw too much of Meka. She was always working on Fig. She was rarely seen or heard until the day we went to the hotel and Black beat her ass. I didn't get why she hated me so much or my child.

"No, I'm not happy, bitch. Where in the fuck did you send my child?"

"I told you! Stop acting like you give a shit. You care about my little sister as much as I care about her."

I narrowed my eyes at her. Hoes referred to other hoes who shared the same pimp as wifey. So I was confused by her terminology. She caught my confused look.

"I'll repeat it if you want me to. Dominique is my little sister. Oh yeah, you never knew. Black was my daddy. Yep. And my mama gave me to him when I was twelve and I been working for him since. So that makes her my sister, bitch! Sad thing is he gonna do her like he did me. Use her up and throw the bitch away. And I'm glad at that shit."

I gasped hella distressed at what she was saying. She was Black's daughter? And if he treated her that way how would he treat my child?

I asked in a shaking voice, "Where is she please?"

"Look I told you what I know. Now you figure the rest out. It ain't gonna matter if you find her anyway." She chuckled.

"What are you saying?" I asked evenly as my heart started to speed up.

"Your precious daughter ain't so precious. She been cracked! She been fucking in a way that rivals you when you were that age. She is a hoe. And a good one and she love that shit. In addition, sweet Cashmere, she had sex with a few of my clients. And we did a threesome with one and like me the guy was infected. Do I need to spell the shit out? Fine I will. I have AIDS!"

"You filthy, scum bitch!"

That's when I lost it, rushed forward, and started throwing blows at the bitch. She fought back, which made it difficult for Caesar to break it up. I pounded and pounded on her.

"Cashmere!" Caesar grabbed me, causing us both to lose our balance and fall backward on the wooden floor. Caesar's head hit the wood floor with a bang, weakening him. That's when the bitch scurried away and ran into another room.

"Cashmere!" But I ignored him, adrenaline pumping through me. I ran toward the hallway searching for the bitch. Her bathroom was empty. Next I ran toward another room; when I opened it I searched for her and the bitch was nowhere in sight.

That's when Caesar came up and grabbed me from behind. "Cashmere, stop. I—"

"Die, you fucking bitch!" Meka rose with a gun in her hand and pointed it at me. Before I could react Caesar shoved me out of the way while reaching for his gun. But it wasn't quick enough and the first stray bullets from her gun hit Caesar making him fall to the floor. I ducked down and snatched his gun from his pocket and started firing shots at Meka until I struck her chest several times. She flew into her wall and slowly with her eyes wide, slid to the floor.

My heart started pounding.

"Cashmere! Give me the gun and get out of here now!" he commanded.

I rushed back over to him. "Are you hurt?"

"It's in my shoulder. I'll live. Trust me. Give me the gun and leave! I'll deal with this."

I hesitated for a second at all the blood I saw but if I got locked up I couldn't save my child so I ran out of the apartment as Caesar told me to.

I jumped in my car and sped until I made it to my house. I didn't know what the fuck to do. Things were so fucked up! And I was fearful as hell that I wouldn't see my child again. This was just too fucking much! Meka being Black's daughter. My daughter possibly having AIDS and being missing. And I had killed Meka and I hoped to God Caesar really wasn't hurt too bad.

Still crying, I pulled into my driveway and put my car in park.

"What the fuck?" I screamed out loud hitting my steering wheel. I punched it several times and cried my eyes out. I felt even more hopeless now that Caesar was hurt; he probably couldn't do anything for me. I prayed that the investigator could help me.

Suddenly someone was knocking on my driver's side window. I looked at my mother.

I rolled down the window. "What?"

"Girl, I been blowing up your phone. Get out of the car and come in the house. I have someone here who can help us."

I did as she said and she grabbed me by one of my arms and pulled me with her at a hurried pace and as she pulled me she said, "I got some good news. I got someone to unlock Dominique's accounts! But we need your help!"

She pulled me into the living room and over to my computer desk. That's when I noticed the guests in the room. One of them was a nerdy-looking older black man. The other was Hank.

My eyes burned into him. I wanted to tell my mom about what I saw but I knew now wasn't the time. And his eyes pleaded with me not to.

"This is Teddy. He's a technician who lives on my street," my mother said quickly.

"Now in order to do this I need someone who is friends with her to log on to their account," the guy said.

"I'm her friend." I quickly logged into my account.

"Now go to your friends list, find her, and click on her page."

I did so quickly but she was not in my friends list. "What the hell?"

"She blocked you. Okay. Give me one second." He pulled a tiny device out of his bag and hooked it into the computer. "This is called Firesheep; it's a plug-in that is essentially a packet sniffer that monitors and analyzes traffic between a Wi-Fi router and end users connecting to the network. Pretty much with this you can hack into anyone's account as long as there is a wireless router." He attached some tiny cord to it and plugged it into his laptop. He did some typing and a few seconds later he had her page open.

I took a deep breath, relieved. A few seconds later, he looked at me and said, "Is this her?"

I looked at Dominique's page in disgust. She had changed her name to Sexy Dom-Dom Mitchell. In her

"About Me" she put: I'm a chill girl and finally I'm happy 'cause I got the bullshit out my life. Anyway fellas you want some of this you know what to do. HMU at prettygirldom@gmail.com. You have to at least have one hundred roses if you want a date. And if any pretty wifeys want to join the stable of a real nigga and you willing to put those pretty toes to the concrete for a nigga who is going to hold you down, hit me up! Serious bitches only!

I scrolled down her page.

"Is there a way for me to see what city she is in?" I asked him.

"If she does a post or post a pic her location will show up only if she agreed to let Facebook access her location." He paused. "And it looks like she didn't."

Shit. I sighed.

There were dozens of pictures of Dominique half naked and posing with a man. And there was no need to guess. It was Black Mitchell hugged up with my child. Pictures of him kissing her and her kissing him. On one of the pics it read underneath: Where I want to be.

I looked away as I felt the tears come on again. It was clear that he was prostituting my child. And she was not the same child I raised.

"That motherfucker," my mother said.

Just then my phone rang. It was Caesar. *Thank God.* "Hello? Caesar, Dominique is with Black!"

"I know; that's why I calling. Meet me at Centinela Hospital now."

Chapter 34

Cashmere

When I walked into the hospital room Caesar was in, although I was anxious for what he was going to tell me I couldn't help but see that he was banged up. His shoulder was in a sling and there were bandages on his leg.

I looked away quickly. Damn I needed his help. "Are you in pain?" I asked.

"Well the doctors managed to pull three bullets out of me. Two in my shoulder and one in my arm."

"Caesar, I'm so sorry I got you involved in this. You could have been killed or arrested. Is she?"

"Dead? Yes. But don't worry. Despite what you feel about her, how you felt in your heart in that moment and what you planned to do to her, at the end of the day it was truly self-defense. No one will ever know you were there. And there is no investigation pending. I took care of it, Cashmere."

"What did you tell them?"

"Cashmere, I'd rather not say because I'm not a dirty cop and I hate dirty cops. But I don't want you in jail. So I lied and pieced a mock puzzle together. I told my boss that I came simply to interview her about the murder of Patrice Wilson. When I saw the bottles of Molly I had probable cause to take her in. I told her to get her hands behind her head because she was going in on a possession charge. However, she panicked and ran in the bedroom.

When I went in the bedroom she started firing. I said I didn't get it being that it would have only been a possession charge. But my boss ran her record and she had several warrants. One is for exposing someone to AIDS. In addition, to find Molly on someone and to be questioning them in regards to someone who dies from Molly would make sense why she would. No one is concerned about her. She is a prostitute with AIDS. In their eyes, she is better off dead. Truthfully I think that she wanted us to kill her. You heard with she said. She was tired of the life. And look how her father did her. But, it's just that given her situation with Black, I feel bad for her. She was a victim. And, well, because that could have been you."

I understood what he said but I didn't feel bad. I didn't. I was a victim and I could have never done what she had done. Expose an innocent child to this life? To AIDS? Life is based on choices no matter how hard it was for you. I also couldn't feel sorry for her because of the fact that she had given my child to Black. "Well just so you know I feel like shit for involving you."

"I wanted you to involve me so don't. And, babe, don't worry about me. I'm okay. My career will be fine. It's just that there is not much I am going to be able to do to help now but give you this." He handed me a folded piece of paper.

I unfolded it quickly and scanned the writing on the paper. There was an address on it and the city was Oakland.

"The investigator got back to me. That is where Black Mitchell is. He actually owns the property. That is the red light district for child sex trafficking."

I took a deep breath. I had to figure out something. But what? Without Caesar I was pretty much lost as to how to get my child back.

"Now you could go to the police. I mean I know some—"

"First off no. The police are the reason I'm in this shit. Why in the fuck would they let him out? He is a murdering piece of shit. And no to getting you involved any further. I have implicated you in this enough. You could have been killed. I will figure out some shit on my own."

He closed his eyes briefly. "I knew you would say that. Cashmere, I know that I can't stop you from whatever you plan on doing. But, baby, just be careful. The Five North will take you all the way there."

"I will, Caesar; don't worry about me. I'll be fine." I leaned over and kissed him.

But as I said it and walked off, I asked myself, how could I promise that? The last time I was in Black's presence I was raped and almost killed. Had my mother not come I and Demarco would have been dead. But I knew I couldn't involve anyone this time in this mess. Caesar had almost died for God's sake. No. I had to do this shit on my own. But as for me, I was more than willing to die to save my child. Which was exactly why I went back home, snuck in the back door of my house to Demarco's old office, and grabbed the nine millimeter gun along with some bullets. I snatched up my purse, phone, and keys as quietly as I could. I didn't need anyone else but Caesar knowing my whereabouts at this point.

Once I had what I needed, I slipped back through my back door and rushed over to my car. I jumped inside and tossed my purse on the passenger seat. Nervously I looked down at my phone as my mother called me. I didn't answer it. I took a deep breath and played with my phone for a second. Visions of what had happened the last time I saw him flashed before my eyes. I knew I was stalling because I was scared as hell to face Black again. He was a cold person. I thought back to how he raped me in front of Demarco. If my mother and the cops had not showed up he would have killed me. I looked at the voicemails I had. I scrolled down until I saw the one from Demarco. I checked the date. It was the same day that he was in the car accident. Thing was I was no longer delusional. I knew my husband was dead. And our marriage was dead long before he was killed in that accident. I had accepted this. But I guessed I was curious as to what the message contained. There was a chance I wouldn't make it back. I didn't want to die not knowing what he had said. Even if it was, "Bitch, die. I hate you and I'm so happy with my new bitch." As the message started I pulled off, my focus on the road ahead of me.

My heart thudded violently in my chest as I stood outside the abandoned house. I was about to face a major demon. A demon from my past and a demon in form: Black Mitchell. But if I wanted my baby back home and safe I knew that I had to do this. But if I could free my daughter trust and believe I would give up my life to do so. I could not believe that this man after all the horrible things that he had done to me was free to walk this earth. And free to ruin more young girl's lives like he had almost ruined mine. But I couldn't let him do that to Dominique.

I crept up the termite-bitten, cracked wooden steps to the house. My nine millimeter gun was locked and loaded and there was another clip tucked in the back pocket of my jeans. I could hear a TV playing from a distance. I ignored the sound and reached out and jiggled the doorknob to see if it was unlocked. It wasn't. The front window had a black sheet covering it so I couldn't see inside. *Damn.*

I crept around to the back hoping I could see some sort of sign of my daughter inside. The sound of the TV got closer and closer as I walked. Each window I passed was closed and was covered. *Fuck it,* I thought. I would just have to bust a window or shoot the door handle off. But as I walked a little farther around the house, I saw a linen blowing out of a window. It was on the right side corner of the house. I walked up to it and saw the window luckily dangled open. I peeked inside what looked like a bedroom. I waited a few minutes for any sort of movement. When there was none, I tucked my gun in my pants band and climbed up the sill.

I smoothly and as quiet as I could slid into the room. I then pulled my gun out of my waist, cocked it, and aimed it should anyone appear. So many thoughts were flying through my head. Part of me wondered in that moment if I should have gone to the police but they were the ones who let Black out to begin with! They cared very little about my problems with this man. They had proven that they couldn't protect me or my daughter. So I had to do this.

I tiptoed out of the bedroom to the hallway. There were two more doors I had to enter. One was the bathroom, which was empty. I took a deep breath and walked to the bedroom. I hoped the sound of my feet on the carpet wouldn't alert him if he was in there. I opened the door with my gun aimed. There were two bodies lying on a bed. As I walked farther in the room, words could not describe the rage, shock, and hurt I felt to see my thirteen-year-old daughter lying down next to Black. And this mother-fucker was pimping my child now! He had destroyed my innocence and now he was destroying hers. She was lying down next to him, his arms were wrapped around her as they spooned. She was dressed in a white nightgown with her feet bare looking so innocent, so fragile. 'Cause my baby was and he probably used that against her. I wondered if he had had sex with her.

I shuddered and closed my eyes briefly. I stepped closer to the bed, toward my daughter. I tapped her on her shoulders and whispered firmly, "Dom. Get out of that bed now."

Her lashes fluttered open and she gasped. When she didn't move fast enough for me, I yanked her little body out of the bed by her arm and shoved her behind me. "Stay," I commanded in a low voice. Truth was I honestly didn't know if she would comply. Now more than ever I wished when I was eighteen with that gun in my old apartment that I had pulled the trigger and ended his life then. Maybe I wouldn't be here now. A sob racked my body.

Black remained asleep but turned on his side, with a snore on his lips. Although I didn't want to do this in front of my daughter I had to.

My gun was aimed at his sleeping form. I wished I had a machete.

"Black Mitchell! Wake your motherfucking ass up!" My gun was aimed at his sleeping form.

As soon as I saw a speck of white in his eyes, as his lashes touched the bottom of his brows I wasted no time in pumping those bullets into that sorry motherfucker as his body jerked to and fro. In fact, I emptied the entire clip. I enjoyed seeing all the bullets pierce his flesh as smoke filled the air and blood started to seep from his body. But still, despite the fact that he was no longer breathing and his eyes were wide, I loaded another clip and emptied it as well, ignoring the terrified screams of Dominique. I smiled at his dead body for a moment; then as my daughter continue screaming I looked over at her tear-soaked face.

I lowered the gun. She stood to her feet.

"Dominique. No!"

Before I could grab her, she ran toward the bed and threw her body over Black's. She started bawling.

I rushed over to her and grabbed one of her arms. "Get off of him, baby!" I started crying. What had he done to my child?

"How could you, Mom?"

"I had to baby. I—"

"You killed my father!"

There was so much I wanted to say to my child in that moment. So much I needed and wanted to explain but in that moment I needed to get her the fuck out of the house before the cops came.

I snatched her up as she struggled against me. At one point I had to backhand her to keep her quiet. But she still struggled against me so I gripped an arm around her neck and dragged her outside to my truck. Once I got her in the truck she tried to get out of the car so I wrapped an arm around her neck and drove off.

Dominique continued to cry and moan during the drive. Truth was I didn't know if I was going to make it back to Inglewood. The cops may have caught on and nabbed me. It was a six-hour drive back. But did I regret blowing his head clear off? No.

I had rid her of Black. She was free from him and nothing else could be worse. He could no longer hurt my child. Even if they caught me and arrested me and charged me. My child was fucking free. But I had to tell her the truth before we were separated. Once two hours had passed and I was not in that city I pulled the car over on a street and yanked her out and shoved her against the car; then I blocked her so she couldn't get away.

"I know. And I know right now you hate me. But, Dominique, what I did, it's for the best. Look at me and know that I love you. That man has been brainwashing you. I will not give my daughter to the streets like I was given to the streets years ago. You will not live that life a day longer; if I have to die or end up in jail to stop it then I will. This love he is offering is not real love and it will hurt you. Blood or not."

"But . . ." She shook her head and sobbed uncontrollably.

Then I noticed: the brand. The tattoo of Black's name on her neck. I looked at the sky and tried to mask my pain. That's not all I saw when I looked into her face. She had a black eye, a busted lip, and when I pulled her gown away from her body she had welts all over her skin.

"Do you think this shit is love? Love doesn't hurt. A person who loves you will never inflict pain, make you cry, make you suffer! If thats love . . . It's not a love you need, baby, any more than it was a love I needed! It almost ruined me. It scarred and almost killed me. It killed my sister long before her heart stopped beating. He would have just used you up and thrown you away. I know I should have told you the truth long ago, that my mother abandoned my sister and me, and I was forced to be a prostitute with my sister, and that yes, I went to jail for murdering her. I never ever set out to kill my sister it was just a horrible accident. In my time with Black he drugged me, raped me, beat me, and got me and my sister addicted to drugs. He is no good I swear to you, baby. He tried to kill me. You have to trust me. You used to trust me. Remember the bond we had. Please trust me again!"

Her words surprised me: "I don't understand, Mom. He promised me he would be different. But he hurt me too, Mom, he hurt me too. I'm so confused." She bawled like a baby.

It was killing me to see my daughter so broken. "What did he do to you?"

"Things to have his love and attention that I thought were worth it. But I just don't know anymore. I was trying to figure it all out, Mom, but I couldn't. Thing is, he was the only daddy I had. So I exchanged that pain he inflicted that night for having him. Because he said he would never leave me. I don't like myself, Mom. And he said no one else would either. But he said he loved me because I was his."

"Listen to me. Think about Meka! Why wasn't she living with you guys when that's all she ever wanted"

She is his daughter. Look how he treated her. He used her up. He would have done the same to you!"

Her eyes were wide when I mentioned Meka being her sister.

"I guess none of this really matters anymore does it, Mom? I'm stuck at square one again." Between sobs she said, "Who's gonna love me now?"

"I will. Listen I know I made mistakes and I should have been honest to you about who your father was and I'm so sorry for that. I'm sorry that I allowed things to get out of control, not standing up to Demarco and forcing him to either be right by the both of us or get the fuck out. I realized that I in some ways was just as weak as my mother was when I was your age. How Demarco treated you had nothing at all to do with you. There is nothing wrong with you, baby. Listen we can start over. Let me fix this." I reached in the car and pulled my cell phone out of my purse and searched for the voicemail I had heard earlier from Demarco. "Listen to this. It's the night Demarco was killed."

The message played: "Hey, baby. I'm calling to let you know I'm coming home. I'm so sorry for all of this. I fucked up. And I been fucking up for a long time. I'm just lucky you stuck by me. You know what, ever since I left, I been doing a lot of thinking. A lot of sober thinking. Trying to make some sense of this bullshit. Trying to figure out why I've been being so angry and filled with so much hatred, directing it at my family. The truth is, I don't hate you. When I look at Dominique I am reminded of that night. And that night is a reminder of what you went through and I couldn't save you. It always left me feeling like I wasn't a man. What I never told you is that the day he raped you, it took away my manhood. I always felt that if I had taken a chance, despite the gun, maybe just maybe he would have never raped you. The time I've been away, baby, I realized I was never mad at Dominique. And it wasn't her I hated. I hated myself. From the day I met you I thought you were a queen, and I wanted to be your champion, your Superman, and I failed you that night. I never forgave myself for it. So my anger that I directed at you and Dom was really the anger and disappointment I felt for myself. I know I told you that when I look at Dominique I see him. But I also realized that whenever I looked at her I see you. And how can I not love something that came from you? And she is so precious, so beautiful, so sweet. Like a little angel float-ing around. I'm sorry for treating her so bad. I love you and I love Dominique and I'm so, so sorry that I have made her feel like I didn't. If you two will let me, baby, I'm gonna come home and fix all of this before it's too late. Before I lose you and Dom. I promise that for all the times I made you cry I'm going to fix it. I'm going to make it up to Dominique too, baby. I'm going to mend her heart, baby. I'm going to be the father she always needed me to be I promise." He started breaking down crying on the phone. Then suddenly there was a loud car horn and a crash sound.

Dominique had her hands over her face. She was crying loudly into them and saying, "I wanted Demarco's love so bad, Mom." She broke down crying hysterically. She looked so limp and so fragile. Her whole body was racked with sobs.

As tears of my own slipped down my face, I grabbed her face between my hands. "Dominique, will you please forgive me and let us start over? Can we please put this behind us? Trust me you will be okay. We will be okay."

She closed her eyes briefly, opened them, and said, "Okay, Mom. Okay."

I pulled her into my arms and we both continued to sob.

Chapter 35

Dominique

"And you just don't even understand that I love you to an amount that is immeasurable and I'd take a thousand bullets for you, little girl." Those words continued to ring out in my head. They were my mother's words, the day she had caught me red handed at the strip club. I felt so many different emotions as we were driving home. The day that I was reunited with Black was nothing like I thought it was going to be. It was the worst three days of my life. For starters, he forced me to get the tattoo and when I said I was scared to he slapped me over and over again. Then once I got settled at the house I jumped in the shower and before I could even put pants on there was a man in my bed nude. Thing was I was confused because Black swore to me that when he got out I would no longer have to prostitute myself. Initially, I thought maybe it was a mistake because Black did have girls out here working for him but not at our house. When I told Black about the guy in my bed, he punched me in my mouth and dragged me by my hair back to the room to have sex with the man. Then guy after guy came. And Black said since I was resisting he was going to punish me. That meant putting me on the block in Oakland to work. After five hours out there he came to get me, brought me home, and beat me up more because according to him one of his other hoes said I was putting in no effort.

I didn't like how he was treating me. He was worse than Demarco. And yes, I was upset at my mother for killing my dad. But deep down the man he had shown himself to be in that one night was not who I thought he was. Then he did something I never thought he would to me. He raped me. And the fact that Meka was his daughter and he abandoned her just didn't make a bit of sense to me. And the things he did to my mother. I realized that my father was the real liar not my mom. I believed my mother when she told me what he had done because of how vicious he was to me. Truth be told a part of me hated her for killing Black and a part of me loved her for doing it. Although I fought her I did it in confusion because they had both hurt me and I didn't know if I was safe with either of them. But now I was starting to think that she saved me from him. And I was safer with her. Because despite her mistakes she continued to fight for me. Backflashes of her getting beat up in the squad car the day she went to confront my aunt flew before my eyes and her words, I could hear them loud and clear now. *"Jail or bullets don't mean shit to me when y'all got my child in those cuffs for some shit she had nothing to do with."*

And she continued to fight for me, for my safety. I thought back to the day she beat up Jada's mother and when she tried to stab Dame. She did this all for me. Because she felt that they had harmed me. My mother had proved in so many ways that she loved me. Even after losing Demarco and having a miscarriage she tried to pull it together for me. I guess I was too much in my feelings to see that everything my mother had done was to protect me. And even her killing Black. I asked myself time and time again why this hadn't been so clear to me before. I guess I either wasn't in a position to see it or I didn't want to see it. Maybe it was both. I thanked God my mother had found me. What if she hadn't and I'd be stuck out there with those other girls at Black's mercy and his black heart? Thank God for my mom. I realized in that moment that my mother no longer needed to ask for my forgiveness. I needed to ask for hers. As my mother drove, I grabbed her free hand in mine and I clutched it. She looked my way, smiled, and kissed my hand. As we pulled down our street, I gasped as a total of five police cars were blocking off our driveway. "Shit," I heard my mother whisper.

They all had their guns drawn. My mother pulled up along our driveway and parked on the street. I saw my grandmother, Bev, and Hank standing on our porch. My grandmother was sobbing.

My mom slipped the gun out of her back pocket and set it on the middle console.

"Get out of the car with your hands up!" they yelled with their guns drawn.

My mother looked down. She closed her eyes tightly. She did as they said with her hands in the air.

Several cops approached her with their guns still drawn. One shoved my mother against the closest squad car to us, and applied handcuffs. As they shoved her in the back of the car, I grabbed the gun, wiped it off on my gown, and rubbed my hands all over it. Then I tucked it in my underwear.

I slid out of the car. I jumped out of the passenger side with my hands up. "I did it!" I yelled loudly. "My mother didn't do it. I did! He kidnapped me and raped me!" I shouted.

My grandmother, Hank, and Bev all looked at me and gasped in shock.

As two officers approached me I continued to yell. "My mother didn't do this. I did! I have the gun in my underwear."

One of the officers frisked me and felt for a gun. When he found it he pulled it out and they applied handcuffs on me as well.

I watched my mom struggle in the back of the squad car. She was shouting and shaking her head but I couldn't hear her. There was no way I was going to let my mother go down for Black's murder. She was protecting me; that's why she killed him and now it was time for me to protect her.

Once I was secured in the back of one of the other squad cars we all drove off while my mother continued to struggle in the back of the car. I looked away and gave one final look at our house. My grandmother covered her face with both her hands and sobbed while Hank comforted her.

Epilogue

Cashmere

I held on to my daughter's hand and tried to look brave when I was cracking inside. So much had unfolded six months ago. It was like a fucking nightmare. Since I had got my daughter home, it was pure hell trying to get my baby back on track. But we had and there was one more thing we had to find out: whether my child had AIDS. When I first brought the subject up to her she broke down crying and said, "Mom, I don't want to know." But I encouraged her to be brave and take the test.

Now two weeks later, we were back at out doctor's office waiting for the results. To be honest, the thought of her having AIDS sickened me to no end. She was now fourteen and the last thing she needed to hear after all that she had gone through was that she had a lifelong illness. I shuddered to think that she did. But despite all the apprehension I had, I didn't want her to worry. And if she did have it I didn't want her to think her life was over.

"Either way, whether you have it or not, Dom, don't worry, you will be fine. They have all sorts of medications that can help you live a long and healthy life. Look at Magic Johnson," I said with a reassuring smile.

But inside I was shitting bricks. The threat of my child having the virus haunted me day and night. But the fact of the matter was that she could very well have it. Meka had it and Dominique admitted that she did sleep with

Meka and a customer at the same time and like Meka had said, both of them were infected. I knew as scared as I was I had to convince my daughter that she would be okay. Even if I didn't believe it.

As the doctor came back in the room I grabbed both my daughter's hands in mine and kissed them. "Remember what I said. You are going to be fine either way."

She gave a small smile and looked up at the doctor. As the short Middle Eastern guy opened the manila file and read the results inside he was quiet and his expression like a poker player. Then he closed it and focused on us.

He took a deep breath and said, "I wish I didn't have to be the one to say this but you tested positive for AIDS."

I closed my eyes briefly as his words rang out in my head.

Damn.

My baby had AIDS!

I blinked back tears, which was hard as hell to do. I looked at my child who sat there frozen. I squeezed her hands. "You'll be fine." It took some serious work for me to blink back those tears.

But my daughter buried her head in my lap and cried like a baby. And although I promised her she would be okay and life would still be the same, could I really promise her that when she was walking around with a deadly virus and she was only fourteen fucking years old?

Fuck! These were the casualties of the game. But my daughter didn't deserve that shit. She buried her head in my shoulder and continued to cry. I comforted her as best I could.

During the ride home, I continued to try to stay calm and optimistic and all I wanted to do was scream. So I babbled the whole way home about all the different types of medications and how she would be fine. But Lord knows I didn't feel that way. I kept seeing images of my daughter being sickly and then in a casket. But I kept a smile on my face and continued to reassure her.

When we made it into the house I held on to my daughter's hand as we walked into the living room. "You okay?" I asked her.

But she jerked away from me and shoved me roughly into the couch. Caught off-guard I lost my balance and fell. Then suddenly she took off running.

"Dom!" I panicked. I chased after her but she was too fast and had a head start. "Dominique! Stop running!"

She ran into Demarco's office that I hadn't had a chance to clean out and get rid of his gun collection. The one that I didn't lock back on the day I went to Oakland.

"Dominique, get out of there!" I tried to open the door but she had locked it. I panicked and banged on the door. "Dominique. Baby, no, don't do anything stupi—"

That's when I heard it. A single gunshot.

I beat on the door and screamed. "Dominique, nooooo!"

"Cashmere. You okay, baby?"

My eyes shot open and I looked up at Caesar as he wiped sweat off my forehead. Then I looked around the room frantically for my child. My heat thudded in my chest. "Where is Dom?"

"I'm right here, Mom." Dominique's sweet face appeared before me. She grabbed one of my hands and kissed it.

I smiled and breathed a sigh of relief. "Shit. I must've just had a nightmare."

"See. I knew you couldn't handle *Hostel*," Caesar said laughing and changing the channel on TV.

Just then someone knocked on the door. "I got it, Mom." Dominique went to the living room door with a huge bowl of Halloween candy.

I could hear the kids yell, "Trick or treat."

It was Halloween night and we stayed home to give out candy.

I smiled and looked at the most adorable little girl in a bumblebee costume standing in my doorway with a couple of other dressed-up kids.

"You are the cutest," Dominique said. She reminded me so much of Dom when she was small. "You get as much as you want," Dominique said.

I chuckled.

"You okay, baby?"

I looked at Caesar's concerned face. It took awhile getting used to how crazy fate was: that my first love popped back in my life.

"I'm okay. But, question."

"What?"

"We had Dom tested for AIDS, didn't we?"

"Yes, baby. Three times and every test was negative."

I breathed a sigh of relief as Caesar patted me on one of my thighs and kissed me on the lips. "We're good, baby. That is over, don't worry."

I smiled and stared at the diamond ring that glistened on my left ring finger. Yes. Caesar was my fiancé. I thought back to how we got here because it wasn't always hugs, laughs, and kisses.

After the ordeal in getting Dom back and finding the police at my house to arrest me for Black's murder, Dominique's statement about killing Black Mitchell somehow managed to stick. And my mother along with Caesar and our lawyer told me to keep my mouth shut. I guessed they knew some shit I didn't. So I for once did and didn't fight them when they bailed me out and instructed me to keep quiet. But my closed mouth didn't last for long.

The night I was bailed out they were all at my house. And I was pissed as hell that Dominique was still locked up in juvenile hall. I started fussing and cursing them all including the lawyer Hank and Caesar paid for. "Y'all worried about me; what about Dom?" I demanded. "She don't need to be locked up."

"Cash, shut the fuck up!" my mother yelled. "Listen to the lawyer; he knows what he's talking about. You don't know shit! They ain't gonna keep Dominique. She got too much dirt on that *black* bastard. You on the order hand, it's different."

The balding black attorney nodded and said, "She's right. Thing is, Cashmere, you will go to jail for life if you confess. Doesn't matter why you went there, what Black Mitchell did, or what you say. You took the law in your own hands and you murdered him. Dominique, however, has a reason: she was raped, branded, held against her will, and forced to sell her body. With the recent release of Sara Kruzan things are much different in cases like these. Laws are changing in regard to child prostitutes. They are not even calling them that anymore. Child prostitution is now being called child sex trafficking. Logically speaking, no child under the age eighteen is able to consent to sex, yet for years and years they have been locked up like criminals. The crime itself is what's happening to them and no one is doing anything about it." He shook his head. "I'm getting off the subject. Thing is I guarantee you that Dominique won't be sentenced to anything. She will be released to you on the grounds of self-defense. Now if you want to go up for this, go ahead, but I can't promise the same thing for you. You are not to confess."

"He's right, Cashmere," Caesar said. "Look, baby, I know you don't want Dominique in there. Her being there will be only temporary. You being locked up will be permanent. You need to listen to the lawyer. If you want to see the light of day, to be there for your daughter."

"Cashmere, just do it," my mom pressed.

I took a deep breath. "Okay." I hoped I wasn't making a mistake.

And they were absolutely right. Neither she nor I were charged with anything. She was underage, and his semen was in her. (Yes. Black had sex with his own flesh and blood.) And she testified that he beat and pimped her. After the court proceedings she was released and returned home and the charges against me were dropped.

Of course it wasn't easy trying to strengthen our relationship. I had to put her in a detox program along with intensive therapy. Fuck school. The first six months home I worked on rebuilding my child. And Caesar, my mother, Hank and Bev were there every step of the way.

And what was hard was after all the drama was over, sitting my mother down and telling her that I found Hank in Meka's apartment. Hank swore up and down that he had never slept with her. After I told her, my mother camped out on my couch. Hank came over every night crying and begging for her to come back to him; he even went as far as having a lie detector test done. But that meant nothing to my mother.

"Motherfucker. Come with an AIDS test!" my mother had told him. And he did and it was negative. Surprisingly my mother forgave him.

"You know if you don't want to go back you can stay here," I told her.

"No. I'm going home to my husband. I wasn't over Desmond and I married him anyway because he was wealthy and powerful. And also it's probably my karma for all the years I fucked around on your daddy and how I abandoned you guys. I'm sorry for that. I know you never forgave me." She broke down crying.

In that moment I made a decision to really wholeheartedly forgive my mother. I think the ordeal also allowed me to finally put my grudge against my mother to rest.

I stopped lashing out at her and disrespecting her. I wouldn't want my child doing me that way when she got older because of my mistakes so I couldn't continue to do it to my mother. Aside from her weed smoking and materialistic mentality, my mother had really tried to be there for me and Dominique. I had to let it go and stop holding her mistakes against her.

Dominique confessed so many things to me that made me want to just break down and cry. From the fact that Mr. Douglas, my neighbor, had been sleeping with my child. Well he was charged right along with Dame for that shit! She even opened up about all the humiliating things that happened to her when Black and Meka had her out there. And me, I held back no punches from my past. It seemed like it made Dominique trust me more because she related to my pain, my story. Because it was now hers. I just thanked God that Dominique didn't resort to cutting and having the anger belted up inside her like I had all these years. But we took things day by day. She was okay despite the hell she had endured. My baby girl was fine, well-loved, and I refused to allow her to be a victim of the streets.

I glanced at the sweet and innocent girl who was clapping her hands and jumping up and down at all the candy Dominique was dumping in her pumpkin and thinking that that innocence should never be taken or destroyed. Yet there are so many girls out there who would be forever victimized for someone else's pleasure or gain. Well I wanted to assist and put a stop to it. So I put my flatiron down to Bev's dismay and partnered up with Caesar. We expanded his nonprofit and opened another office in Oakland. I didn't want what happened to me, Dom, or other girls across the country to continue to happen.

Caesar brought me back to the present by kissing me on my cheek and making me blush.

Who knew he could take away the pain after losing Demarco and allow me to love again? It was crazy that after all those years Demarco was holding on to guilt about Black raping me. Yet in all those years, I never looked down on Demarco nor blamed him for my rape. But he blamed himself. It's funny how if we had actually sat down and had that conversation, maybe things that transpired between us including his death wouldn't have. But who knew. It's also possible that no matter what I said or did to ease his mind and reassure him it wasn't his fault it wouldn't have changed how he felt about himself as a man and thus how he treated me and Dominique.

At the end of the day, I knew I would always love Demarco but I had to move forward with my life, and let all aspects of the past go, so I did. Because despite the mistakes and my past, I knew I deserved love and happiness just like anyone else. And Caesar was now my new love and a love I hoped would stay. One thing about this love was that it was never painful. Every single ounce of it felt good, wholesome, and pure like I was a thirteen-year-old girl all over again. And I thanked God my daughter was there to witness every minute of it so my words on the freeway would always ring out true and she would see the complete opposite of the supposed love that Black offered her that never really was love. Now she knew the difference. And she would grow up knowing she deserved the same and nothing less. I thanked God for that.

Dominique closed the door and hopped on the couch next to me. She buried her head in my lap and said, "I love you, Mom."

"I love you too. Who wouldn't love Dom?"

She laughed and snuggled closer as I dozed off.

Crazy part was that when I reflected on my life it seemed like a dream and the dream I just had seemed like reality. But it wasn't. With Black gone, Dominique and I were finally free from the past. Now and always.

The End

Karen Williams is the author of *The Demise Of Alexis Vancamp, Hail Mary 1 and 2, Sweet Giselle, Aphrodisiacs: Erotic Short Stories, Thug In Me, Dirty to the Grave, The People Vs. Cashmere, Harlem On Lock.* She also contributed to the anthology *Around The Way Girls 7* with her story "Diamond In The Sky," and "He's With Me" in the anthology *Even Sinners Still Have Souls Too.* She also writes as Braya Spice and released *Dear Drama* in 2012. She graduated from California State University Dominguez Hills with a bachelor's degree. She works as a Probation Officer and lives in Bellflower, CA, with her daughter, Adara, and her son, Bralynn.

ORDER FORM
URBAN BOOKS, LLC
97 N18th Street
Wyandanch, NY 11798

Name (please print):_____

Address: _____

City/State: _____

Zip: _____

QTY	TITLES	PRICE
	16 On The Block	$14.95
	A Girl From Flint	$14.95
	A Pimp's Life	$14.95
	Baltimore Chronicles	$14.95
	Baltimore Chronicles 2	$14.95
	Betrayal	$14.95
	Bi-Curious	$14.95
	Bi-Curious 2: Life After Sadie	$14.95
	Bi-Curious 3: Trapped	$14.95
	Both Sides Of The Fence	$14.95
	Both Sides Of The Fence 2	$14.95
	California Connection	$14.95

Shipping and handling: add $3.50 for 1st book, then $1.75 for each additional book.
Please send a check payable to:
     Urban Books, LLC
Please allow 4-6 weeks for delivery

ORDER FORM
URBAN BOOKS, LLC
97 N18th Street
Wyandanch, NY 11798

Name (please print):_____

Address: _____

City/State: _____

Zip: _____

QTY	TITLES	PRICE
	California Connection 2	$14.95
	Cheesecake And Teardrops	$14.95
	Congratulations	$14.95
	Crazy In Love	$14.95
	Cyber Case	$14.95
	Denim Diaries	$14.95
	Diary Of A Mad First Lady	$14.95
	Diary Of A Stalker	$14.95
	Diary Of A Street Diva	$14.95
	Diary Of A Young Girl	$14.95
	Dirty Money	$14.95
	Dirty To The Grave	$14.95

Shipping and handling: add $3.50 for 1st book, then $1.75 for each additional book.
Please send a check payable to:
Urban Books, LLC
Please allow 4-6 weeks for delivery

ORDER FORM
URBAN BOOKS, LLC
97 N18th Street
Wyandanch, NY 11798

Name (please print):_____

Address: _____

City/State: _____

Zip: _____

QTY	TITLES	PRICE
	Gunz And Roses	$14.95
	Happily Ever Now	$14.95
	Hell Has No Fury	$14.95
	Hush	$14.95
	If It Isn't love	$14.95
	Kiss Kiss Bang Bang	$14.95
	Last Breath	$14.95
	Little Black Girl Lost	$14.95
	Little Black Girl Lost 2	$14.95
	Little Black Girl Lost 3	$14.95
	Little Black Girl Lost 4	$14.95
	Little Black Girl Lost 5	$14.95

Shipping and handling: add $3.50 for 1st book, then $1.75 for each additional book.
Please send a check payable to:
Urban Books, LLC
Please allow 4-6 weeks for delivery